The Baron's

Folly

The Baron's

Folly

The Stratford Family

KELSEY SWANSON

Cover Design by Erin Dameron-Hill, EDH Professionals

The Baron's

Folly

The Stratford Family

KELSEY SWANSON

This is a work of fiction. Names, characters, places, and incidents are products of the author's imagination or are used fictitiously and are not to be construed as real. Any resemblance to actual events, locales, organizations, or persons, living or dead, is entirely coincidental.

No parts of this book may be used or reproduced in any manner whatsoever without written permission, except in the case of brief quotations embodied in critical articles and reviews.

Cover Design by Erin Dameron-Hill, EDH Professionals

To my mom, for being a shining example of a lover of romance novels, for helping foster my love of the library, and for never realizing that the only real punishment would have been to take away my reading materials.

Chapter One

London, April of 1816

Lady Lillian Stratford peered over the cut crystal edge of her punch cup in a weak attempt at nonchalance as she scanned the crush gathered in the ballroom belonging to the Earl and Countess of Haverford. The brilliants woven into the hair, strung from the necks, and affixed to the rainbow of the gowns adorning the peacocking women created flashes of dazzling light vying for her attention. Lily, however, was not distracted by bright and flashy; she was searching for—

"What are you doing hiding in this corner?" She could hear the smile in the deep, familiar baritone. The mere sound of the grin was infectious.

Lily spun on her heel and came face-to-face – rather, face-to-crisp white cravat – with Jeremy Balfour, Baron Shefford. Her eyes skimmed the familiar, amazing breadth of his shoulders in his formal jet-black jacket and the contrast of the snowy shirt and cravat against the tanned skin of his face. The corners of his dark eyes crinkled mirthfully in response.

"Waiting on a rather inconsiderate dance partner, Lord Shefford," Lily replied as he took her free hand, bent at the waist, and brought her gloved knuckles to his lips. She tried to ignore how attuned she was to the warmth of his breath through the creamy satin. He looked up at her from his bow with another easy smile.

"I should think any scoundrel who leaves a lady such as yourself waiting should be drawn and quartered."

"I am inclined to agree with you," she laughed as he righted himself and freed the cup of noxiously sweet punch from her hand, smoothly placing it on the silver tray of a passing servant.

"Then I shall have to find some way to pay penance for my tardiness."

Without another word, he folded her hand in his and placed it on his arm as he led her to the space in the center of the grand, glittering room that had been cleared for dancing. Other guests were finding their way to the floor as well. He'd made his appearance with perfect timing because the orchestra struck up the first lilting waltz of the evening as the couples all took their places. His large hand spanned her back as he effortlessly guided her and spun her to the cadence of the tune. Lily relaxed into his practiced direction and allowed the rest of the room to fall away.

"You nearly missed the dance, Jemmy," Lily whispered in a pitch for only his hearing after their first turn around the floor. Though she was trying to disguise it, Jeremy's attuned ear caught the tautness of her anxious undertone. He gave Lily a reassuring wink.

"I've not missed my dance with you since your debut and I wasn't about to start tonight." He gazed down intently into her clear green eyes—eyes that, in his youth, he'd fancied a man could trip into and never be freed—in an effort to convey his sincerity. "You needn't have worried, Lily," this last, spoken much more softly, lest any near-by prying ears catch the familiarity.

The intimacy was born of years of history – twenty-three of them, to be exact. Their families possessed neighboring estates in Kent; their fathers had grown up and attended university together. It was a plan of sentimentality from the earl and baron's respective wives that their offspring should be nursery playmates. Lily's elder brother, George, and Jeremy had been born mere months apart; Lily, four years later; and her younger brother, Simon, the year following that. Jeremy had remained an only child—the heir without a spare—and viewed the Stratfords as his second family. Lily's brothers were as good as his own blood. Part of that bond meant he also guarded and looked after Lily as a sister.

Somewhere along the way, however, Jeremy's young, hormone-addled brain forgot that fact and he began to see Lily as more.

Much more.

At first, he'd dismissed it as being a randy youth obsessed with anything remotely resembling the curves of a woman. He wouldn't have been the first young man to develop an attraction toward a friend's sister only to outgrow it when he came of age and saw what the rest of the world had to offer. To his mutual surprise and chagrin, his attentions refused to waver, and Jeremy was forced to admit to himself that his closeness and companionship with Lily had developed into genuine feelings.

Feelings that he was wise enough to recognize would not, could never be realized.

As the sole son and heir to an ancient barony, he had been raised a practical man. This is, of course, not to say that he hadn't accomplished his fair share of hell-raising—the professors of Eton and Oxford still cringed whenever the Balfour and Stratford names were mentioned—but he had not been brought up with the knowledge that a younger brother could step in should anything happen to him. Nor had he been afforded the security of deep pockets.

Despite the age and respect afforded to his family's title, the Balfour legacy did not come with a large annual income. Their properties largely relied upon livestock and farming; some poor investments a couple of generations before had whittled away at their holdings to barely anything above whatever was entailed and unable to sell to the highest bidder. In the eyes of the *ton*, the only thing holding them aloft of the title of "genteel poverty" was their rank. Lord only knew what they would say if they saw Jeremy out in the fields with his tenants, repairing stiles and assisting in the harvest.

In truth, Jeremy cared naught for what opinion others might have of (dear heavens!) a lord getting his hands dirty. His remaining tenants were fed and comfortably housed—which was, unfortunately, less than could be said of many of his peers—and they respected him and appreciated his assistance. This had been a great matter of pride for Jeremy's father and was now a mindset by which he also lived and worked.

While this gave him mental and moral comfort, it, unfortunately, did not fill the coffers to the level which would allow him to move amongst the same circles that his closest friend, George Stratford, Viscount Sommerfeld, inhabited. It also did not make for the most enticing draw on the marriage mart. There would come a time when he was old enough to compromise and a woman with a sufficient dowry would be tolerable enough to wed.

But that woman would never be the one currently in his arms.

Jeremy had always been privy to several truths: There was no other path for him in his life than becoming the next Baron Shefford, he would do his best to uphold the standards set by his father, he desired Lily every waking moment of his existence, and she was destined for greater things than being the wife of a near-impoverished, lower-ranking peer.

Unfortunately, this last unquestionable truth did not stop his gaze from drinking in the sight of Lily in a dress so blue it could have been woven from the fabric of the sky…the brilliant flash of her gaze as she caught his eye…the twin, milky swells of perfect flesh just above the ribbon-trimmed edge of her gown.

He supposed a man never did quite outgrow the amorous inclinations of a randy youth.

Jeremy found himself missing the small beauty mark which normally sat above her heart. Her mother made her disguise it with rice powder whenever they went to these functions, but Jeremy didn't see it as an imperfection. He found it enticing, to say the least; tantalizing and erotic if he were ever to admit its true effect upon him. Smaller than a ladybug, the freckle usually sat an inch or two above the edge of her bodice, and the way it danced when he made her breathless with laughter nearly undid him every time. He had grown quite fond of that little mark.

Lily did her best to focus on the sensation of Jeremy holding her in his arms as they glided across the floor, but the tiny hairs on the back of her neck refused to stop standing on end. The pinpricks of eyes upon her caused her skin to crawl uncomfortably. This ball was much larger than Mother had said it would be… Lily did not do well in such large crowds. She didn't know if it was the fact that she'd spent so much of her childhood in the relaxed setting and quiet atmosphere of the country, but events of this size made her heart race; she always inevitably felt as if she could never quite get enough air in her lungs to keep her vision from tunneling.

She was tugged back from the beginning of a panic as Jeremy's thumb moved side to side on her spine in a motion meant to reassure her. He'd known her long enough that she was sure he could recognize the faraway look that came over her whenever she began to retreat inwardly. She did her best to smile at him, but she knew the effort was lacking. Jeremy didn't seem to mind. That ever-present grin tugged at the corner of his mouth once more.

He cut such a dashing figure in his formal clothes. The tailored jacket fit him so well it looked as if he'd been poured into it. The starkness of the white complimented the sun-bronzed skin he'd earned with long hours of riding and even more time spent surveying his properties with his tenants, heedless of blazing sunlight. The solidness of his arm beneath her fingers was anchoring her to the present moment enough to give her racing mind a slight reprieve. But her speeding heart was another matter entirely uncontrolled.

"People may think I'm holding you against your will if you don't start enjoying yourself," he jested. This time, her smile was genuine. Even though they were no longer children, Jeremy hadn't been able to stop teasing her, and she hadn't been able to stop using her pet name for him.

To be fair, he never complained.

"Everyone knows you aren't holding me hostage, Jemmy. Indeed, I think people would believe something was wrong if you *didn't* dance with me." He inclined his dark head in agreement as he spun her into another turn.

This much was true. Lily had been crippled by nerves leading up to her debut. Jeremy, knowing her fears were due in large part to the crowd, and reasoning the rest was due to the girlish paranoia that no one was going to ask her to dance, had taken her hands in his and pledged to dance with her all night if he had to.

*****

"What about all the other nights, Jemmy? What about the other balls? You cannot possibly hope to save me from all of them," Lily despaired as panicked bile began to rise in her throat. "I cannot ask that of you, nor can I expect such a commitment."

She'd begged her mother to postpone her debut – practically fallen to her knees in supplication to avoid just this scenario. Her mother had dismissed it as girlish theatrics and ordered her to clean up so they wouldn't be late for the modiste. For Lily, however, it was anything but a simple tantrum. She would have given anything in that moment to be merely dramatic. Instead, she was terrified to the point of collapse.

For a girl who had happily breathed the fresh country air and passed her days in the comfort of a close circle of family and friends, the mere notion of a crushing ballroom, the judging eyes of hundreds of strangers, was quite literally nauseating.

Jemmy had made a rather fortuitous arrival at their London residence and found her wringing her icy hands, fighting back tears as she stared at the chair recently vacated by her mother. His plans with George were instantly forgotten, and he'd drawn her to the chaise and sat beside her to listen to what had upset her so.

It wasn't that her young heart didn't flutter at the thought of this dark, dashing young man deigning to escort her – *her* – in such a manner…she was present enough to recognize the foolishness of just such a promise.

Jemmy would get bored.

His heart was in the right place, but he was a young buck of two-and-twenty and he had his own engagements to handle. She did not doubt that he had much better things to do than follow her around to assuage her anxieties. She'd no doubt he intended to follow through – for a short while at least – but despite how he continued to insist that he would be there for her as long as she needed him, she didn't want to get her hopes up. This wasn't some country dance, but her first Season.

After several minutes of her arguing the futility of such a promise, Jemmy took her hands in his own. Their heat and the roughness of their callouses felt more intimate than she ever could have imagined. His fingers squeezed hers and forced Lily to meet his gaze.

The sincerity in his dark chocolate eyes nearly stopped her heart.

"Try me."

*****

Her fears about not being asked to dance had been unfounded and she'd only been able to have one turn with Jeremy on the night of her debut. Still, each time she'd felt the terror welling up inside of her, he seemed to appear at the periphery of her vision—like some benevolent angel sent to reassure her. He had been easy enough to spot as he'd already been a head taller than all the other men in the room.

There had been a silent agreement between the two of them from that night forward. Lily penciled in Jeremy's name on her dance card beside the first waltz of each event. Men quickly learned that this dance was, without fail, always claimed in advance, and the *ton* had come to expect the sight of the two of them spinning their way through the first waltz. Jeremy unfailingly made his appearance shortly before the dance was slated to begin, whisked her onto the dance floor, and stayed nearby in the crowd as long as she needed him to. Some nights he left shortly after the dance ended—most often when

one or both of her brothers were in attendance. Others, he would offer
to stay and escort her and her mother or other companions home well
into the wee hours of the morning. He'd become so attuned to her
needs and anxieties over the years that she didn't even have to verbal-
ize if she was feeling faint from the crush of the crowd or required
rescuing from a particularly pushy guest. Jeremy never hesitated to
draw her away from the uncomfortable situation with the right excuse
and the perfect amount of finesse.

Gradually, Lily became more comfortable in social settings; she
needed Jeremy's rescue less and less often and his presence at these
gatherings was becoming shorter, but that didn't mean she didn't miss
his company. She knew he did not care for the formality of these sorts
of things, though. He was much more comfortable ensconced in the
country on his estate, managing his lands and seeing to his tenants.
Still, he made the journey to London for the Season, took up residence in his townhouse, did whatever else it was titled men did when
in Town, and attended these functions solely for her. Lily couldn't
help but feel a little thrill at the thought that this man was so committed to a silly childhood pact that he'd suffered through five years of
parties and balls.

Lily experienced a familiar tug on her heart that only became
stronger when his formidable eyes met hers. She didn't know when
the fluttery feelings for Jeremy had worked themselves into a buffet-
ing wind, but there was currently a hurricane throwing itself around in
the pit of her stomach. She'd kept the girlhood fancy for her brothers'
oldest friend carefully guarded and hidden from the incessant teasing
she no doubt would have suffered from her siblings. Instead of wither-
ing with time, that little leaf had grown strong and a flower bloomed
within the protective, nurturing walls of her heart. Lily was now so
much more than physically attracted to Jeremy—though there was no

denying he was considered more than mildly attractive by many a well-bred lady; she heard as much in the retiring rooms of these soirees—but she also knew he was kind, loyal, always willing to laugh and smile, and treated every living thing with care and consideration.

The older Lily grew, the more she learned to appreciate a man who treated his dogs as more than commodities. It might be argued that he could, conceivably, treat his wife the same way—seeing her as something to enrich his life rather than something to be placed on a shelf and dusted off when company came. It was a rather low bar to set if she was honest. But it was easier to understand if one had spent as much time in the presence of the male members of the *ton* as Lily.

In addition to the appreciative whispers of Jeremy's female admirers, Lily was also exposed to compliments of the dashing figure the two of them cut; him dark and her fair, his powerful form juxtaposed to her petite fragility. A fair portion of those women fully expected Jeremy to offer for her, and some even dared ask if she'd heard talk of any impending engagement.

This was the point at which Lily always put a stop to her wild-running daydreams.

For all she was aware, he was treating her like a beloved sister and had no feelings for her above and beyond that. She'd kept her desires hidden for so long that she was afraid of what revealing them might do. Even if he did not feel the same way, she suspected Jeremy would take it in stride and let her down gently. Her brothers, George and Simon, on the other hand…

She didn't want to think about the mocking. She didn't think she could handle that on top of a pulverized heart and shattered fantasies.

Instead, Lily convinced herself to settle for that one dance with Jeremy each evening they attended a function. She locked every encounter away in that secret place in her heart to be revisited in the quiet moments alone in her rooms.

As the waltz swelled and died away, Lily was reminded of just how short those times were. She allowed Jeremy to lead her off the dance floor and he skillfully maneuvered her to a less crowded portion of the room against a window overlooking the moon-washed courtyard. She was grateful for the space to breathe because, as she turned to look back out over the ballroom, it seemed the crowd had grown even larger.

As if sensing her returning nerves, Jeremy squeezed her gloved fingers with his own and she turned her attention back to his face. There was a small ridge in his nose where George had broken it when they'd played at fisticuffs when they were teenagers. He'd inherited his mother's raven-dark hair—continually cut slightly longer than was the fashion, as if he was always a couple of weeks too late for a trim —and his father's eyes, so deep and fathomless they almost appeared black. Bold, dark slashes of eyebrows made his already-expressive, well-cut features even more so. And, oh, when he smiled…his whole countenance lit up and small lines creased the outer edges of his eyes. She could well imagine how nicely he'd age as the years passed.

Standing this close to him, Lily could see the underside of his chin and the small red mark left by the slip of his valet's hand. No matter how close the shave had been a few hours earlier, a slight shadow was already beginning to appear on the chiseled planes of his jaw.

Another quick squeeze of her fingers told Lily that he'd caught her staring. She immediately averted her eyes and willed herself not to flush, which served only to turn her flesh a deeper shade of pink. The vibration of Jeremy's chuckle danced up and down her arm. Lily cleared her throat as daintily as possible and tried to change the subject.

"One would think, after all these years, I could manage a simple ball on my own," she said somewhat wistfully.

"I don't blame you," Jeremy replied gently, surveying the swelling crowd.

A gentleman in black dress clothes opened a French door to admit his female companion into the fresh night air. Jeremy wondered if that wouldn't be a bad idea. The crowd had certainly grown ever since he'd arrived and the air was cloying with a hundred different perfumes, melting wax, and sweaty bodies. If he was feeling the effects, he knew Lily must be bordering on another panic.

"I wonder if Lady Haverford thought to limit the number of guests to that which would actually fit inside her townhouse," he continued, bemused; all the while watching Lily to make sure she was steady and calm. Their conversation seemed to be helping.

"But one must not risk offending anyone by not extending an invitation," Lily intoned in an excellent imitation of her mother's singsongy falsetto she adopted each time she felt she was imparting an important bit of knowledge upon her only daughter. Jeremy grinned; he'd heard that tone more than a time or two.

"Heaven forbid one's guests might want to *breathe* at a ball."

Lily cracked a genuine smile at his sardonic tone and Jeremy did his damndest to ignore the warmth that smile released low in his stomach…and continued to spread lower still.

He peered at Lily out of the corner of his eye and was struck, not for the first time, by how truly breathtaking she was. It was not just the gown – she could have been wearing a maid's frock and apron and he was certain she would still have shone as brilliantly – it was her smile and the light in her eyes. He would do anything to make her laugh; he always had.

A compliment was on the tip of his tongue, but the arrival of the Countess of Aldborough, Lily's mother, stopped him from making that grave mistake. He released Lily's hand. He couldn't have known how immediately she felt and mourned the loss of his comforting warmth in that small, guarded part of her heart.

"My Lady Aldborough," he smiled and bowed over her proffered hand. "What a pleasure to see you, and what a vision you are this evening."

The countess laughed off his compliment with all the familiarity of a woman who was like an aunt to him. "You're truly dangerous with that flattery of yours, Jer—Shefford." She caught herself quickly, still not entirely used to addressing him by his title. The weight of the pause was felt by everyone in their small corner of the ballroom. "And how is your mother?" the countess attempted to redirect the conversation with all her years of practice with social niceties. "I attempted to call before we left Kent for the Season, but I was told she was not receiving."

Jeremy stood a little straighter as he was reminded of the weight of the obligations he'd inherited following his father's recent death. He might have taken some solace had he known how Lily's fingers ached to reach out and hold his arm, to comfort him as he had her so many times before.

"Mother is improving; she is no longer in deep mourning. I can speak to her about starting to receive visitors again if you like?"

"Oh no!" the countess objected, fluttering her hands like flustered doves. "I couldn't impose."

"It's no imposition," Jeremy reassured her. "It would be good for her to have visitors…especially you." He gave her another of his warm smiles to impress his sincerity upon her. This seemed to reassure the countess. Her soft features, a slightly rounder version of

Lily's, relaxed immediately. She clearly missed her friend but was hesitant to intrude upon a grieving household stunned by abrupt death.

"That would be lovely, thank you." She patted him gently on the forearm, seeming to forget herself again, and turned to her daughter.

"I think we've monopolized Shefford's attention enough for now. Let him mingle. Besides…I have someone who is looking forward to speaking with you." Neither Jeremy nor Lily bothered to correct the countess's assumption, but they exchanged a knowing look – both of them well aware that Jeremy would duck out as soon as he was able to do so. A glance in their vicinity would prove his presence had drawn the attention of a number of his aforementioned female admirers, eager to catch his eye despite the speculation that his ancient estate wasn't as financially secure as most.

"Thank you for the dance." Lily tipped her head in gratitude she needn't explain any further to him.

"Always a pleasure," he replied with all sincerity.

Jeremy watched the two women—near remarkable copies—walk away and become swallowed by the press of the crowd. His heart skipped a beat for Lily, knowing her anxiety would return with crushing force. He stared intently after them and listened for any sound that might indicate she needed him; however, his vigil was soon interrupted by a hearty slap on his shoulder.

"I knew you'd show your ugly face here sooner or later!" George, Viscount Sommerfeld and Lily's brother, clapped Jeremy's shoulder again in greeting.

"I didn't realize you were coming tonight," Jeremy grinned and greeted his friend with a firm handclasp.

"What? And miss this lovely mob?" Sommerfeld gestured sarcastically to the undulating crowd around them. "I came to support Lily; Simon did too. I couldn't believe he stepped away from his books long enough to attend." His green eyes, similar in shape and shade to Lily's, scanned the crowd for the youngest Stratford son. "I swear, if he found his way to the duced library and hid away amongst the books on tonight of all nights, I'll pummel him. I don't care how old we are."

"Support Lily?" The more Sommerfeld spoke, the more Jeremy got the distinct impression he had missed some important conversation.

He didn't doubt the love the Stratford brothers had for their sister, but for Sommerfeld to say he attended an event *for* Lily; and for Simon to abandon his studies for a frivolous evening? That was damn near unheard of. Sommerfeld gestured vaguely toward a column on the far side of the ballroom, indicating that he'd finally located his younger brother.

"Good, he hasn't found the library yet. Pray he doesn't before midnight."

"What happens at midnight?" Jeremy's tone had become slightly more urgent. Sommerfeld finally took note of this and turned to him, a frown furrowing his fair brow.

"I'd forgotten. You don't know, do you?"

"Know what?" Jeremy's concern for Lily was growing at an unreasonable pace. He knew her brothers wouldn't allow anything terrible to happen to her, but they weren't always the most understanding sort when it came to her anxieties.

Sommerfeld gestured out to the center of the dance floor.

The crowd parted in a parody of Moses's Dead Sea.

And there, Jeremy saw Lily.

"To whom are you taking me, Mother?" Lily asked more as a way to distract herself from the press of people around her than out of actual curiosity. She willed her lungs to slow and carefully counted each breath, just as Jeremy had shown her when they were children. The methodical practice aided in grounding her when she felt as if her head might explode.

Her mother linked her gloved arm through Lily's and patted her daughter's wrist in what was meant to be a reassuring manner. Lily tried to take what little comfort she could in the gesture; her mother just didn't understand her "apprehension" in social situations. Where Lily's pulse was racing with anxiety, the bright fuchsia flowers pinned into the countess's elaborate hairdo were fairly vibrating with excitement. Two more different women as mother and daughter would be difficult to find.

"You'll see, dear!" Her mother didn't seem able to contain her enthusiasm and her voice began its sing-songy lilt.

Lily had been distracted enough by her mother's behavior that she hadn't realized she was being led to the center of the dance floor.

Nor had she realized the crowd made way for her as if she were visiting royalty.

Nor had she noticed all of the pairs of eyes watching her very expectantly.

Now she did.

The familiar sense of dread began in the pit of Lily's stomach.

Don't be sick.

Please don't swoon or be sick all over Countess of Haverford's nice polished floor in front of all of these people…

She tried to breathe slowly, but her vision began to tunnel nonetheless. She suddenly realized how quiet the ballroom had gotten. Well, not silent, per se, but the cacophony of chatter had died to an excited, expectant buzz and the music had halted.

"Lily," her mother urged and squeezed her hand, wrenching Lily back from the brink of panic. "May I present The Most Honorable

Marquess of Townsend? He requested a more formal introduction."
Her mother's beaming smile as she looked from her daughter to the
marquess was not as reassuring to Lily as, perhaps, it should have
been.

As she held out her hand like a well-trained marionette, Lily
couldn't help but scan the edges of her line of sight for any glimpse of
Jeremy. She needed his eyes—they would be her lifeline in this
swelling ocean of humanity. She didn't immediately see him and
couldn't risk seeming rude enough to turn her back on a marquess to
look; even in her panic, she'd been too well-trained to create a scene
with such a slight.

Instead, Lily made a valiant effort to fight back the rising panic
and pasted what she hoped was a convincing smile upon her face.

"I am pleased to meet you, my lord," she ground out, hoping the
words didn't sound as wooden as they did to her own ears. The niggling voice in the back of her head wondered if all of these people
were waiting with bated breath to witness this introduction, but she
quickly brushed it aside as an absurd idea.

The marquess bent over her hand in a flourishing bow and pressed
his lips to her silk-covered knuckles perhaps a moment or two longer
than was proper.

"I assure you, my lady, the pleasure and honor are all my own."
When he righted himself, he smiled the reserved smile of a high-rank-
ing peer and Lily realized, even in her haze of panic, that she recognized him. Vaguely. They'd never spoken until that very moment, but
he'd certainly attended some of the same balls, musicales, and large
dinner parties she and her family had. She remembered his blond hair
and clear blue eyes, trim build, and uncommon fitness for a man who
was likely nearing his fortieth year.

Lily's spinning, floundering mind was interrupted by the appearance of her father at her side, his silver hair and laughter lines less reassuring in that moment than she would have liked. He smiled down kindly at his only daughter and said, "Lily, my dear, Lord Townsend and I have been speaking and negotiating over the last several weeks. We've come to an agreement I believe everyone will find most acceptable."

The mirth in her father's eyes did nothing to slow the dread that was blooming in various vital locations of her body like blood from shrapnel. Her heart's pace redoubled.

The marquess lowered himself to one knee.

He produced from his pocket something glittering and gold.

Lily barely heard his proposal over the crescendo of blood in her ears.

Chapter Two

No.

Jeremy's heart crashed into his stomach. Rather, it must have plummeted further than that because he could no longer feel the blasted organ's beating. He narrowly resisted the urge to press a hand to his chest to make sure he hadn't expired as a result of the blow he'd just been dealt.

He'd known it was coming, in a way.

He'd always known Lily had to marry and he'd believed that her parents—despite the families' connection and deep affection for one another—had always planned on marrying their beautiful daughter to some lord who was ranked above them, not below them.

Like a baron.

The only daughter of an earl was born and bred to be a bargaining chip in the grand game of society. She was a pawn to forge alliances, to help set her brother up when he eventually inherited the earldom, and she would bear a son who would play a role in the country's future – not one whose sole pride and joy was a small corner of Kent.

He'd been keenly aware Lily could never be his, but the sting of reality was still too fresh—still standing in front of him—for rational thought to take any sort of foothold. He barely registered the sound of Sommerfeld's congratulatory applause—the similar cheers gradually rising around them to fill the already stifling ballroom with even more nauseating closeness. Jeremy was hyper-focused on the fair-haired man standing and sliding a ring on Lily's finger.

The air froze heavily in his lungs when the man rose and continued to possessively hold Lily's fingers in his own, turning to take in and nod a regal thanks for the joyful attention surrounding them.

*****

"Jem?" George had stopped clapping and was eyeing him in the queerest way. Dimly, Jeremy wondered if he'd noticed the stricken expression on his face or the bloodlust in his eye. He was certain the tension in his body rolled off of him like waves on a shore, hammering upon everything within reach and then grasping for more.

He squeezed Jeremy's shoulder in an effort to shake him from his unnervingly keen analysis of the scene that had just unfolded before them.

"Jeremy," George repeated, raising his voice to be heard above the rising din of well-wishes.

Jeremy's head whipped around, but he doubted Jeremy saw him. George pulled his hand back as if avoiding a bite from a rabid dog, and then brushed at the sleeve of his coat to hide his unease at Jeremy's unanticipated reaction."What say we go congratulate the new couple, hm?" he asked, affecting a nonchalant tone. Just then, a servant carrying two trays stacked high with a diminishing pyramid of crystal goblets of sparkling wine passed by. George swiped two glasses and held one out to Jeremy.

"Congratulate?" Jeremy asked as if he'd passed the last several minutes in a stupor.

"Yes, Jem," George replied, a concerned note to his voice, as he peered into his friend's eyes, searching for a glimmer of the friend he knew. Jeremy accepted the proffered flute, but Sommerfeld took note of the white-knuckled manner with which he held the fragile stem of the glass. He pressed forward, attempting to maintain some normalcy in the conversation. "This is, after all, a surprise engagement party. Mother and Father have been collaborating with Townsend and Lord and Lady Haverford to coordinate this for weeks. Lady Haverford is, after all, a cousin to the marquess and you know she never passes up the opportunity to be touted as the hostess who pulled off the event of the Season. She was the one who suggested the public proposal, I believe. The marriage agreement was prepared and finalized earlier this month."

Jeremy looked back to where they'd watched the event unfold, but the happy couple had been swallowed up by the crowd once more.

"Come now," George continued to try to urge his friend away from the outskirts of the room. "Father's going to make a toast. You should be upfront with me, with the family. You are family too, Jem." His smile was wasted on Jeremy, for he was already lost somewhere deep inside of himself. George doubted there was ever a time he'd seen Jeremy's eyes darker, more unnerving than in that moment.

He cleared his throat and turned, hoping Jeremy would follow suit, but he made it no more than three strides before there was a sudden crack and the tinkling sound of shattering crystal from behind him. He whirled around to find Jeremy gone, the nearby French door hanging ajar, a shimmering puddle of sparkling wine and fragments of crystal mixing with a healthy splash of bright red blood. Servants in Haverford livery scrambled to clear away the mess before any of the ladies were disturbed by the scene.

It was in that moment, however, that George finally allowed his mind to come to the grave realization that the niggling suspicions he'd had for years were, in fact, truth.

"You bastard," he breathed with an incredulous laugh and raked his hand through his hair in disbelief.

Jeremy was in love with Lily.

The next morning was Jeremy's purgatory and hell all rolled into one; he was trapped vacillating between disbelief and the need to remind himself that Lily's betrothal to another man had been bound to happen sooner or later.

He'd just anticipated more time to prepare himself than a surprise engagement afforded.

Jeremy had foregone a hack after vacating the ball the previous night. He didn't think it wise to lock him inside a moving box with all of the raging emotions vying for a place of prominence inside of him: anger that he now well and truly could never have the one thing he'd desired most for nearly his entire life; emptiness at the loss of one of his closest friends; and even a tinge of relief that the inevitable had happened and maybe, just maybe, he might be able to move on with his life and let go of Lily.

Because that was exactly what he had to do.

He had to let go of her now.

After much prowling and pacing the cobbled streets of Mayfair, he'd finally stalked up the steps to his townhouse. The tidy white stone facade and symmetrical lines did nothing to comfort him.

Once inside, his butler, Hampton, attempted to greet him and take his hat. Though only a temporary hire from an agency while he was in residence, the butler was efficient and dedicated in a way one would expect from a long-time employee. This, however, didn't prevent him from raising a bushy black brow when his master had no hat or coat to hand over.

Jeremy had cursed beneath his breath and asked, without explanation, that a footman be sent to the Haverford townhouse to retrieve his belongings. He'd then stalked upstairs to his chambers. Only then had his valet, Charles, taken note of his injury.

"My lord! We should send for a surgeon," the wiry, prematurely-gray-haired man had said as he propped Jeremy's hand above his head, pressing toweling linen to the wound to staunch the flow of blood. No doubt there was a trail of it leading from the Haverford's townhouse all the way to his front door, like some sort of macabre breadcrumbs.

Jeremy had declined to summon the surgeon once the bleeding slowed. Instead, he'd gritted his teeth and allowed Charles to clean the shards of crystal from the wound, pour spirits into the gash, and, instead, tightly bandage the hand. He'd suffered far worse and survived. Hell, he'd felt more banged up from watching Lily accept another man's proposal than he had from the damage inflicted by the crystal goblet.

After replacing his starched evening clothes with a linen shirt and comfortably-worn breeches, Jeremy relieved Charles for the evening, gathered the brandy decanter and a cut crystal glass—one *without* a stem—and seated himself at the desk in his study where he promptly drank himself into a stupor in the one place he had no memories of Lily.

No matter how much brandy he imbibed, he couldn't cleanse his addled mind of the image of Lily's face. It seemed to be branded behind his heavy eyelids; her open arms awaited him in oblivion.

Jeremy awoke that next morning to the hellish cacophony of pounding on the front door of his modest townhouse. The beams of light streaming through the gap in the curtains framing the ceiling-high windows were daggers piercing his throbbing eyes, continuing onward through the back of his skull. He pressed his forearm against his eye sockets and attempted to sit up, but the motion nearly made him ill. He promptly lay back down with a heavy *thunk*.

He wasn't in his bed.

Where the hell was he?

Torn between wanting to gain his bearings and fearing the blinding daggers from hell that were the rays of sunlight, Jeremy groped around with his good hand and felt the carved wooden foot of a chair. Taking careful, shallow breaths, he caught whiffs of old wood smoke, leather, and warm parchment. He was still in his study. A scratch at the door interrupted his clumsy investigation.

"M'lord?" came the housekeeper's cautious voice. It wouldn't have been the first time since the old baron's death that the household would have tiptoed around him after a night of heavy drinking, and— even though Jeremy didn't want to think about it at the present moment – he had the distinct feeling it would not be his last. "M'lord, Viscount Sommerfeld is here to see you. Shall I tell him you're indisposed?"

Before Jeremy could reply he heard his friend's muffled voice call to him from the hallway. "I know you're in there Jem. We need to talk."

A groan escaped his lips and, in that moment, he hated Sommerfeld. He hated the whole bloody Stratford family. They had dangled

Lily in front of him for nigh on four-and-twenty years and tore her from him without so much as a warning. They called him family, yet he couldn't help but feel a knife of pain at being so detached from an announcement of this great import.

Not that he expected to be consulted, mind you. A part of him resented not being given even a moment to mentally prepare himself. He didn't care one whit if that made him selfish.

Or irrational.

Or childish.

If a man couldn't be these things in the safety of his own head, then what was the world coming to?

Mrs. Hallsworth, refusing to be cowed by a viscount – bless her soul – repeated herself more loudly, "Shall I tell him you're not receiving callers today, m'lord?"

Jeremy could easily imagine Sommerfeld's irritation through the wooden barrier of the mahogany door and it made him feel a little better.

Only marginally.

"Enter," Jeremy rasped from his parched throat. He listened as Mrs. Hallsworth opened the door for George, and then winced as she shut it slightly harder than was necessary before spinning away in a flurry of skirts and petticoats, the keys on her chatelain jangling like church bells in the hollows of his skull.

"Jem?" Sommerfeld sounded puzzled.

"What?" Jem demanded, finding a bit more of his voice this time after he cleared his throat.

"Wh…where are you?"

"Here, you bloody idiot." He felt the vibration of George's footsteps on the floorboards beneath his back. There was a pause.

"You do realize you're under your desk?"

"Under my...?" Jeremy sat up and cracked his head against the underside of the enormous desk that had once been his father's and his grandfather's before him. His eyes flew open on impact and a fresh wave of flaming, hellish pain set his brain afire. He let fly a particularly virulent and colorful string of curses and dropped back to the floor. He wished he'd paid more attention in Latin because he would have gladly added those curses to the mix.

There was the grating scratch of metal-on-metal as his friend closed the drapes and drowned the room in blessed darkness. Jeremy cautiously opened one eye and then the other. The pain was less crippling this time around. He kicked the chair away from the desk with a scrape and slid from beneath the furniture, trying to work out how he'd gotten there. His hazy brain was of no help, but the goose egg on the back of his skull and rug burn on his lower back hinted that he may have passed out in the leather-upholstered chair, went limp, and slid down beneath the desk, hitting the back of his head against the seat of the chair on his way down before connecting with the unforgiving floor.

"You look as if you were run over by a hackney with a gin-loving jarvey," Sommerfeld remarked, bemused.

"Thank you for describing exactly the way I feel; I hadn't realized," Jeremy snapped as he ran his good hand along the back of his head to make sure he wasn't bleeding there as well. He did his best not to wince as he tested the tender skin and unintentionally stretched the bandaged wound on his hand. Sommerfeld set aside his silver-tipped walking cane, crouched down, and held out a hand to his prostrate friend. Jeremy eyed the appendage for a few heartbeats before clasping it.

"Easy now." He slowly helped Jeremy to his feet and steadied him as he winced and gained his bearings. Jeremy's bare foot knocked against something cool and hard. The empty brandy decanter lay on its side, spinning drunkenly from the contact. He felt a fleeting loss at having been too stupid not to choose a lesser-quality drink with which to drown his unfortunate emotions. He half expected he was still more than a little bit sloshed from the excellent vintage.

Jeremy attempted to scrub the blurriness from his vision and was finally able to focus on his friend's face. The concern he saw there was more than a little disconcerting. His green eyes belied a sympathy Jeremy had only ever received one other time: when his father had died of a bad heart nine months ago.

His stomach flipped uneasily at the memory.

"Don't look at me like that," Jeremy grumbled brusquely as he batted Sommerfeld's hands away. "This isn't the first time one of us has walked in on the other piss-drunk. At least I've got my clothes on." As an afterthought, he stole a glance down to make sure he was, indeed, decent. Though clothed, he was more than a little rumpled and there were several spots on his once-pristine linen shirt where brandy had splashed out of the decanter and missed the glass.

Maddeningly, Sommerfeld said nothing, so Jeremy moved past his friend and made his way over to the sideboard where he knew (hoped) there was another decanter of brandy waiting. The key for the sideboard was still in the lock on the cupboard, telling Jeremy that he'd sure as hell tried to get to the other bottle. Some kinder angel must have smiled upon him in his drunken disgrace because he'd been unable to get the key to turn in the sticky lock; the other brandy decanter was waiting for him, full and untouched. He snagged it from the cabinet, set it on the sideboard, and began preparing another drink. The smell of the brandy caused another current of nausea, but he swallowed back the bile and told himself it would help ease the morning-after discomfort.

"Jem…" Sommerfeld cautioned from behind him.

"Oh, how rude of me," Jeremy said, choosing to ignore the tone of his friend's voice. "Would you care for a drink?" He held up the glass, but George shook his head.

"Jem, it's half past nine in the morning."

Ignoring the comment, Jeremy swallowed the fiery liquid in one great gulp. He savored the burn as it seared its way down his throat and spread its embers with languid fingers in his stomach. He poured himself another glass and turned back to his friend.

"Hair of the dog, and all that…" He mumbled as he strode over to one of the great armchairs and dropped into it, instantly regretting the abrupt motion. Sommerfeld continued to eye him like some grotesque specimen in one of his younger brother's scientific books. "Would you cease your pitying looks?" Jeremy snapped. "I've not grown a second head. Can't a man get a little foxed once in a while?"

One of Sommerfeld's sandy brows quirked upwards in response. "A little foxed?" George scoffed. "And, pray tell, why did you feel this need to get so foxed that you passed out beneath your desk?" He strode over to Jeremy and perched himself upon the other armchair facing the crackling fireplace. It appeared a small favor that the char maid had lit the fire, never realizing her employer lay unconscious beneath the furniture a few feet away—the mornings could be rather chilly this time of year. Sommerfeld leaned forward and rested his elbows on his knees, all the while eyeing Jeremy with that gallingly condolatory veil over his eyes.

Jeremy had to avert his gaze before he gave in to the temptation to strike him. He knew Sommerfeld was just being a good friend; he didn't deserve to be the recipient of *all* of Jeremy's frustrations and jealousy. Instead, Jeremy stared into the amber liquid in his hands and rolled the glass between his palms, warming it and keeping his idle hands busy. Idle hands were never good for Jeremy, especially not when he'd been drinking. A few juvenile bar fights and scrapes were a testament to that.

He weighed his options in the silence that followed Sommerfeld's inquiry. To admit the truth was pointless. The only purpose it would serve would be to generate an intolerable ribbing from Sommerfeld and create a blow to Jeremy's pride. Plus, he'd spent one too many evenings regaling stories of youthful debauchery with Sommerfeld... His friend was smart and Jeremy doubted he would appreciate the knowledge that his closest friend had been secretly hoping all of those other women had been Sommerfeld's own younger sister—that the reason Jeremy had a "type" consisting of light-haired, green-eyed, slightly built women was because of Lily. She'd always driven his fantasies, even from the very beginning.

The only thing left was to blame it on his father's untimely passing. Jeremy hoped it didn't damn him to place the responsibility for his recent debauched actions at his father's grave, but, at that moment, brimstone seemed preferable to the possibility of alienating his closest companion.

"You'd drink too if you were riding with your father, watched him clutch his chest and fall from his mount, dead before he hit the dirt." He hoped the insincerity wasn't as obvious to Sommerfeld as it was on his tongue. The lie tasted even worse than if he *had* been sick.

The corner of Sommerfeld's mouth twitched while Jeremy availed himself of what he hoped was another nonchalant swig of brandy.

"You know I loved your father as family, Jem...don't disgrace his memory by blaming his death for your current, miserable state."

Jeremy leveled his most intimidating glare – the look he'd learned from his father – at Sommerfeld, but his friend remained unfazed.

He'd grown up with the old Baron Shefford's stare as well, and he'd known Jeremy his entire life; he wouldn't back down from that look.

Realizing Sommerfeld was far from relenting, Jeremy sank back into the comfortably-worn upholstery and eyed his friend. "And why do *you* think anything else might be at the cause for my 'miserable state?'"

There was another pause as if Sommerfeld was wondering whether or not to divulge his suspicions. Jeremy's stomach made another unpleasant flip when he registered the uncharacteristic seriousness on Sommerfeld's face.

"I know," George finally said with heavy solemnity. Jeremy clenched his jaw against the realization that he made a grave mistake in his inability to control his emotions the prior evening. "I *know,*" Sommerfeld repeated with more vehemence. "I know about Lily." Jeremy fought the urge to wince at the sound of her name. It was more than a little disturbing that her name, once so sweet to his ears, could now strike him like a weapon. Would that dull over time, or be just as keen a decade from now? He hoped for his sanity, and his liquor stores, that it would lessen…

"And what do you know about Lily, Georgie, hm?" he demanded acridly, his pain making his tone more defensive than he'd intended. "What could you possibly believe you know about her that would have anything to do with me?" his tone fell dangerously low, warning Sommerfeld he was treading in precarious territory.

"I've had my suspicions over the years—and I *know* you know to what I am alluding, so don't bother pretending you don't. I just want you to answer one thing for me, as my oldest friend…" A pregnant pause ensued. "Did you touch her, Jem? Did you ruin Lily?" The accusation—presented in such a calm, cool fashion—made Jeremy's blood heat to boiling in less than a second's time. It was all he could do not to smash his fist into George's solemn face.

"How dare you even ask such a thing?" Jeremy roared as he shot to his feet. The sound and abrupt movement nearly made Jeremy sick, but he choked it back with a firm knuckle pressed to his mouth and regained his equilibrium. Sommerfeld stood as well, wisely not wanting to be at a disadvantage in case the drink got the better of Jeremy and it came to blows. They may have been the closest of friends, but that didn't mean they were unaware of how hard the other could punch.

"You know I must ask, Jem!" Sommerfeld's arm slashed through the air to gesture at Jeremy. "She's my sister, for Christ's sake!" He shoved a rough hand through his blond hair, mussing his normally immaculate appearance. "What am I supposed to think when you re-act the way you did last night? No man who loves a woman as a sister would have stormed off in such a fashion, leaving a trail of his blood like—like a beaten dog."

Jeremy heaved a deep breath and set his glass on the small table situated between their chairs.

"I never touched her," Jeremy began as calmly as he could. "I have far too much respect for her and love for your family to do something like that." Jeremy's eyes searched his friend for any sign of warmth. "You should know that," he added coolly after several tense seconds.

Finally, Sommerfeld scrubbed the back of his neck and dropped back down into his chair. Jeremy did the same.

"I know…" Sommerfeld sighed heavily.

For the first time, Jeremy noticed how weary his friend appeared. There were dark circles beneath his normally lively green eyes. He must have left his townhouse without bothering to allow his valet to shave him because a shadow of light brown stubble coated his jaw. It was so unlike the Sommerfeld to enter public in such a state. He must have been up the entire night at the engagement celebration and then pacing until morning wondering how he was going to confront Jeremy, leaving the house as soon as it was no longer a truly ungodly hour. "It's just...I had to ask."

The exhaustion was now apparent in his voice; perhaps made more evident by his relief that he didn't have to call out his best friend and duel for Lily's honor – not to mention the issues that would no doubt cause with Lily's new fiancé...

The concrete realization that Lily had a fiancé struck Jeremy like simultaneous blows to the gut and side of the head. His skull screamed against the pressure of his brain, and his stomach roiled with the unpalatable thought. He screwed his eyes shut and pressed the heels of his palms into his throbbing eyes.

"So, if you haven't...touched Lily, then you must, at the very least, feel something for her," George began gently, followed by a sardonic laugh. "No 'brother' would have reacted the way you did," he added very matter-of-factly.

Jeremy immediately reached for his drink and tossed it back. He needed the encouragement for this conversation – one he thought he need never have.

"You sound as if you've had more than minor suspicions."

"You teased her incessantly when we were children, and that wouldn't be out of place—Lord knows we all put her through enough misery—but I watched it develop into some kind of affection." Sommerfeld shrugged. "You do dote on her, Jem. You humor her imagined panics—"

"They're not imagined," Jeremy growled.

Sommerfeld held up his hands in defense but didn't amend his earlier statement.

"I've been asked if you'd offered for her yet, you know? Several gents at my club had their eye on her, but they preferred not to step on your rather formidable toes if she was yours."

Jeremy's brows rose at the unexpected admission. He'd apparently been much more transparent than he'd previously believed.

How embarrassingly pathetic.

"Not wanting to put you in an awkward situation by letting them believe you were committed to her, I always quelled those rumors – stamped them out before they even got to you. I convinced myself you'd come to me if you felt that way about Lily…" If Jeremy wasn't mistaken, he could hear a hint of sadness in Sommerfeld's voice. A little blade of guilt was dragged across his conscience.

The two of them had grown up sharing everything; they had the same education, schoolmates, and hobbies, they'd even shared a woman a time or two in their wilder days. And there Sommerfeld sat before him feeling as if he'd been left out of one of the biggest secrets of Jeremy's life. Jeremy couldn't blame him for feeling stung by the omission.

He heaved a heavy sigh before speaking. "You're right. I care for Lily as more than a sister…I have for almost as long as I can remember—"

"Why did you say nothing?" George demanded hoarsely.

"She was not meant for me!" Years of frustration began to pour into Jeremy's tone. He stood abruptly to pace the room. "If our families had desired something of the sort, then it would have been mentioned long before now. If *Lily* had desired such an arrangement, she would have indicated so. Your parents clearly planned a better match for her than the son of a baron; even the son of their closest friends. Lily *deserves* a better match than I. I cannot give her the grand lifestyle Marquess Golden-And-Rich can provide. I can tell you he's a better match and I don't even know the bastard."

"So you love her then?" Sommerfeld effectively stalled his rant like a shot to an ill-fated grouse.

Jeremy froze for several heartbeats.

"Love is a weighty word."

"If not love, then you cared for Lily enough that you considered marriage?" Sommerfeld pressed.

The grim set of Jeremy's jaw served as a sufficient reply.

"Jem…" Sommerfeld groaned and dropped his head into his hands.

"I realize it's ridiculous!" Jeremy threw out his arms in exasperation, trying not to feel insulted by his friend's obvious disapproval. "That is why I never said anything. There was no sense in mucking up the families' relationship by making it awkward. What was I going to do? Offer for Lily and have your father turn me down? I'll be damned before I'm humiliated like that. I'm no marquess, but I'm a peer of the realm, nonetheless."

Sommerfeld shook his head without lifting it from his hands. "That's not it at all, Jem." His blond head lifted slowly and he finally met Jeremy's eyes. His voice dropped to a very serious timbre as he spoke, "*Everyone was waiting for you to offer for her.*"

Jeremy could only stare at Sommerfeld and wonder if his half-drunk ears had heard him correctly.

"We are none of us blind, Jem! You were doing a piss-poor job of hiding your feelings if you didn't want them to be known.

"Why do you think my parents waited this long to marry Lily off? She's three and twenty; she should have been married with at least one child by now. Each year they waited, hoping you might come forward and offer. When that never happened, they assumed you'd met someone else or that they'd misjudged your affections…and, dammit, I helped things along by swearing you never said a word about having any designs on Lily.

"I saw your behavior as they all did, but I let my belief in our friendship overshadow my gut feeling that you cared for her—I truly believed you would have at least mentioned something to me. They only agreed to the marquess' offer because you never stepped forward, Jem…not because they didn't think you were good enough." Sommerfeld sighed heavily. "Our families wanted the match, but they wanted *you* to want it as well. No one was going to force you into a marriage you didn't want; not with a woman everyone believed you loved as a dear little sister. They didn't want to back you into such an uncomfortable arrangement. When an offer wasn't forthcoming and after she hadn't expressed any real preferences to anyone, they arranged a match for her."

Jeremy reached for the arm of the chair as the full weight of the words sank in, still nearly missing the seat as he dropped down.

"My God." He felt numb, and not in the pleasant way alcohol usually ushered along.

Sommerfeld took in Jeremy's dumbfounded expression and gave him a sad smile. "I would have been happy to call you my brother in truth, but now it would seem you've made a hash of things with your misguided nobility." George stood with another weighty sigh. "I think I'll take that drink now," he said, retrieving Jeremy's glass. "And I'm sure you could use another as well."

Chapter Three

Lily was not in much better shape than Jeremy the morning after the Haverford ball and ambush proposal – for how else could she describe the event but as an ambush? She felt rather like a victim of a surprise attack.

As she lay in her bed that morning, following her night of sleepless pacing, she cursed the fact that she had no access to even a spot of claret to calm her nerves – brandied tea would have been far preferable, but she'd learned long ago from George that their father kept the side tables locked tightly to prevent pilfering. Her racing mind had not ceased its brutal pace since the unexpected proposal, and what she wouldn't give for some relief from the creeping shadow of despair hovering at the periphery of her thoughts.

Not for the first time she raised her hand and stared, bewildered, at the cluster of diamonds and gold adorning her finger. Even her unpracticed eye could recognize the craftsmanship and likely cost of such a piece. But, rather than the thrill most other Society women would feel in her position, Lily felt like an imposter of the worst sort.

The echoes of shock had nearly deafened her to her father's toast congratulating her on the engagement (during which—purely by the grace of God—Lily narrowly escaped a mortifying fainting spell induced by the weight of all those eyes upon her). Afterward, William Monmouth, Marquess of Townsend – *Townsend,* she reminded herself how he'd bid her call him simply "Townsend" now that they were engaged to be married—had explained how he'd watched her over the past several months and decided with her beauty, charm, and "affable disposition" that she would make his perfect marchioness. He'd shortly thereafter contacted her father and the two of them made arrangements and negotiated the terms of her dowry over the ensuing weeks.

"Isn't it such a lovely surprise?" her mother had asked, excited to the point that her voice reached an entirely new register. Lily could only stare dumbly at the ring on her hand and count the minutes until she could feign exhaustion and be taken home; that was if a true case of the vapors didn't strike first. She couldn't breathe, she couldn't think with all those people staring at her and vying for the opportunity to congratulate her on the advantageous match. Especially when, in reality, she'd had no part in this. No say. Nor any desire to be thrust into such a situation.

After having the silent hours and peace of early morning to mull it over, Lily recognized how, logically, she should be pleased. What girl would not wish to be a marchioness? Her mother had quizzed her on the peerage enough that Lily recognized the weight the Townsend title bore. Being the wife of such a man would give her social standing and influence the likes of which she'd never dreamed…then again, nor had she ever desired those things.

Still, Lily experienced an undeniable sting in her heart. Her parents had not so much as mentioned their machinations to her. No sooner had she been formally introduced to the man than she'd had this ring thrust upon her finger and been announced as his betrothed. In front of an enormous crowd. She imagined now that this was how chattel at auction must feel if the poor beasts were aware of their lowly circumstances. Nothing about it sat well with her.

Despite the excitement and crush of the crowd—or, rather, because of it—Lily's eyes had been drawn to look for Jeremy's tall, dark figure on the outskirts of the ballroom. She'd been able to catch a brief glimpse of him as he ducked out one of the doors leading to the veranda – there'd been no mistaking the breadth of his retreating shoulders. Lily's heart had sunk further. Her hands and feet went numb until she could no longer feel the weight of the marquess's ring on her finger. She doubted Jeremy had even stayed long enough to witness the proposal. If he had, then surely he would have stayed to congratulate her? Surely he would have been there to help guard her against the swarming crowd?

But, no.

That was no longer his job.

It had never been his job; not really.

Lily heaved a heavy, unladylike sigh and hoisted herself from the bed to ring for her maid. It was still early, but it was not helping her nerves any by remaining locked in her room, pacing and talking to herself like a batty old spinster.

Once she'd changed into a pale pink sprigged muslin dress trimmed with white lace and her maid had plaited and tamed her wavy golden hair into a smart knot at the nape of her neck, Lily went down to break her fast in the conservatory. She bounced down the stairs in an attempt to inject some levity into her heavy thoughts and heart, her footsteps muffled by the thick runner covering each step.

If she could bring herself to let go of her girlish fantasies of love – her infatuation with Jeremy—then, perhaps, she could eventually get on well with Townsend. If she could convince him to respect her fears of crowded spaces, then…maybe he'd allow her to spend more time in the open air of the country. Surely such a man owned at least a few country homes. Lily wasn't picky. She needed only the air and nature to feel truly at home.

Yes.

That had to be the compromise that would make this work. She'd speak with Townsend and get him to understand what a trial it was for her to be in Town—that it was no small dislike of social functions which made her feel this way, but a physical terror which crippled her if not dealt with properly.

And she'd give up her silly infatuation with Jeremy. She didn't have a choice.

As much as it would pain her to do so…as much as she would feel the loss of his presence in her life and the role that he'd adopted…it was something that must be done.

When she reached the bottom of the curved stairway, she collided with a large figure turning the corner from the library.

"Georgie!" she exclaimed breathlessly; he caught her shoulders in his hands to steady her…though he seemed to need more steadying than she. Lily squinted up into his face and noted the glassy sheen to his bright green eyes. "Have you been drinking?" she accused. It was impossible not to smell the spirits on her brother's breath as he held her mere arms' distance away from his chest.

"Lily!" he laughed, seeming either not to have heard her inquiry, or ignored it entirely. "My little sister, the soon-to-be marchioness." He smiled his lop-sided grin and rubbed her upper arms affectionately. "How does the bride feel this morning, hm? I bet you can't wait to start the wedding planning." George turned and linked her arm with his; correctly assuming she was coming down for breakfast and guiding her to the conservatory. She was still unused to seeing her elder brother in residence. A typical bachelor and heir nearing his thirtieth year, George had rented rooms on St. James's Place for quite some time; however, he'd spent the last several weeks at Stratford House while the papering on the walls was being redone. Lily had come to enjoy a measure of solitude with George on his own and Simon away at university. Though she loved both her siblings, having a brother around once more to pester her wasn't the most ideal of circumstances.

The sliver of clarity and optimism Lily had begun to feel quickly withered away. She should have guessed that her engagement would have been all anyone wanted to discuss.

"Actually…I'm just trying to absorb the entire situation. It was all rather unexpected."

"That was the plan. Mother and Lady Haverford thought you might get a thrill from the surprise engagement. I understand Townsend was rather keen to have it at the ball."

Lily nearly tripped over her own feet. "They…Mother and Father encouraged such a public spectacle?" Lily experienced a slowly growing sense of betrayal.

She'd known her family believed her panics to be overreactions, but she hadn't thought they discounted her feelings entirely—let alone that they'd be so unwilling to respect her that they'd condone the proposal as it had happened.

First, they planned her future by betrothing her to a man to whom she'd never actually spoken, and then they allowed that man to make a very public spectacle of what was usually a very private event.

"You seemed to handle it well enough," George replied dismissively as they entered the conservatory. Servants alerted by Lily's maid had already worked to prepare breakfast. A single place was set at the small wrought iron table, but another place-setting was laid quickly and seamlessly as soon as they noted George was accompanying her. He led Lily to her seat and then took his place across from her. Footmen bearing trays of toast and fruit approached; they offered softboiled eggs and tea. Lily took her time selecting a triangle of toast and coating it in strawberry preserves. She watched from beneath her lashes as George waived away all offers of food, but accepted the strong, dark breakfast tea.

"Might I ask where you ran off to this morning?" she prodded while he added four lumps of sugar to his cup and stirred more vigorously than was perhaps necessary. Like most little sisters, she considered herself a master at needling her brother where it bothered him most.

Instead of answering, however, George proceeded to take a long, scalding draught of tea. She supposed he really must not want to discuss his inebriation with her if he was willing to suffer a burned mouth and throat.

Lily barely resisted the urge to smile and, instead, took a small bite of toast. As the only sister to two brothers, she'd long since perfected the art of waiting out their stubbornness. She was very good at being patient. George would finish the tea sooner or later and then he'd have to answer her question.

Or not.

"Are you happy with the match, Lily?" His eyes searched her face with such intensity that it unnerved her. The suddenness of the change in topic threw her with the same jolting effect as being tossed from a horse.

"I—I do not really know the marquess, so I do not feel as if I am qualified to answer that just yet." Seeing that this did not assuage whatever curiosities George was feeling, she added, "I'm sure Mother and Father wouldn't have made the match had they not believed I'd be content. Someday..."

George leaned back in his chair and signaled for more tea to be poured. The next comment was uttered with negligent nonchalance: "Is there...no other match you might've preferred?"

Lily nearly choked on the bite of toast. The dry bread lodged in her throat as she frantically reached for her teacup and inhaled an unlady-like gulp.

"What?" she sputtered. "Why would you ask that?"

It could have been the tears in her eyes from coughing, but Lily would almost have sworn that George's mouth tipped slightly in a sad smile. "Just curious, I suppose."

Lily dabbed at her mouth with her napkin, taking those few precious moments to decide how to respond. Mentioning Jeremy would only earn her ridicule from her elder brother. And it was entirely pointless, besides. Jeremy was her friend, while she was engaged to another man. Saying anything now would prove utterly useless except to cause her a headache to go with her heartache. Lily sat up straighter in her chair and used her most convincing tone. "No one in particular."

George's catlike green eyes examined her very intently over the rim of his teacup, but she refused to squirm beneath his interrogation. The tea and conversation seemed to be taking effect because his eyes were slowly beginning to return to their usual sharpness.

Hoping it did not make her as much of a coward as she felt, Lily finally broke their eye contact and turned to the wall of windows. Through the great panes of clear glass, warm morning sunlight was filtering into the conservatory, glazing each potted plant and frond a brilliant shade of verdant green. Lily loved this room. It was her fa-vorite place in their townhouse because it reminded her of their country home. Other than the nearby parks—which, depending upon the time of day, were often congested—there was so little green and even less fresh air in London.

To think she'd begun this Season with the hopes for a quick, relatively tame round of the usual events; anticipating a quick return home to Kent. She was, after all, becoming a bit long in the tooth, so to speak, as far as unwed women were concerned. A few more years and she'd have been considered firmly upon the shelf and might have been able to get away with rusticating in peace.

Her nature wasn't antisocial in the least; in fact, it had been remarked upon by more than one matron that she was possessed of a kind, uncommonly honest and cheerful disposition. She could attend a small dinner party, a quaint gathering of close friends, and, depending upon the turnout, even the odd country dance. But no matter how she'd cried as a young girl or how often she'd been physically overcome with terror in a crowded room, her mother had refused to believe her daughter was experiencing anything other than youthful defiance when she attempted to beg off an event.

To brand Lily with anything resembling a nervous condition could spell social disaster.

So, her parents and even George continued to shove Lily out of her comfortable corner of Kent, deny the truth of her feelings, and grudgingly promise her a few quiet months in the country in return for a good performance in Town during the Season.

All Lily wanted was to be home.

As much as she enjoyed this conservatory, it held no candle to the rolling fields of green and wildflowers in Kent. Bridleton Manor was her true home. The home of her heart and her soul.

Unbidden, memories of Jeremy wove their way through her thoughts of her family's country estate. He'd been as much a fixture of her childhood as the dirt beneath her fingernails after spending the afternoon picking wildflowers; the late-afternoon rains briefly misting the sheep-laden fields; the smell of leather and musty parchment of the library.

It made her heartsick to think that she'd never relieve herself of this grief that nothing would ever be the same, because she would certainly never be able to recall a single important childhood memory in which he didn't feature.

Her reverie was halted as a servant entered and offered George a calling card on a small silver salver. George polished off the last of his tea and took the card. Skimming it, his sandy eyebrows rose – in surprise or amusement, Lily was unsure—and he bid the servant to show their guest to the parlor and inform him they would join him presently.

"Who has arrived?" Lily asked, confused. It was barely half past eleven in the morning—still fairly early for any callers as far as the *ton* was concerned. George stood and offered her his hand.

"You'll see, dear sister."

Chapter Four

Jeremy tapped the silver-capped head of Sommerfeld's frivolous walking cane against his shoulder as he stared out the window of the blue parlor in Stratford House. He still remembered the day his friend had purchased the cane as a joke prop back when they were at university. Unfortunately for everyone else, Sommerfeld had taken a liking to it. Now, he carried the dratted thing everywhere…and tended to forget where he left it after a few glasses of brandy. Jeremy held the weighted handle up to his face. The snarling lion's head was crafted with impressive detail and the eyes were filled with chips of garnet. It was entirely unnecessary for a man not even in his thirtieth year and in perfect physical condition in the prime of his life. Then again, Sommerfeld had always enjoyed the attention of affected eccentricity.

Jeremy had noticed the sodding cane shortly after his friend had taken his leave. Jeremy sat in his study glaring at it, weighing the choices of finishing the drink in his hand or taking a cold bath and a strong tea, making himself presentable, and heading over to Stratford House to return it.

The latter option afforded the opportunity to bump into Lily.

It was another fist to the gut to realize that those times would come ever more infrequently—if at all after she was wed. He didn't know a man alive who would be lax about his wife carrying on a close relationship with a bachelor.

Jeremy promptly set down his full glass of brandy, stoppered the decanter, and called for the maids to draw a freezing bath and have his valet make sure his jacket was pressed.

Little more than an hour later—after being ill only once from the past twelve hours of overindulgence—Jeremy turned at the creak of the door and in walked Lily and her brother. The sight of her released a fresh wave of pain and anger, like grinding salt into an open wound…with shards of glass for good measure. He clenched his jaw against the crashing emotions—an attempt to dam the rising, suffocating tide of words he'd always wanted to say and now would certainly never allow to cross his lips. He'd drown beneath them before he ruined the future which lay ahead of her. Instead, Jeremy focused on the only thing upon which his eyes could focus: Lily.

To him, she'd always been beautiful, but she seemed to glow that morning; maybe because he knew she was well and truly out of his reach now. People did tend to see the beauty in things they knew would forever be outside of their grasp, didn't they?

The dusty pink of her frock made her dewy skin rosy with health and life, and it didn't take much for his imagination to stray to an all-too-familiar territory in which he pictured that flush on every inch of perfect, pale flesh. Her golden hair was swept back behind her head, leaving her swan-like neck deliciously naked and unadorned. Her wide mouth with its full lips smiled when she saw him, causing his stomach to perform a familiar flip. With her coloring and her petite, slender form, she would have been considered the model of an English Rose, save for that mouth. There was no delicate Cupid's bow that popular poets seemed so inclined to immortalize in their writings. Rather, her mouth was expressive with full, pink lips, and when she smiled…her whole face lit as if from within. Jeremy had always been grateful she'd never mastered the demure coyness of the other debutantes and, instead, smiled with her soul and revealed a flash of pearly teeth.

Of their own volition, his eyes darted down to his favorite little freckle on the top of her breast, and he thanked God for small favors when he was greeted by the dainty mark of his fantasies.

"There's my cane. I knew I was missing something, but I couldn't figure out what it was." Thankfully, Sommerfeld interrupted Jeremy's daydream before it progressed any further.

"Right, yes," he cleared his throat as he tossed the cane up and caught it about the middle. "I thought you might need this, you know, for your bum leg and all."

"Bugger off," Sommerfeld chuckled and took the walking stick. They'd long since given up trying not to curse in Lily's presence – probably because they quickly learned they could be out-cursed by a creative thirteen-year-old chit.

Jeremy turned to Lily and inclined his head in greeting. He modulated his voice very carefully when he spoke to her.

"Lily…I hear congratulations are in order."

She didn't give him a verbal reply, but Jeremy knew her well enough to recognize that her grateful smile did not quite meet her eyes. The usual glitter in her emerald irises was dulled.

He took her hand to kiss her middle knuckle out of habit, but what he found there stopped him mid-action. A cold, circular cluster of diamonds flashed mockingly in the morning sunlight. The bauble was undoubtedly a literally shining example of her new fiancé's wealth and stature.

It was also quite obviously well out of the range of anything Jeremy could ever have afforded while still managing to keep on his current staff at both his London townhouse and country estate.

For years.

He recovered in what he hoped was a relatively smooth manner and turned to Sommerfeld. "Our little Lily, a marchioness! Who would have thought?"

He bowed over her hand and released her without kissing it. While a perfectly acceptable exchange in the eyes of Society, it still felt as if a bit of him chipped off in the process.

Lily clasped her hands tightly in front of her, covering the ring with her right hand. The setting bit into her opposite palm, but she welcomed the sting. Anything to help take her mind off of how different Jemmy seemed that morning. She felt silly about it, but she experienced the lack of his kiss on the back of her hand as keenly as a missing limb.

Did he think they were no longer permitted to be friends now that she'd been betrothed? The thought cut her deeply.

She turned to her brother and watched as he toyed with that useless cane of his. Suddenly, everything clicked together. George had left the cane home the previous evening before they went to the ball – only after their mother demanded he do so upon threat of histrionics – and the only way it could have gotten into Jemmy's possession was if George had gone over to his townhouse earlier that morning.

Her eyes narrowed as she looked between the men. George was remarkably soberer since she'd first bumped into him and Jemmy seemed, well, like Jemmy. Composed. Polite. Charming. A closer inspection, however, revealed faint shadows beneath his eyes. His features were drawn as if sleep had eluded him. Something about him seemed amiss even though he was groomed and dressed for a proper Town call. He'd donned an impeccably knotted white cravat, brushed blue jacket, gray waistcoat and breeches, and tall shiny black boots.

It was entirely inappropriate, but, not for the first time, Lily found herself admiring the cut of those breeches and pondered the solid muscle required to fill them out thusly. No doubt all the riding he did afforded him the benefit of such a shape. Lily felt a flush creeping up her throat and she placed her hand over the warming flesh. How improper for her, a betrothed woman, to be ogling him thusly. Unwanted betrothal or not, she had to get herself under control. She was an engaged woman, whether or not she wished to be.

She wrenched her eyes back up to his face, though her flushing skin was given no reprieve. His raven-wing hair curled at his temples and fell long enough to brush past the collar of his coat. As always, her fingers itched to know whether it was as soft as it appeared.

The hum of conversation died away and Lily realized both of the men in the room were looking at her as if waiting for a response. Her throat flushed an even deeper shade of pink and she chided herself for her improper examination of Jeremy.

"I beg your pardon?" she asked as she attempted to regain her composure. Jemmy smiled his heart-stirring smile and kindly repeated himself.

"I mentioned it's a lovely morning and thought I would invite you and your brother to take some air in the park. Georgie here doesn't feel up to the outing." He knew very well she couldn't resist any opportunity to enjoy a bit of air and sunshine, even as hazy as the London air often was.

"Yes, please!" Not needing any further encouragement, Lily clapped her hands together and made to leave the room for her bonnet and pelisse. "You stay and rest, Georgie. I'll ask Mary to join us."

And with that, she hurried off in a flurry of excited skirts to round up her maid.

Jeremy was staring after Lily when there was a tap on his shoulder. The snarling silver lion's head of Sommerfeld's cane was resting there.

"I hope you know what you're doing, my friend," he said soberly. Jeremy brushed him off.

"I'm a man grown; I think I can handle this situation."

Sommerfeld quirked a brow as if to say *? Because I didn't see very good coping skills earlier this morning.* Jeremy rolled his eyes. "I'm saying goodbye, Georgie. At least let me have that much." He eyed Jeremy for a moment before clapping a sympathetic hand on his shoulder and exiting the room without another word.

Half an hour later, Jeremy helped Lily step down from the hired hack. The Stratford butler had offered to ready the carriage for their outing, but she'd declined, arguing it would have taken longer to prepare the staff, animals, and the conveyance than it would to stop a passing hackney. If he'd needed one more reason to adore her, then her practicality and eagerness to spend time out of doors were just a few more tallies in that column. Unfortunately.

They settled into a comfortable pace and Lily's maid, Mary, followed them at a distance close enough for a sense of propriety, but far enough that she couldn't overhear their conversation.

With each step they took on the path, the gravel crunching beneath their feet, Jeremy experienced the chilling realization he was growing ever closer to relinquishing Lily forever—whether she realized it or not. It left him feeling gutted and hollow. In time, he knew he'd feel her loss less keenly. Or so he hoped. He'd likely move on enough to do his duty, marry another woman with a small, but helpful, dowry, and get a couple of children on her.

And he and Lily would likely hardly ever see one another again.

There would be no more summers spent split between their close-ly-situated ancestral homes. No more relaxed picnics near the river. No more of Lily's bright, easy laughter filling the halls.

She'd likely hardly set foot in the Stratford country estate in Kent again, let alone visit his own home, Rosehall. He made a mental note to send her gentle silver mare to whatever new country estate her husband held, and Jeremy had an inkling there would be more than one.

"You're so quiet, Jemmy," Lily commented lightly, halting his dour train of thought.

He looked down at her face, still glowing in the morning sunlight filtering through the misty sheet of London clouds. He couldn't help but smile down at her. God how he would miss this; this easiness… how comfortable the two of them were together. He doubted if he spent the next fifty years with another woman as his wife, he'd never capture the same experience. There was something to be said for af-fection fostered in the cradle.

"You seem to have recovered a bit better than my brother from whatever trouble the two of you got yourselves into this morning." A beautiful, mischievous smile spread across her face, revealing her even, white pearls of teeth. Jeremy couldn't stop himself from return-ing it. He should have known she'd figure it out – she was an ex-tremely intelligent, observant woman. "Aside from your hand, that is," she said as she nodded at his bandaged left hand.

They strolled past another couple and each pair nodded polite, silent acknowledgments.

"It would seem we neither of us is quite past the age where we don't get into trouble now and again," he finally replied; for what else was there for him to say? That his injury had been due to his inability to cope with witnessing her engagement? That her brother had come across him after a drunken stupor induced by grief and rage? That he'd confessed to a lifetime of loving this woman before him? And that he'd only just learned that he could have had it all, had he not been such a bloody coward?

Her emerald-hued eyes bore into him. She knew there was more to the story—she knew him too well to believe his pathetic excuse – but he did not bother to elaborate. Instead, he placed his hand over her much smaller one currently hooked about the crook of his opposite elbow. Her eyes broke their inquisitive contact and she turned her attention to the path they traversed. The angle hid her face beneath the curved brim of her beribboned bonnet. She'd donned a pelisse several shades darker than her dress, and he'd donned his doeskin gloves, but Jeremy remained attuned to the whisper of heat seeping from her flesh to his palm. Jeremy did his best to swallow past the tightness in his throat.

There were a good number of people visiting the park that morning and Lily seemed to be managing her panic well. He knew she usually did better in the open air and not crammed into an overstuffed ballroom with hardly enough space to move one's elbows.

He wondered somewhat wistfully if her fiancé would take his place during the first waltz, or if she'd free up the dance entirely for some stranger to claim. Would he protect her and comfort her if her panic set in?

He gave himself a strong mental shake. This was none of his business. Though the words were like glass on his tongue, he knew he needed to try to inject some normalcy into the outing.

"Have you given any thought to when you might want to have the wed—"

"Might we not discuss the wedding?" she cut him off brusquely. "Or the engagement?" Her eyes pled with him in a way that wrung his heart like a sopping cloth. "Please?" she asked more gently. He patted her hand in assent, though she surprised him by continuing.

"It has not been a full day since it happened and it seems to be all that anyone wants to talk about with me. I'm not...I'm not sure enough of how I feel about it to reply to the queries with any certainty. I don't even know the marquess..." she trailed off. Jeremy could have been mistaken, but he thought he noted a hint of melancholy. Part of him wanted to latch onto it—the part that had burned for so long to have more than a friendship with Lily—but the rational side of his consciousness told him it would only kill him in the end.

"Then we shan't discuss it," he said firmly. Their boots crunched along the gravel path as they continued on in companionable silence. As much as he loved the sound of Lily's laughter, these pleasant quiet times would be some of the most missed.

As teenagers, they'd once spent an entire week reading together in the library of Rosehall to pass the rainy late-spring days. To be more accurate, Lily had done most of the reading while Jeremy watched her over the edge of the book in his hands; periodically flipping pages so it appeared as if he were making progress. He doubted she was aware, but Lily pulled faces when she read. She would smile, tug that full lower lip between her perfect teeth, and press her fingertips to her mouth when she read something particularly moving. That week had been a mixture of pleasure and torture. Together, in the peaceful house with their families engaged in similarly quiet, rainy-day activities, it felt as if the two of them lived alone. The incessant rain created a cocoon around Jeremy's intimate little fantasy and he knew in that moment that he was well and truly lost.

Lily interrupted his musings with a sudden, light laugh. "Do you recall how you once pushed me in the stream because I wouldn't leave you and Georgie alone when you were trying to fish?"

The clarity of the memory was startling, given the fact that it was not one he'd dusted off in many years.

Jeremy experienced the warm fragrant breeze of the early summer morning as it dragged gentle fingers across his cheeks. He'd likely been no more than fifteen, which made Lily eleven years of age. Home on break from school, he and young Sommerfeld were busy engaging in the delights and freedoms cherished by so many privileged sons of their class: hell-raising, the enjoyment of flirting with pretty young women in the village, riding, and occasionally fishing at the stream which fed the secluded lake on Shefford property.

The sun wasn't yet high enough in the clear blue sky to make for poor fishing, so he'd been eager to enjoy the peace and show up Sommerfeld in a little competition. They'd long since doffed their coats and rolled up their fine linen shirtsleeves. Jeremy knew his mother would have his head if he wrecked another of his good shirts. She was already fretting that they'd have to provide him with several new wardrobes in the coming year if he continued the same rate of growth he'd achieved in the last six months alone. While Sommerfeld was still slightly taller than he, Jeremy's frame had begun to fill out and he showed signs of being unfashionably tall and muscular. Not ideal for the ballroom, but perfect for hands-on country living, and this suited Jeremy just fine.

"First to three wins?" Jeremy asked as he fiddled with his line.

"Loser has to streak bare-arsed across the West fields," Sommerfeld chuckled mirthfully at his wit. Jeremy's nose wrinkled in distaste. Half of Rosehall overlooked those fields. Someone was bound to catch an eyeful of whichever one of them lost. His mother would be exasperated, but likely chuckle over it later with his father. Jeremy would be surprised if Sommerfeld's mother, the countess, didn't take to her bed from shock and embarrassment. However, if any of the maids saw, that was something else entirely. It was one thing to chat up a pretty girl, but he was still young enough to be bashful at the prospect of baring it all for anyone to see and gossip about.

He might have protested the stakes more had he not been so confident about his fishing abilities.

The young men clasped hands and prepared to cast their lines just before a cacophony of snapping branches, a yelp, and a flurry of startled wings disturbed their peace. Both of their heads whipped around, already knowing what they would find.

"Aren't you supposed to be having lessons?" Sommerfeld groaned and scrubbed a hand across his face.

There, in a heap on the ground attempting to untangle her skirts and scrape a tangle of golden curls and leaves from her face, was Lily.

"You promised to take me fishing with you," she accused, huffing a lock of hair from her eyes. "It makes it difficult to follow through on your promise when you sneak out of the house early." The glare she sent her brother made Jeremy grateful for the first time that he was an only child.

Sommerfeld planted a hand on his hip and jabbed the base of his fishing pole in the spongy earth, showing no sympathy for his younger sister—who had lately taken a spill from a low-hanging tree limb—as she scrambled to her feet and plucked twigs from the fabric of her pinafore and frightfully yellow dress. Jeremy spotted several snags which would surely make the countess vibrate with irritation. She loathed the fact that her only daughter preferred frolicking out of doors, bothering the older boys to no end, to her lessons in manners and deportment. Jeremy couldn't blame Lily and, whereas Sommerfeld wanted nothing more than to escape his sister's hounding, Jeremy felt a pang of sympathy for the lack of choices and freedoms she was allowed. He, for one, would have preferred death over memorization of Debrett's, tea etiquette, and needlework.

"If you have a break from lessons, then why can't I?" Lily asked, planting her fists on her own slim, girlish hips.

"Because I'm on break from school," Sommerfeld sighed. "You take your lessons at home; it's not the same thing."

"Well," Lily grumbled, making her way over to them and poking through the basket in which they carried their supplies; "I don't see why it should be any different."

"Of course you don't," Sommerfeld snapped as he toed the lid of the basket shut. Lily snatched back her hand. "Go home, Lily."

She glared up at her elder brother and, with the indignant righteousness only truly achieved by the very young or the sincerely stupid, she reiterated, "You. Promised."

"Just let her stay," Jeremy chimed in, forestalling further sibling squabbling. In reply, Sommerfeld rolled his eyes and went back to readying his pole; Lily grinned up at him, her emerald eyes glittering with gratitude. She was still only a child and already showed signs of the beauty she would become, and much of it lay in her genuine smile and the kindness of her heart…when she wasn't trying her hardest to drive them mad.

Lily scurried over to the other side of Jeremy—better to be further away from her brother—and peered over the grassy edge of the riverbank.

"What are you using for bait?" The question was directed at her shimmering reflection.

"I have a lure," Jeremy explained patiently, holding the line for her to examine the jig he'd crafted from bits of string and scraps of bright feathers from one of his mother's old hats.

"A lot of good that'll do for him," Sommerfeld snorted while readjusting his uncomplicated set-up with a curved hook and small piece of cheese pilfered from the kitchens. He swore there was nothing better than the simplicity of this rig.

"We'll see about that," Jeremy countered.

"W-will you really run naked through the fields if you lose, Jemmy?" Lily's cheeks, still rounded by childhood, were aflame as she asked the question. Of course, she would have overheard their challenge from her perch in the nearby tree. Jeremy felt his face begin to warm. He did the only rational thing a fifteen-year-old lad could do: He laughed off the question, told Lily she really could be a nuisance, and shifted his hip just enough to send her backward one step and into the chilly stream with another yelp.

"I was an ass," Jeremy growled more to himself as his mind returned to the present. "We were lucky you didn't drown."

"Don't be so dramatic. The water was barely to my waist."

"Still."

They continued a few more paces before she spoke again. "I wish I'd known this past summer would be my last in Kent."

The admission caused an ache to radiate from deep inside Jeremy's chest.

I, as well, he thought morosely.

"Perhaps I can visit in spring when the lambs are due?" she asked hopefully. The glitter in her emerald eyes was so like when she'd been a child that it caused him physical pain. It was a miracle he was still upright.

"You're always welcome. Always." Jeremy firmly pressed his hand upon hers once more to convey everything he couldn't vocalize. He knew Lily's favorite time of year was when the pastures were filled with bouncy white lambs, unsteady on their gangly limbs and bleating for their mothers. To be fair, the lambs always seemed enamored of her as well. She'd resembled a mother duck with a trail of her offspring following her unquestioningly. He couldn't blame them. If she held his head cushioned in her lap and stroked his hair, then he would probably have followed her like that too. (Who was he kidding? He already did that...)

"It still won't be the same. Not really." This time, Jeremy was certain there was sadness in her voice. Whether it was for the loss of her relative freedom as an unwed young woman, the fact that she wouldn't be spending summers with their families any longer, or – damn his pathetic hopefulness—because she would not be seeing as much of him, Jeremy was unsure.

Whatever hollow reassuring words he'd been about to say died in his throat with the growing thunder of approaching hoofbeats. Unless he was mistaken, someone was riding at a reckless pace in a park full of people; and, from the sound of it, he was coming right toward them.

With only a second to react, Jeremy yanked Lily to his chest and held her against the length of his body. He spun them away just as a horse and rider burst through a copse of bushes to their left. The animal's shod hooves scrambled on the gravel path and Lily's maid released a scream of surprise behind them. The black-clad rider sawed on the reins as the horse hit the grass and skidded. He turned the great black beast in tight circles and had the gall to laugh as he apologized for the near miss.

"Forgive me! Goliath is a bit tightly-strung and I didn't realize there was anyone on this path."

"Are you bloody insane?" bellowed Jeremy.

Lily could hear as much as she felt the hammering of Jeremy's heart against her cheek; its thumping pace matched hers almost beat for beat, though she doubted the reasons were the same.

The near miss with the horse and rider had been shocking, but, against all logic, the experience of Jeremy's warm, taut body pressed against the length of her was an even greater surprise. He had one steely arm around the middle of her back, clutching her to him as if he was afraid she'd be ripped from him. His other hand cupped the back of her head, nestling her face against the hard wall of his broad chest. Lily closed her eyes and reveled in his scent—a mixture of warm male skin, leather, and soap. Very no-nonsense and unpretentious, just like Jeremy.

"I beg your pardon?" the rider asked from above them; his tone indicated disbelief that his earlier apology hadn't sufficed.

Still, Jeremy held her against him.

Protecting her.

She recognized in the time between one heartbeat and the next that she would probably not have another chance to do so, so Lily carefully unclenched one of her fists and splayed her fingers, pressing her palm against his abdomen. Beneath the layers of his waistcoat and crisp undershirt, she felt more warmth and powerful muscles. It would appear that the only soft part of Jeremy was his personality when confronted with helpless animals.

"You're lucky no one was killed. Allowing a horse like that to have his head in a public park filled with pedestrians? Only a poor rider or an idiot would allow such a thing." Jeremy had whipped out his most authoritative tone; something Lily had never experienced. His timbre dropped and his voice rumbled against her cheek, setting free some as-yet undiscovered part of her. An irrational thrill raced up and down her spine. She could feel the coiled tension against every point of her that touched him.

He felt dangerous.

It was exciting.

Jeremy, seemingly reminded of her presence by her shiver, finally freed Lily from his embrace and stepped back. He didn't release her; probably afraid she might swoon.

Quite the contrary.

She felt more exhilarated and alive than ever before.

She reached up to readjust her bonnet and noticed her hands were trembling. Jeremy's dark eyes didn't miss her shaking fingers and he took her gloved hands in his own. No doubt he mistook it for fear, but the heat beginning to spread throughout Lily's body said otherwise.

"M'lady!" Mary rushed up to them. "Are you all right?"

"Yes, Mary. I'm fine," Lily replied more breathlessly than she'd intended.

"My Lady Stratford?"

Lily turned and looked up at the rider…and into the face of her fiancé.

Chapter Five

If Lily hadn't been shocked by a careening horse nearly trampling them, then she certainly was by the fact that her new betrothed had been the one steering the beast.

"Lord Townsend?" Lily was still attempting to shake the Jeremy-scented fog from her brain. Townsend dismounted and steadied his side-stepping horse. The great black beast tossed its head in impatience, the whites showing in the corners of its fathomless eyes. Gripping the reins with a firm hand, the marquess walked the animal in one final circle before approaching them.

"I did not realize it was you. You appear overwrought; I do hope you were not overly frightened," Townsend offered, though he did not turn from his horse, giving it several firm pats on its thick, sweating neck.

Lily shook her head in response. She didn't think he would be so calm if he knew her physical reaction had been to another man and not the horse.

Then again, if she were wise, she probably should have been equally afraid of both.

That morning, the marquess was dressed in buff buckskin breeches and tall polished riding boots. His well-fitted black riding jacket gleamed with golden buttons. His dark blond hair was windblown from the ride, and a few strands of silver streaked back from his temples and lent him a dignified air. For a man nearing his fortieth year, he was an objectively fine physical specimen. His nose was perfectly straight and his high cheekbones spoke of centuries of good breeding; his ice-blue eyes were piercing and intelligent. However, he did nothing to stir her blood like the darker man at her side did. Lily shoved away the comparison and prodded her manners to the forefront.

"May I present William Monmouth, The Most Honorable Marquess of Townsend?" She held out an upturned hand, gesturing to Jeremy, "My lord, this is a family friend, Jeremy Balfour, Baron Shefford—" She was stunned into abrupt silence when Townsend snatched her hand and bowed over it, pressing a lingering kiss to the sensitive flesh on the underside of her wrist.

It was an extremely intimate, possessive gesture for having only been formally introduced less than twelve hours prior—regardless of any marriage agreement. Lily was mortified, but not so much as when the marquess eyed Jeremy and spoke with his lips still hovering just above her flesh.

"I'm Lady Stratford's betrothed."

Jeremy saw nothing past the scarlet red haze clouding his vision.

He'd been close to pulverizing the man for nearly maiming or killing them, but nothing compared to the blinding rage he experienced when the man kissed Lily's wrist. He was one breath away from roaring at the unfairness of it all. How many years had he dreamt of what it would be like to taste her racing pulse on that very same tender patch of skin?

Unfortunately, his good breeding forced him to incline his head in greeting rather than knock the man's teeth in. "A pleasure." Jeremy wasn't certain his tone was convincing. He felt a little kick of pride when Lily snatched her hand back from the man.

What would the marquess make of his betrothed on a stroll in the park with another man? Jeremy knew he wouldn't stomach such a thing if Lily were his; let alone the murder that would follow if he'd caught another man embracing her. He filed away the memory of Lily's soft curves against him for later and crossed his arms over his chest.

Either it didn't bother the marquess or he thought a baron was no contest to the dangling carrot labeled "marchioness," but the man didn't seem the least disturbed at having found Lily with Jeremy.

"Enjoying the morning?" he began genially. "The fresh air is very becoming on you," the marquess complimented Lily, those pale eyes of his sweeping the length of her body.

Jeremy's fists clenched reflexively.

"Thank you, my lord, I—"

"How fortuitous that we've met here," he said, cutting Lily off. He corrected his antsy horse with a tug on the reins. "I was going to call upon you at your home later this afternoon, but you've saved me the trip." He shot her what Jeremy supposed was intended to be a devilish smile. Jeremy's skin crawled. "I've received an invitation from my cousin to visit him in his home in Venice. He's generously offered for us to stay for a portion of the honeymoon. The only catch is that we will need to be married in six weeks' time if we're to join him while he's still in residence there."

As in tune as he was with Lily's every move and word, Jeremy immediately noticed how her hands clasped together in a white-knuckled grip; the corner of her mouth twitched downward for a fraction of a second before she propped it up once more.

"So soon?" she asked. "I was hoping we could…get to know one another a bit better before the wedding…" The marquess waved her words away as if they were as inconsequential as a gnat.

"We have the rest of our lives to get to know one another." This seemed to be all the explanation he felt was necessary. He patted his horse on its velvety black nose before moving to mount it once more. "I'll send a note round to your parents and inform them of the situation. I trust you'll manage the planning without issue. I look forward to seeing what you design."

Jeremy watched Lily's shoulders slump a fraction of an inch and it made him ache.

"You will not be taking part in the planning?" she asked in a small voice that gutted Jeremy. All he could do was stand and watch. He technically had no business being there for this conversation, let alone commenting.

"Of course not!" Townsend laughed as he held the horse – anxious now that it had the weight of a rider on its back once more – in check with a tight rein. "I have business of my own to which I must attend. Surprise me. Spare no expense!" With a cursory nod in Jeremy's general direction, he released the horse and kicked it forward. They were off in a scramble of gravel and clumps of grass.

*****

Lily had been so deflated after Townsend took his leave that she'd asked Jeremy to escort her back to the townhouse. The reality of her situation penetrated her more deeply the closer they got to her home. Not only was she engaged to a stranger, but she was going to marry said stranger in only a matter of weeks. She hadn't had a traditional courtship and now even her betrothal would be rushed. Would nothing about this situation afford her any measure of comfort? She realized this was the reality for many women of her class, but she'd always hoped for more for her future—however naively.

Of course, Jeremy had noticed her silence and attempted to cheer her up on the way to the townhouse with some amusing commentary on the people they passed in their hackney, but Lily could not be motivated to participate in any banter. What had her well-meaning parents gotten her into?

It was early afternoon by the time they entered the parlor to find George and their mother in residence. George had his hat in his hand and appeared to be preparing to leave.

"Lily, dear!" Her mother stood and held out her hands to her daughter, beckoning her closer. "How are you this morning? Does it all still feel like a dream?" Her voice somehow managed to grow in volume, yet remain dreamy and wistful. Seemingly seeing Jeremy for the first time, she acknowledged him with a warm smile over Lily's shoulder, "Hello, Jeremy!" She slid into her habitual use of his given name in this informal setting. "Thank you for taking Lily for some air." Lily did her best not to feel like a spaniel who'd been taken for a trot in the garden.

"It was my pleasure," he replied before he and George exchanged grim, conspiratorial nods.

Lily glanced at Jeremy and her chest throbbed. She wondered if every one of the strings attaching him to her heart would ever be completely severed. The tangled web had been woven of years of affection and companionship and she didn't know if she would ever find her way out.

"We bumped into Townsend on our walk," Jeremy added suddenly. There wasn't time for Lily to analyze the glance George shot him before their mother began her string of questions.

"Oh, did you, now? And how is he? Does he seem excited about the wedding? We've been planning the proposal with him for weeks now, you know; he's had his eye on you for some time."

Lily felt an embarrassed flush rise to her cheeks. She smoothed out her skirts and traced the pattern on the rug with her eyes. "He has asked to set the wedding date for six weeks from now…so we can join his cousin in Venice during the honeymoon." Lily watched her mother's face shift from joy to horror and back again.

"So soon! But, how will we ever complete such a task in that amount of time?" She began short bursts of pacing to and fro as her words rambled on. "There are flowers and a *dress*, the wedding breakfast, invitations, goodness! The banns must be read immediately if we're to get them all in by the time of the wedding." It was a wonder her mother's legs didn't get caught in her skirts from all the spinning and turning. Was this a lesson she'd missed during finishing? Because Lily sincerely doubted she could accomplish such a feat.

"He said to spare no expense," Lily tried to add helpfully, but her mother continued to talk over her in her well-intentioned chatter.

"A list! I must begin a list." She looked at George, but he held up his hands to ward her off before she could enlist his assistance.

"I'm to meet some friends at my club," he laughed nervously. I'll leave the two of you to your planning." The countess hardly seemed to hear him and turned back to Lily.

"We will have to contact the marquess and obtain his schedule. He'll need to be present for some of the preparations."

"He's not going to help, Mother." Those words finally stalled her mother's chatter.

"Well of course he will, love," her mother laughed breathlessly, dismissing Lily's comment as an impossibility.

"If I may?" interjected Jeremy as he strode further into the room; he had always been so good at making sure Lily's overbearing family didn't dismiss her. "Townsend indicated he had business that would take him away from the wedding preparations." She resisted meeting Jeremy's eyes.   That had been a rather polite way to put her betrothed's dismissal of all that went into planning a Society wedding.

"Oh…" Her mother dropped heavily into the striped blue sofa. It was a testament to the weight of the blow that she sat with less than her usual grace. "Well, that is…a bit of a disappointment. I didn't think he would want to partake in every bit of the planning, but he should at least have some say on the menu…" Her voice trailed off.

The ensuing silence was filled with a hodgepodge of emotions. Lily watched George put up his indifferent mask—the one he wore when he knew it was wiser to remain silent than comment—and Lily had a very difficult time reading the grim set of Jeremy's mouth. A muscle twitched in his jaw though the rest of him seemed relaxed. Lily, herself, was becoming terrified at the prospect of wedding a perfect stranger and having to go through this process knowing so little about him and what he expected of her—above the basics, that is. Her mother just shook her head and fluttered her hands.

"We'll get on without him. I'm sure it'll still be lovely," her mother said, seemingly more to console herself than anything.

"I'll help."

Chapter Six

Three sets of eyes flew to Jeremy and, this time, the silence was a stunned one. Lily narrowed her eyes when she caught George giving a nearly imperceptible shake of his head as Jeremy began to elaborate.

"My solicitors expect me to be in London for another couple of months anyway. I've nothing better to do while here." He walked over to Lily's side. She nearly shivered when he placed his large hand on her back. "I'll serve as escort and make sure the wedding doesn't end up too...lacy." He smiled down at her and Lily swore her insides became warm pudding. Apparently, helpless animals and *weddings* brought out Jeremy's softness. Lily was undecided as to whether she preferred this doting demeanor or the exciting hardness she'd felt earlier that morning.

"Didn't you mention needing to return to Kent at the end of the week? Something about a tenant border dispute?" George asked Jeremy, a very strange edge to his voice.

"No," Jeremy replied with adamancy. "It's been handled."

The countess clapped her hands in delight, seemingly oblivious to the inexplicable tension Lily was now certain was boiling beneath the surface of Jeremy and George's friendship.

"Then it's settled! Won't you drop by tomorrow afternoon and we can start working on the guest list, hm?"

George stomped across the room and took hold of Jeremy's bicep.

"Lovely," her brother fairly growled. "Come with me for a bite to eat, Jem. I'd love the company."

Lily knew Jeremy could have easily shaken off her brother—though George was slightly taller, Jeremy had easily three stone on him—but he allowed himself to be steered rapidly toward the door. He bade the two of them a quick goodbye and Lily was left alone with her mother.

"Wasn't that kind of him?" her mother asked.

"Indeed." Lily stared at the empty air where Jeremy had been standing, pondering the curious generosity she'd just witnessed.

What man subjected himself to wedding planning willingly?

Especially when it wasn't even *his* wedding?

Even though she'd pondered it nearly incessantly, Lily still did not have an answer to that question by the following morning. The only possibility she'd reached was that Jeremy had decided on martyrdom and sainthood.

Lily pondered the merits of being burned at the stake as her mother chattered on about the tragic scarcity of French lace. She poked a strawberry cap around her breakfast plate and tried to imagine herself in the beautiful gown her mother described, studded with seed pearls and silver embroidery as she walked down the aisle of the parish in Wrothsborough, the country town sandwiched between the Shefford and Aldborough lands.

She'd never pictured herself getting married anyplace but that little stone building with its beautiful rainbows of stained glass, and meeting her husband at the altar. She'd look up into his face. Her heart would do a funny little flip, letting her know she was doing the right thing by marrying this man and laying her future in his hands. He'd smile down at her and, cheekily, wink one of his dark chocolate eyes–

No.

The marquess had blue eyes.

Jeremy had dark eyes.

Lily gave herself a little shake. It was time to give up those girlish fantasies.

"Did you hear me, Lily?" Her mother's voice startled her so much that she dropped her silver fork with a jarring clatter.

"I'm sorry?" She quickly picked up the utensil and felt an immediate sense of guilt. Here her parents had done their best to make her an advantageous match; her mother was currently working to give her the most beautiful wedding possible in such a short period; and Lily sat there daydreaming about another man. She felt like a child caught doing something naughty, causing a blush to creep up the back of her neck.

"The music, dear. I was wondering if you would prefer to have a harp or a quartet?" Lily opened her mouth to say she didn't have a particular preference, though she'd always loved the violin; however, her mother continued to talk without giving Lily a chance to respond. "I'm concerned a harp may not be grand enough…"

Lily stopped listening.

Her mother continued talking.

And this was the unfortunate way in which the remainder of the morning proceeded.

The prior afternoon hadn't been all that pleasant for Jeremy either. After he had all but been dragged from the Stratfords' townhouse by Sommerfeld, he wrenched his arm free and stopped at the foot of the stairs leading down to the street. Sommerfeld whirled on him and thrust the lion head of his walking stick into Jeremy's chest.

"What the actual bloody hell are you on about?" Sommerfeld hissed. "Do you enjoy torturing yourself? Or do you believe I derive some sick pleasure from watching you do it?"

Jeremy stared down his friend for several tense heartbeats before shoving that blasted cane away from him.

"This is not the place." Jeremy prepared to turn on his heel and have the nearby footman hail him transportation back to his town-house, but the Aldborough carriage in burgundy and black with a matched set of high-stepping bays rumbled up in front of them instead.

"Then get in, will you?" Sommerfeld gestured roughly to the vehicle. When Jeremy made no move to comply, he added, "Get in the ruddy carriage, Jem. You are an idiot if you think you can confess to me what you did and then pull that stunt in front of my mother and sister. I'll not let you sink yourself and take my family down with you. You may be my oldest friend, but my blood comes first."

Jeremy shot his friend a glare that would have shriveled a lesser man's soul, but he stepped up into the carriage and dropped his weight onto the rear-facing seat. The carriage rocked as Sommerfeld climbed up after him and sat in the seat opposite. The door was secured and they lurched forward through the din and bustle that was Mayfair.

"I do not need to explain myself to you, George," Jeremy said. There was a blatant warning in his voice, though he addressed his friend informally.

Kelsey Swanson

"Quite the contrary," Sommerfeld replied as he, unconsciously, used his thumb to circle the mane of the lion on his cane. "I have a vested interest in making sure Lily has the best match possible. If your involvement threatens the contract already in place, then I have to put a stop to it.

"You had your chance, my friend," Sommerfeld added somewhat sadly, more gently than he'd begun. "You didn't claim what was right in front of you, and now we, all of us, must live with what has come to pass. I'm going to be the Earl of Aldborough someday and it is part of my duty to ensure Lily is secure. Allowing you to step on Townsend's toes is counterproductive to that aim."

A fit of all-too-familiar anger and frustration began seething inside Jeremy's chest. "The man doesn't give a damn about Lily. You should have seen him today. The cocky bastard was riding roughshod through the park and nearly trampled us. I don't like the way he looks at Lily either."

"Naturally," Sommerfeld interjected in a bemused tone and sat back against the plush seat.

Jeremy didn't dignify the comment with a response.

"He all but told her he had better things to do than plan their wedding. She looked so stricken, George; I couldn't allow her to feel that." Jeremy watched his friend's features soften. Though not always the most understanding of brothers, there was no denying Sommerfeld's love for his sister. "Think about it. You've signed her life away without her knowledge or consent to a man she's now encountered twice; at least a full half of those conversations have been unpleasant for her. She won't even have the opportunity to truly get to know him before she's wedded and…bedded." Jeremy nearly choked on the last word. If his skin crawled at the memory of Townsend kissing Lily's wrist, he didn't want to know what would happen if his imagination wandered further. "If I can give her familiarity and comfort – no matter how small – during this time, then who am I to deny her?" Jeremy leaned forward and rested his elbows on his knees, turning his hands palm-up in a timeless gesture of helplessness.

"So you're going to willingly subject yourself to all the fresh hells entailed in planning a wedding, on top of practically handing over the woman you love to another man?"

"I never said I loved her."

George shook his head and turned to look out the window. "Now I know you've lost your mind."

Jeremy rapped on the grand door of the Stratford townhouse at two o'clock the following afternoon. If he was going to go through with this farce, then he might as well be prompt.

The elderly butler, Edwards, was as efficient as ever even though he'd appeared dusty and creaky even in Jeremy's youth. He was immediately shown through the entryway crafted from large, peach-toned marble tiles, corinthian columns, and intricate archways above each door to one of the smaller sitting rooms near the rear of the residence.

The atmosphere was overwhelmingly feminine, making Jeremy feel decidedly out of place in a situation where his discomfort had already been astronomical. The walls were papered in powdered blue with a pattern of shepherdesses interspersed with floral bouquets, and the impossibly dainty chairs and sofa were upholstered in a complimentary shade of ivory entirely impractical anywhere other than the home of an earl.

Jeremy's eyes were instantly drawn to Lily standing in front of the window, cast in a halo of warm afternoon light. She was tapping the fingernail of her index finger against her teeth—a nervous habit she'd developed long ago—as her mother sat at a small writing desk nearby, filling the silence with the furious scratching of quill on parchment.

Jeremy drank in the sight of Lily in those precious seconds before Edwards announced him and she was alerted to his presence.

The desire to press his lips to the furrow in her brow made every joint in his body ache. She'd donned a light green morning dress free of frivolous trimmings and the spun gold of her hair was tied in a simple knot at the base of her neck. He'd seen her in this dress before and knew the simple skirt, without the cumbersome layers with which women were so taken, was free to graze the gentle curves of her hips as she walked. The artfully scooped neckline would afford him a fair glimpse of her décolletage and, of course, his favorite freckle. It took every ounce of willpower within him to prevent his mind from sliding to a much less innocent place. To him, she looked even lovelier and more tempting in her ease than she had at the ball a few nights prior.

Jeremy wondered what he'd done to God to deserve such torture.

He'd known being around Lily was going to be difficult, but why did she have to look so damned delicious?

The countess stopped her scribbling and Lily spun when his title was announced in Edwards's raspy voice. The unfiltered glow of joy upon Lily's face nearly undid Jeremy; she looked both elated and re-lieved at his arrival. Urging his knees to remain steady, Jeremy strode into the room and greeted the ladies. He did his best to ignore the ring on Lily's finger as he kissed the back of her hand.

"Thank you for coming, Jemmy," Lily said, and then added be-neath her breath; "Mother has been working tirelessly on this guest list and I don't know how much more I can take."

Jeremy smiled and squeezed her hand reassuringly, letting her know he would do his best to make this easier for her.

"And how goes the planning thus far?" he asked her mother with decided cheerfulness and went to look over her shoulder at the columns of names she'd copied. Almost immediately, she launched into a stream of questions – asking his opinion and then answering for him all within the same breath. A quarter of the way through, Jeremy glanced up and caught Lily watching him. She smiled and rolled her eyes as if to say, *See what I've been going through?* He winked at her and then looked back down at the countess' papers.

Sometime later, after much pacing (by Jeremy) and relatively one-sided debate (by Lily's mother), the countess finally stood from her desk and turned to her daughter. At some point, Lily had taken up a seat on the sofa with her legs curled beneath her in her skirts. It was a testament to her mother's distractedness that she was allowed to sit in such a way and not be chastised.

Jeremy was struck by how small she appeared. She held an embroidered pillow to her stomach and the weariness in her expression was worrisome. He realized, not for the first time that afternoon, that Lily had spoken up very little. In place of her voice, which her mother so often drowned out, he'd looked to her and conveyed Lily's infrequent opinions to the countess; remaining adamant where Lily would have been un-maliciously trampled by her mother.

Jeremy strode over to the sofa and claimed the cushion beside her, hoping both that his proximity would assuage whatever was bothering her, and the furniture would bear his added weight. He ached to take her hand in his, to pull her into his arms and hold her close, to press his lips to the crown of her head and tell her it would all be all right.

"I think we finally have an acceptable list," the countess began. "Of course, there will be some additions from the marquess—I'm sure he has more friends and family he would like to attend—but our side of the church and most mutual acquaintances should be accounted for." There was a pause while she tallied up the names. "Three-hundred and forty-six."

Lily shifted beside him. She was clutching the pillow to her chest as if it were the only thing keeping her weighted on this earth.

"Three—three hundred?" she squeaked.

"And forty-six, dear," the countess added with a flourish. "Of course, that is just the preliminary number. There will be more once we send the list round to the marquess. He'll no doubt have some additions of his own," she reiterated.

Lily's knuckles turned as pale as the pillow in her arms.

Jeremy hadn't realized how many names they'd run through. Lily's crippling fear of large crowds in enclosed spaces would paralyze her; and on her wedding day of all days. The flippancy with which her mother had placed Lily into such a situation soured his stomach. Lily deserved to be protected, to be respected and cherished. Instead, she was a marionette to be dressed and danced down the aisle, obedient to those tugging at her strings, regardless of her own thoughts and desires. No bride should have to suffer so on her wedding day.

It was also the one time he most certainly wouldn't be able to stand up and help her through it.

"That is a rather large number of invitations," Jeremy began cautiously; trying to gauge the best way to make the countess understand that Lily simply wouldn't be able to survive an event of that size.

Not to mention, he was not the bridegroom. He had no *real* say in anything.

"Well of course it is! Everyone will want an invitation. One must not risk offending anyone by not extending an invitation. We don't want Lily to commit social suicide before she even takes the title of marchioness."

There was a mouse-soft whisper beside him. Lily stared unblinking at the rug. She'd hung her head and pressed her mouth to the pillow. The mere thought of being forced into a situation with that many people had caused her to retreat within herself. Jeremy doubted she was even aware he was still sitting beside her. What he wouldn't give to gather her into his arms and stride out the door—to take her away from all of this.

She made another sound and he leaned in closer to hear her; he couldn't help but inhale deeply the light scent of lavender soap from her skin.

Wrothsborough.

That was the village between their family's country estates. Jeremy pondered that for a few moments. Why would she be saying such a thing? What did it have to do with the wedding preparations; with the guest list? Then, it struck him. Weddings and their following breakfasts were typically hosted by the bride's family. He looked back at the countess.

"The parish at Wrothsborough might accommodate fifty at most. Where is everyone else to sit?" The countess laughed airily as if it had been a silly query.

"We cannot have a wedding of this caliber at a country parish. We'll have it here in Town, of course. All the shops and vendors are here anyway. And, with such a constraint on time, we would be hard-pressed to find many who would be willing to travel out there before the end of the Season. The parish is lovely, but not suitable for *this* wedding."

The countess had begun detailing how she would send 'round an inquiry at St. Margaret's when Lily stood silently. The pillow fell forgotten from her lap and, wordlessly, Lily slipped from the room.

"Lillian!" the countess called after her daughter before turning to Jeremy. "I apologize for her rude behavior. I do not know what has gotten into that girl."

Jeremy did his best to remain polite; knowing the countess cared for her daughter and was entirely well-meaning, if a bit dense.

"It's quite all right. I'll just make sure she's well and then take my leave. Perhaps she's just a bit overwhelmed at the prospect of being a marchioness." Jeremy bowed out of the room without waiting for a response, taking advantage of his family's long-standing relationship with the Stratfords and knowing she would forgive his brusque departure.

Jeremy stepped into the hallway just in time to catch a glimpse of mint green fabric darting into the room he knew to be the library. He heard the door click shut as he made to follow her. She wouldn't be able to lock it without one of two keys held by the countess and the housekeeper.

He turned his ear to the door and listened for a minute. When he heard nothing, he knocked gently on the mahogany barrier. There was no response. He rapped a bit more loudly.

"Lily, it's Jem. Might I enter?" This still didn't earn him a response. Prodded by his desperate desire to make sure she was okay, he placed his hand on the gleaming bronze knob and entered the room.

Lily had curled up in one of the overstuffed armchairs by the fireplace. Propping her elbow on one of the arms, she rested her heavy, buzzing head in her hand. There, Jeremy found her as she willed the room to stop spinning. She watched him from beneath the fringe of her lashes as he entered as quietly as his large frame allowed and gently pressed the door closed. He stood watching her in silence for a moment before he approached her as one would a nervous filly. Lily lifted her head.

He'd been a remarkably good sport over the last several hours; not once showing frustration, annoyance, or impatience. His good humor had remained through it all. Now, his demeanor had shifted to one of seriousness and concern. For her.

He looked so handsome that afternoon. Though he'd been freshly shaved when he'd arrived, even a few hours' time had afforded that shade of stubble to begin its re-emergence. The dove-gray of his jacket contrasted becomingly with his dark coloring. Her heart skipped an unbidden beat as he crouched in front of her and gently took her hand in both of his.

His piercing dark eyes examined her with an almost unnerving intensity as he looked up at her. It was an unusual sensation, looking down into his face. Lily realized for the first time how long his kohl-colored eyelashes were. She knew ladies of the *ton* who would have killed for less upon themselves.

"Are you well, Lily? I saw how taken aback you were by the number of guests…"

"It's not just that, Jemmy." She stopped, not entirely certain how to proceed without seeming like a little girl throwing a tantrum.

"Then what is it?" he urged her gently.

Her brain became hazy again when the thick pad of his thumb began to trace the fragile bones in the back of her hand. A honey-warm curl of what Lily could only think to be desire began to unfurl low in her body. His nearness was not helping her senses recover at all.

She gently repossessed her hand, though the sensation of his touch left her feeling as if she'd been branded. She stood and walked over to one of the ceiling-height bookcases lining every wall of the room. The silent space smelled comfortingly of leather and old paper. She aim-lessly traced the spine of a red, gilt-trimmed tome with her fingertip.

"I know it seems silly, but I'd always rather fancied that my wed-ding would be at the parish in Wrothsborough. We grew up going there but—I suppose my mother is right. It's unsuitable. I need to give up on my childish fantasies."

"It's not foolish." She was surprised by the adamancy in his voice. The heavy thud of his boots told her he'd strode over to stand behind her. Lily could have sworn that she could feel the heat radiating off of him. "Nothing you desire is foolish. I'll try to reason with your moth-er over the guest list."

Lily whirled on Jeremy. "You heard her, did you not? I am to be a marchioness. I must have an event worthy of such a title," she inject-ed her voice with false pretentiousness, which Jeremy doubtlessly found very transparent. "There will be no parish wedding. There will be no quiet ceremony with only the people I love. There will be no getting to know my intended husband before the wedding. And I will be expected to endure those hundreds of eyes upon me as I am mar-ried to a man whom I do not know." She hesitated before continuing; admitting to another aspect of her anxieties she had yet to voice aloud. "What if I cannot do it? What if I am all wrong for the title of mar-chioness? I will be expected to be graceful and refined; a brilliant hostess in charge of running events where three-hundred guests is a common occurrence."

"Lily," Jeremy said forcefully, commanding her to meet his eyes. "Don't you ever feel as if you're not good enough, or that your desires are unworthy of consideration. You are far more than that man de-serves—than most men deserve." Lily's pulse stalled. "Your kind heart is the biggest I've ever known. You're intelligent and witty. You're beautiful, Lily—inside and out."

She experienced a blush that heated her face to an uncomfortable pinkness at the comment. She was unused to hearing such flourishing compliments from Jeremy and she wasn't quite sure what to make of them.

Having a brother like George meant she wasn't deaf to whispered stories of exploits – her peers did so enjoy a good rake. Her time out in Society afforded her even more access to the delighted tittering and rumors amongst women. She wasn't blind to the fact that Jeremy had flirted and interacted with other women; the man was darkly handsome and she was under no false belief that he'd lived like a monk. She just wasn't used to being on the receiving end of such attention from him and couldn't help but wonder at its sincerity.

Her pulse resumed at a break-neck pace, Lily tried to look away from Jeremy's boring gaze, but he stalled the movement with a gentle, hooked finger beneath her chin.

"Look at me, Lily."

She couldn't help but comply. She swallowed convulsively when faced with the fire in his eyes. She'd never been this close to him before—not even when dancing. His breath mixed with hers in a sweet cloud between them. She didn't know how she hadn't seen that his eyes were not merely a flat dark brown, but the pupils were rimmed with a color she hadn't known existed in nature. The smoldering amber captured her and refused to let her go. She couldn't blink, let alone turn away. Her heartbeat redoubled as Jeremy leaned in a fraction closer. His shaky exhalations were excitingly close to her and his face occupied her entire field of vision. She instinctively took a step back, but he had her caged against the bookcase with one arm propped against the shelves and the other under her chin. She knew she could have ducked and he would have let her escape, but – if she was honest—she didn't want to be free. She'd waited countless years for this attention; spent sleepless nights pondering what it would be to have Jeremy this near to her. His hands and mouth were what filled her dreams.

"God, you're beautiful," he repeated in a voice that sounded almost pained.

"Jeremy," she released his full name on a sigh.

And, as if taking this as his sign to claim what he so clearly desired, Jeremy's mouth was suddenly on hers.

He kissed her.

Chapter Seven

Jeremy's self-loathing for succumbing to his impulse very quickly gave way to the glorious realization of one in the long list of fantasies he'd secreted away for nigh on a decade.

Lily was even sweeter than he'd dreamt; she tasted of tea and strawberry preserves. Her soft, full lips remained motionless at first – perhaps from shock. Jeremy prayed to God and every other deity he could think of that it wasn't from revulsion.

One of those higher beings must have heard him because Lily sighed against his lips and began to kiss him back. She was tentative at first, but she'd always been a quick learner.

That's my girl.

Emitting a low groan of approval, he tilted her head up and to the side for better access and drank her in. His tongue gave a testing pass of her lips and a white-hot flame of desire shot through him when she gave a little moan of what could only be desperate need. Her fingers flew to his lapel, but, rather than pushing him away, however, she fisted her hand in the fabric and boldly pulled him closer. Jeremy's groin hardened painfully quickly, a pounding rush of blood escaping his brain for less logical, more impulsive climes. She was more responsive, more eager than he ever could have dreamed.

When she parted her lips for his tongue's passionate onslaught, Jeremy nearly lost what little control remained. An involuntary growl rumbled in his throat as he pressed the length of his body against her softness. Lily was trapped between him and the unforgiving bookcase...and Jeremy was damned if he was going to let her go now. He wanted her to feel in his kiss, as he stroked her tongue with his, how beautiful he believed her to be. He needed her to read how desirable he found her in the gentle caress of his thumb on the rabbit-fast pulse in her throat. Years of unrequited yearning poured through every point of contact between them.

His hand moved from the bookcase and, as if of its own accord, snaked around her slim waist and wrenched her against him more tightly. Jeremy relished each of her curves, the hills and valleys, as her breasts were crushed against the hard wall of his chest.

She whimpered lightly when his mouth left hers. The little sound sent a fresh wave of desire straight to the growing crisis barely contained by his breeches. God, she made him feel like he was seventeen again – incredibly nervous and excited, thrilled beyond containment. But this was better. This was *Lily*.

She wound him up fair to breaking with her innocent kisses and he feared his already fragile control would snap.

No matter how he tried, Jeremy, however, could not control himself. His lips found the sensitive, flushed skin where her jaw ended and throat began. His tongue darted out to taste her rapid pulse and he kissed his way down to her collarbone. She gasped and shivered at the new sensation.

"Lily. My Lily." Jeremy groaned and reclaimed her mouth with his own. Some rational part of his mind managed to break through the fog of pent-up lust and reminded him that she was *not* his Lily. She was wearing another man's ring.

With an uneven breath, Jeremy broke their contact and released her as if he'd been burned.

What had he done?

Jeremy abruptly pulled away from their embrace and his lapel slid through Lily's weakened fingers. She returned to her senses as if moving through molasses, and blinked away the haze of passion that had filled her head. The expression on Jeremy's face was concerning.

"Jem. What—"

"I should not have done that." He raked a trembling hand through his raven hair. Lily couldn't help but notice how he refused to meet her eye. Had she done something wrong?

She was inexperienced to be sure—the sum of all her knowledge of kissing amounted to this one experience with Jeremy—but she didn't think it had been terrible. She'd rather thought he'd been enjoying himself from the way he clutched her to his body. She hadn't known if he was ever going to let go.

She hadn't wanted him to.

He looked as if he needed reassurance, so Lily took a step toward him. Jeremy retreated two steps and heaved a weighty breath.

"I only meant…to let you know that you shouldn't discount yourself. You're entitled to your opinions and desires," he said slowly, all the while focusing on something near Lily's left shoulder. A sinking sensation in the pit of Lily's stomach rid her of whatever warm feelings remained from their embrace.

"So you didn't *mean* to kiss me then? It was some sort of terrible accident, like a trip and fall?"

"No—Yes—I don't..." Jeremy shook his head, seemingly at a loss. He rubbed the back of his neck and finally met Lily's eyes. "I wanted to kiss you. I shouldn't have given into the impulse."

Her stomach gave a flip and she pressed her palm to her abdomen to still it. "You wanted to kiss me?" she asked slowly, as if repeating the words would better help her to comprehend what had transpired. If she wasn't mistaken, there was something akin to pain in Jeremy's intense eyes.

"I assure you it won't happen again," he replied with nauseating gravity.

There were several minutes of pregnant silence. Steeling her resolve, Lily finally whispered, "But...I quite liked it." She regretted the words as soon as they passed her lips.

She prayed he wouldn't laugh and spurn her comment as infantile. Of course she'd liked it. Nothing had ever made her burn as his mouth and the crushing pressure of his body against hers had – not even those late nights when sleep eluded her and she dared to slide her hand down beneath her night rail and touch that most private of places; that secret spot at the juncture of her thighs which, even now, throbbed with liquid heat. It was clear to Lily now that Jeremy saw her as a woman. No man would have kissed her thusly, otherwise.

Jeremy gave a strangled groan and advanced one step before checking himself. His eyes screwed shut with the effort.

Lily pulled her lower lip between her teeth and tasted Jeremy there. Spice and a touch of brandy. She, in her naïveté, could not have known how erotic he found the gesture.

"Be that as it may," Jeremy's words sounded forced when he finally spoke, "it can never happen again."

Even though it was agonizing, Lily knew he was right. She wore another man's ring on her finger and the ink was dry on the betrothal documents. But why, oh why, did he have to wait until *now* to kiss her? If she wasn't mistaken, that had been desire she'd glimpsed in his eyes. She gave a disbelieving scoff at the absurdity of it all.

She spends decades pining after a man who waits until she's well and truly betrothed to someone else to give her a proper kiss. She couldn't decide if this amount of irony was appropriate or obscene.

"You're right, Jemmy."

He winced as if she'd struck him with a physical blow.

Several tense heartbeats passed before he cut her a stiff bow, turned, and left the room. The silence he left in his wake was deafening.

Jeremy arrived at his townhouse in a fury. God, how he needed to hit something. He'd oscillated between disbelief that he'd finally given into his desires and kissed Lily, and rage at his stupidity and the unfairness of the situation.

He let himself through the front door before the butler could do so and slammed it shut behind him. The cracking sound echoed through the foyer. Before the reverberations died away Jeremy cocked his arm and, rather stupidly, punched the mahogany door. The ensuing stream of curses that followed rivaled that of the one from the prior day.

"M'lord!" Mrs. Hallsworth exclaimed from behind him.

"What?" Jeremy demanded and whirled on her, shaking out his hand and hoping he hadn't broken anything.

Mrs. Hallsworth had known Jeremy his entire life and she wouldn't be intimidated by a fit. Stoically, she pulled a plain, clean handkerchief from the pocket of her apron and held it out to him.

"Please do try not to bleed on the rug; the maids will have a difficult time cleaning those stains."

He stared at the handkerchief for a moment before heaving a sigh and taking it. He pressed it to his mashed knuckles to staunch the blood. The palm of his left hand was still freshly sliced open and now, at the very least, he'd split open his right hand. This infatuation with Lily was going to kill him if he wasn't careful.

"What is it, Mrs. Hallsworth? As you can see, I'm not really in the mood for solving crises."

"That's good then because I wouldn't call Lady Shefford's arrival a crisis."

"My mother is here?" Jeremy's head perked up.

"She is. And she's probably heard your arrival, so you'd best reassure her that all is well." The older woman eyed his matching pair of injured hands.

"I'll purchase another handkerchief to replace this one," said Jeremy, feeling all the world as if he was a young boy being chastised for rash behavior. She waved off his offer.

"Handkerchiefs I have. Another position as a housekeeper is hard to come by. Do take care of yourself, m'lord." With that, Mrs. Hallsworth moved to show him to the cozy green parlor where, no doubt, he would find his mother.

He stepped into the room and instantly regretted not having his valet clean and bandage his hand. The first glimpse Lady Shefford had of her son in nigh on two months involved him raging and bleeding. Jeremy's sense of guilt only deepened. What wouldn't he give for a sinkhole to open up and swallow him… That had to be the most appropriate end to this hellish day.

His mother stood abruptly and the little book she'd had propped in her lap fell to the floor with a gentle thud.

"Jeremy! What happened dear?" She rushed over and immediately took his hand in hers. As she did so, he found himself wondering when she'd gotten so thin. Even the wedding band on her finger slid around as she fussed over his hands. More silver had worked its way through her hair, once so dark and glossy that it shone blue in the sunlight.

Everyone had been affected by the sudden death of Jeremy's father and they all missed him terribly, but none so much as his mother. They'd been married when she was seventeen and Jeremy knew his parents had come to love one another with a fierce devotion relatively unknown in the *ton*. His parents' love had been one of little touches and reassurances; Jeremy thought this might be why her hands were constantly moving now. Without his father to touch and fuss over, she was lost.

New lines had carved their way on the outer edges of her dark blue eyes and around her mouth, grief had altered her irreparably, even in this relatively short amount of time. Her waist appeared impossibly tiny and she still wore a simple gown of dark gray for mourning.

"I'm fine, Mother. I didn't realize you were coming for a visit?"

"I received your note about Elizabeth's desire to see me and it made me realize how remiss I've been as a friend." She was speaking of the missive he'd sent to their Kentish estate. His mother had ensconced herself in solitude in the country after his father's death; he'd let her know Lily's mother was growing concerned and missing her friend. "The physicians felt that it would be good for me to start seeing friends once again. They hope the exertion will encourage my appetite, but they worry overmuch." Despite the levity in her tone, Jeremy remained skeptical. The sadness in her eyes didn't speak to sincerity.

"I am inclined to agree with them," he said. His mother stopped dabbing at his gashed knuckles.

"Now Jeremy…"

"Now Mother," he mimicked her tone, and she couldn't help but smile. She took the chance to change the subject.

"Are you going to tell me what is going on with you? From the looks of it, you've been rather accident-prone as of late."

Jeremy gently took the handkerchief from his mother and gestured for her to be seated. He took his place in a chair across from her. He should have known she would be able to read the exhaustion on his face.

"What is wrong, my dear? What has happened?" Her concern was growing by the second.

He finally had the chance to ask his mother a question that had been burning deep inside him for several days now. He'd lost his patience for beating around the bush.

"Were you hoping I would offer for Lily Stratford?" he asked bluntly.

Her eyebrows rose in surprise. "We'd always hoped the two of you would have affection for one another. It was a silly dream of Elizabeth's and mine that the two of you would marry—ever since she gave birth to the girl. We thought you two were wonderfully close for so long, but you never came to me or your father and expressed an interest in extending an offer."

He'd believed it when Sommerfeld explained it the other day, but hearing it from his mother felt like a sucker punch to the jaw.

"So no one cared that she was my social better? That I couldn't possibly provide her the life which was her birthright?"

His mother leaned forward and spoke in a very sincere tone. "I'm sure it may have been an issue had you been anyone else, but you were *our* son…and no one could help but love you, my charming boy. You are nothing if not the product of your father and it's in your nature to do everything for those you care for, no matter the sacrifices or work you must invest. That cannot be said of many men in your position."

Jeremy gritted his teeth against the welling sense of betrayal. He stood and began to pace the width of the room.

"Why? What does this have to do with anything?"

"Do you know," he ground out, trying to remain civil with his mother; "that Lily, as of two days ago, is engaged to be wed to the Marquess of Townsend?"

"Oh, it's done then! I shall have to call on Elizabeth to see how the planning is going!"

"It's going bloody wonderfully, Mother," he said with a vicious, sarcastic lilt to his voice. He halted his pacing and was too enraged to yet feel guilt over his mother's stricken expression. He couldn't recall a time he'd ever cursed in front of his mother. "Did no one think to *ask* me if I would have wanted to marry Lily? Did no one think to ask Lily what *she* wanted?"

Her hand flew to her mouth as the realization dawned. "Jeremy. You don't mean…?"

He had to look away from her for fear that the barely contained frustration would boil over. "It does not matter any longer. She'll be married in six weeks' time and gone."

"And…what does Lily—"

"She knows nothing," he snapped. Jeremy wasn't sure that was entirely true; not after the kiss they'd shared in the library that afternoon. But it could mean "nothing" as long as he didn't allow the circumstances to repeat. "And no one will tell her," he said gravely.

"Does anyone else realize?" she asked, tears clouding her eyes.

"Sommerfeld guessed it some time ago but assumed like everyone else that I would have mentioned something. In reality, I believed myself too far beneath her touch to even hope for." Jeremy dropped into the chair once more. He closed his eyes and let his head fall back, not so much as wincing when the bump on the back of his skull collided with the wood. He welcomed the dull ache. He deserved it for his cowardice.

"Dear God," he heard his mother whisper into her hand; "what have we done? I'm so sorry, my love. So sorry." The realization that their family's lack of communication had, perhaps, broken her only child's heart crushed any other words she might have said.

Late that night, Jeremy dismissed his valet for the evening and began undressing on his own. His bandaged hands made him frustratingly clumsy as he unwound his cravat and slid off his jacket. He couldn't wait to be back in the country where he didn't have to wear all those damnable layers.

He and his mother had eaten a simple, somber supper of cold chicken and an assortment of cheeses and fruit Cook had managed to scrounge up on short notice. The conversation had been largely dominated by his mother while she vacillated between tearful apologies and trying to convince him to allow her to say something to Lily's mother, to which his response had always been a resounding "No" due to the uselessness of it all. It was done. Their fates were sealed.

Stripping down to his skin, he strode over to the large four-poster bed, slid beneath the coverlet, and extinguished the sole source of light. It was an unseasonably warm night, so no fire had been lit. The room was thrust into complete darkness and, without the irregular popping of burning logs, silence.

Unfortunately, being emotionally drained didn't equate to instant sleep, and Jeremy was left staring into the heavy void of the pitch darkness.

Even closing his eyes did not help his situation; doing so only caused the memories of his kiss with Lily to return with surprising vividness. And his body responded with a vengeance.

His recollection of her breathy sighs, the sweet taste of her mouth, and the feel of her soft body against his caused a powerful wave of lust to rush to his groin. He was instantly hard and throbbing. With his eyes closed tightly, Jeremy was able to take the images from memory to fantasy. If he couldn't have Lily in real life, then this would have to suffice.

Jeremy reached beneath the coverlet with his less-injured right hand and wrapped a firm grip around his aching cock. In his mind's eye, he was hiking up the skirts of Lily's light green dress. She moaned his name like she had earlier today—no childhood nickname, *his* name—when his fingers found her wet and ready for him. He stroked his member slowly at first from tip to base, increasing the pace as the fantasy gained momentum.

He was tasting Lily's lips, kissing that maddening little freckle on the top of her breast. Then he was inside her, pinning her against the bookcase with her shapely legs wrapped around his waist; pumping into her with years of pent-up lust.

His chest heaved as he worked his cock in rapid, desperate motions; climbing ever closer to the oblivion of release.

He growled deep in his throat when he finally tumbled over that ledge. Panting, he flung his left arm over his face and gave into the aftershocks of his orgasm. She was still there behind his eyes, waiting for him with a sated smile and lips tasting of tea and strawberries.

Chapter Eight

Two days had passed since their encounter in the library, but Lily still caught herself pressing her fingertips to her lips in moments of deep thought—as if feeling for a brand Jeremy's mouth had left upon hers. Her mother had needed to snap her back to attention more than once throughout their wedding planning meetings.

Jeremy hadn't returned, nor had he sent word of when he would do so. Part of Lily knew it was for the best – that she was a betrothed woman and would do better to keep her lips to herself – but the other part of her ached to know what would have happened had Jeremy not come to his senses. She'd gone back and forth between feeling so wrong for betraying her fiancé—even though this was certainly no love match – and, somewhat torturously, wondering for just how long Jeremy had wanted to kiss her. She didn't dare to hope it had been as long as she'd wanted to kiss him.

"Lily, dear; don't forget your gloves. We're going to be late for the florist if we don't leave immediately," called her mother from the foyer. She must truly be impatient if she broke one of her own rules and raised her voice enough to be heard above stairs.

Lily descended the stairs and smoothed the pleated skirts of her dark plum-colored gown. She tugged on her dove-gray gloves and accepted her reticule. Pausing at the mirror near the front door, she tugged at a lock of hair near her temple and tried to set it to rights, making sure the rest of the waterfall of curls were behaving themselves. Then, she caught sight of a rather grim young woman looking more as if she were going to the hangman's noose than a florist's shop with a fathomless budget.

That wouldn't do.

Lily was able to paste on an acceptable smile after only a couple of attempts.

"Don't you look lovely, dear," her mother complimented her warmly, but the words fell hollow on her ears.

There was a knock at the door before Lily could thank her. Edwards moved past them to answer it.

Lily didn't need him to announce their guest; she knew the dark timbre of Jeremy's voice anywhere.

It haunted her dreams.

A pleasant chill ran up and down Lily's spine as Jeremy entered the townhouse behind his mother, Abigail Balfour, the Dowager Baroness Shefford. Lily's mother gave a cry of delighted surprise and immediately embraced her dearest friend.

"Abigail! I'm so happy to see you; what a lovely surprise!" They clung to one another, conveying their joy, sorrow, and everything in between through touch, as only close friends are capable. Lily's eyes flitted to Jeremy at that thought, but he was already smiling and staring at her over their mothers' heads. His eyes began to smolder, causing her breath to catch in her throat; her nipples peaked and tingled with awareness. She tore her eyes from his and focused on their mothers.

The older women finally broke their embrace and Abigail turned to Lily. Lily offered her a warm, welcoming grin in return and walked into her open arms. Despite her somber mourning dress, she still smelled lightly of violets and dusting powder. She closed her eyes and savored the moment. There was something rather comforting about it all – that some things would remain the same despite how much it felt as if her world was falling apart.

"Oh, Lily! You're stunning!" Abigail held her at arm's length and swept her up and down with her warm blue eyes. Lily was careful not to meet Jeremy's eye once more; fearful that his gaze had grown even more intense now that she was nearer.

It was then Lily noted further changes in Jeremy's mother. Always a slim woman, she seemed dangerously so now. The wrinkles at the corners of her eyes were deeper, but so, too, were the ones bracketing her mouth. Smiling seemed to have been an infrequent occurrence over the last year. Sorrow had changed Abigail's appearance in ways that would mark her forever, carving new lines of sorrow and dulling her once radiant beauty. Lily's heart ached for Abigail's loss, but concern for her well-being overshadowed it. She turned a troubled glance toward Jeremy, but his expression was inscrutable. Surely he must see the worrisome alterations in his mother? Could this be his way of seeking help to bring her back to her usual self?

"Congratulations on the engagement, my dear," Abigail continued, though there was an odd gleam to her eyes which hadn't been there previously. "I'm sure the wedding is going to be spectacular and you will be the most beautiful bride."

Lily thanked her demurely and stepped back; still unsure about meeting Jeremy's eyes.

"I wish we could catch up, Abigail, but Lily and I were about to leave for the florists. We have only five-and-a-half weeks now to get everything together for the big day, you know," said Lily's mother regretfully. She knew how her mother had been so desperate to comfort Abigail over the last months since the death of Jeremy's father. Her despondency and mourning had been so great that this was truly the first time they'd seen her since the funeral. Now that they were finally together, Lily was loath to separate them. She was about to tell them that they could always reschedule the meeting with the florist when Jeremy spoke up.

"I can accompany Lily," he offered lightly. "I did promise to assist with the process, did I not?"

Lily stared up at him, but he steadfastly refused to meet her gaze.

What is he on about?

"I don't know…" hemmed the countess. Abigail reached out and squeezed her hand.

"Let them go, Elizabeth. Jeremy will take care of her. Have a footman or Lily's lady's maid attend them for propriety's sake. You and I have so much to catch up on; I've missed you my dearest friend," Abbigail pleaded. That seemed to be the push her mother needed.

"All right, then," she capitulated. "If Jeremy is offering his assistance, then who are we to decline? The driver has the address."

Somehow, without so much as asking Lily what she would care to do, she was thrust into the care of Jeremy and whisked away to the carriage. Always an issue, this habit of not bothering to ask Lily what she wished was quickly becoming a raw nerve with her.

Unsure where to look, Lily opted for the scenery outside of the window rather than the large man taking up nearly the entire seat opposite her. The carriage hit a missing cobblestone and rocked. His knee collided with hers and a spark of awareness flared inside of Lily. She shifted a little further into the corner of the cab.

Jeremy chuckled. "You're not scared of me, are you? I promise not to pounce."

Lily blushed and finally turned to face him. He looked dashing that morning – groomed and brushed, pressed and filling the carriage with his scent of leather and soap. How could he behave so nonchalantly after what had happened? Perhaps he hadn't been as moved as she had been?

No, that was impossible.

If shaking hands were any indication of desire, then he'd been moved back in the library, indeed.

"I'm not afraid of you, Jemmy," she replied and folded her arms over her chest.

"Oh, you're not?" He spread his legs wider and pressed his knee and the lower half of his leg against hers. Lily scooted up against the side of the cab and crossed her legs at the ankle.

"Any further and you'll be traveling *outside* the carriage," he commented with a smirk.

She declined to respond and his easy smile withered slowly like a flower shocked by unexpected frigidity.

"I can take you home if you're truly uncomfortable," Jeremy offered, reaching up to rap on the roof of the carriage to have the driver turn around.

"No!" Lily said, stalling his hand in the air. "That is, I just…I have a difficult time thinking when you're that close to me."

"Is it your panics?" he asked, suddenly concerned. His leg instantly retreated a respectful distance. She shook her head.

The realization of what she meant dawned on Jeremy slowly and his grin followed suit. He scratched at his temple and then winked at her. "I have a similar problem, myself." He leaned forward and said in a conspiratorial tone; "Especially when you look as lovely as you do right now." The admission caused Lily's heart to jump halfway up her throat, but she schooled herself to remain calm in appearance.

"You seem so nonchalant," she all but whispered.

Jeremy shrugged and leaned back into the cushion as they bounced along in the well-sprung carriage. "Just because that is what I show the world does not necessarily mean that's what I feel."

"And how do you feel?" Lily blurted out, not quite knowing what boldness had suddenly come over her. "About the other day...about the library?"

A mischievous glint shone in his dark eyes. "What happened in the library?" he asked innocently.

Lily scoffed. He was trying to make her say it. He wanted her to put into words what he did to her...what he made her feel...when she wasn't entirely sure there were such words in her vocabulary.

"You know perfectly well what happened." A heated blush crept up her throat to her cheeks; made worse by the fact that Jeremy seemed to be enjoying her torture like he had when they were children.

"I seem to have gotten a rather nasty bump on my head sometime in the past few days, so I am going to need you to refresh my memory." His grin was wicked.

"You kissed me," Lily blurted out. "Thoroughly."

Jeremy's expression sobered. "You have much to learn if you believe that to be a 'thorough' kissing."

Lily's spine felt as if it had been transformed into hot pudding. "I—I thought you said it was never going to happen again."

"It won't," Jeremy replied with finality and turned to look out the window at the passing shops and traffic.

The ensuing silence was not one of their most comfortable. Something had shifted between them in that library and Jeremy seemed at war with himself over it. That battle, in turn, made Lily more than a little confused and unsure over how to handle the mixed signals she was receiving. He'd tease and flirt with her one moment and then, seeming to catch himself, he would shutter himself from her. Not for the first time, Lily pondered what he'd told her in the library, that her desires and opinions were of import and that she was not to discount herself. She mulled this over all the way to the florist.

When they rolled to a stop in front of the shop, Jeremy helped her disembark and they, followed distantly by Lily's maid, Mary, entered the narrow, well-kept little brick building. The group was instantly assailed by a wall of fragrance; an amalgamation of hundreds of varieties of flowers, exotic and domestic. Practically every surface – even much of the walls – was covered in vases and pots of cut flowers in every shade known to nature. It felt almost as if the entire shop had been crafted from blooms...a house of flowers. Irises, lilies, carnations, roses, and dripping greenery surrounded them, making Lily feel as if she'd fallen into a magical world where fairies and pixies could appear at any moment.

Their little party was quickly greeted by a friendly, mousy young woman, the daughter of the proprietor. She dipped into a deep curtsey.

"M'Lord Townsend; m'Lady Stratford?"

Jeremy was warm and gentle when he corrected the girl. "No, miss; Baron Shefford. I am a friend of the family."

To the girl's credit, she didn't question the strangeness of the situation where another man, unrelated to the bride, was helping her choose her wedding flowers. She gave a quick, sincere apology and showed them to a little glass room in the back filled with hothouse flowers—only the best for the marquess's wedding. Here were colors and veritable explosions of roses Lily didn't recognize. Exotic, strange-looking orchids dripped from above as if reaching down for Lily's attention.

Jeremy's resolve to keep his distance from Lily was once again shaken when he experienced her unabashed amazement at the florist's shop. Her emerald eyes danced and seemed to take on the rich hues of the plant life surrounding them. She'd always loved nature and flowers, so it was no surprise to Jeremy that she would be entranced by the shop. His familiarity with her didn't make it any less enjoyable for him to watch.

They'd left Mary in the main room of the salon and the proprietor's daughter had abandoned them to browse while she retrieved her mother, so it was just the two of them in the hothouse. He watched with unveiled pleasure as Lily flitted like a hummingbird from one flower to the next.

"I didn't know nature made this color!" she exclaimed over an orchid in a shocking yellow tone with a deep burgundy throat. The varieties of the orchids and other hot-climate flora were no doubt imported from South America and other tropical climes. Lily went next to a pale pink bloom that bore a startling resemblance to the delicate folds of female genitalia and delicately caressed the fragile petals in appreciation of God's craftsmanship.

Jeremy cleared his throat and captured her attention; she released the bloom.

"Do you see anything that would suit your vision for the wedding?" He hoped his voice didn't sound as strangled as he felt.

"These are all beautiful," she said without turning to meet his eyes, "but you are assuming I have a vision; which I do not." Lily walked over to a small wooden table in the center of the room and seated herself. She continued to stare up at the flowers hanging from the ceiling, as an astronomer would the stars.

"Of course you have a vision," Jeremy said gently as he claimed the other chair. "Surely every woman has some idea of what she would like her wedding to be?"

She finally met his eyes. "You do recall that my desire for the parish in Wrothsborough was deemed insufficient, do you not? Mother has made it clear that I need to make plans on par with what is expected of a future marchioness; and, thus, anything I might have imagined is irrelevant."

Had he tried, Jeremy couldn't have stopped himself from reaching over the table and taking her fragile gloved hand in his.

"Forget the expectations...forget what your mother said you *should* have...what do *you* desire?"

You, the word came unbidden to Lily's mind. A wave of heat rushed through her body like an unstoppable tide.

Instead, she said, "Wildflowers. Chamomile, bluebell, centaury, scabious."

Jeremy's knowledge of flowers wouldn't have filled a thimble, but he'd listened to his mother enough to recognize those were all varieties that filled the fields in Kent. Lily had grown up picking those flowers every summer, collecting armfuls of the blue, purple, and white blooms and haphazardly arranging them in tin cups as a little girl is wont to do. He squeezed her hand, realizing that she had, indeed, been dreaming of her wedding since she was a child; no one had ever really bothered to ask. The knowledge caused a fresh stab of pain and guilt to infiltrate his chest.

Lily looked down at their joined hands and, for the first time, she noticed that Jeremy had foregone gloves and was wearing more bandages than when she'd seen him last.

"Both of your hands are injured! What do you keep doing to yourself?"

He pulled his hands back and shielded them beneath the table. His response was evasive. "I seem to be rather accident-prone as of late."

She would have pressed him further, except Mrs. Goodwell, the owner of the florist shop, entered the room and curtseyed her greeting.

"D'you see anything that pleases you, M'lady?" she asked Lily, but Jeremy spoke up before Lily could reply.

"These are all quite lovely, but the lady would prefer something a bit more domestic. Do you have any wildflowers? Particularly the kind native to Kent?"

Lily had cared for Jeremy for the duration of her life. She'd admitted to herself that she had an infatuation and, yes, desired him as a woman does a man. But, looking back on it later, Lily would pinpoint that moment as the time she fell hopelessly, earth-shatteringly in love with Baron Shefford.

It was mid-afternoon by the time they left the florist shop. The shopkeeper had been unable to hide her disappointment that she couldn't persuade Jeremy to allow more extravagant, exotic arrangements to grace the wedding, but he'd been insistent upon Lily's choice of flowers. If the marquess had the nerve to comment on the choice, then Jeremy would tell him where to go.

He handed Lily up into the carriage and followed close behind. She smiled at him from beneath her long blond lashes in a way that made his breath hitch deep in his chest. He hardly noticed it when the carriage jerked into motion.

"Mother is going to be mortified," Lily snickered lightly.

"Place the blame on me." Jeremy smiled back. "It would not be the first time you did so," he said, recalling a particular incident with a broken vase and a gangly seven-year-old girl with golden braids to her waist.

"You're willing to face the wrath of my mother for me?" She laughed airily but sobered when she saw his seriousness.

"Indeed."

Several moments passed, filled only with the clatter of wheels, shod hooves on cobblestones, and London traffic. That was, until Lily stood as best as she could in the cramped space, turned, and claimed what little space was left beside Jeremy on the rear-facing seat. He eyed her warily and did his best to ignore the quickening of his pulse at her nearness; her lavender scent which lingered on her skin even after their hours spent in the florist's shop. He stiffened as she did the unthinkable: She reached up cupped his cheek in her hand so he could not move, stretched up, and placed a heartrendingly tender kiss on his jaw.

"Thank you," she whispered against his skin; "thank you for standing up for me. Thank you for being my advocate when no one hears my voice; for knowing me better than I sometimes know myself."

He turned to look at her and was met by those fathomless, rich green eyes. He opened his mouth to speak, but her hand tightened on his face and pulled his lips down to collide with hers.

The simultaneous shock and pleasure of her mouth overtook Jeremy. His eyes slid shut as he once again tasted that forbidden nectar of tea and strawberry preserves. Her tongue gave a testing swipe of his lips and he emitted an involuntary groan. She was an astonishingly quick study, but he knew what must be done.

Reaching up, he covered her hand with his, gently removed it, and forced himself to pull back. Lily's eyes were closed; her lips, parted. A becoming flush tinted her throat and cheeks. That little freckle on her breast heaved with her every breath. Her eyelids fluttered open after several breaths passed and their kiss did not resume.

"What are you doing, Lily?" The words sounded strained even to his ears.

"If you need to ask that question, then I must be truly terrible at kissing," Lily replied with a little self-deprecating laugh.

Jeremy shook his head. "You know what I mean."

She blinked up at him and he caught a disturbing glimpse of determination flaring in her eyes.

"I'm doing exactly what you told me to do. I'm taking stock of my desires and I've finally come to realize that I am worthy of whatever I put my mind to. I'm going after what I want." The matter-of-fact tone of her words sent a bolt of lust throughout his body.

"What about Townsend?" Though the words pained him, the last shred of decency inside of him made him ask the question.

"If I am going to be expected to live in a loveless marriage for the rest of my life—to never again have someone who knows me as well as you do and cares for me as you have all these years—then I cannot knowingly, willingly consign myself to such an existence without at least experiencing one thing I've dreamt of."

The air from Jeremy's lungs was involuntarily expelled with great force as if he'd been punched in the gut. Was she admitting to feeling something for him, or was it something else?

"Perhaps you're simply experiencing some trepidations over the wedding?"

She shook her golden head, her curls bouncing as she did so. "You're misunderstanding me, Jeremy." She pressed her hand to his face once more and forced him to meet her eyes. Her voice trembled when she spoke next—with nerves or excitement, he couldn't quite tell. "You are what I desire."

Those words caused his fragile restraint to snap and Jeremy crushed his mouth to hers. Lily's hand slid back into his hair as they took turns devouring one another. Jeremy drank deeply from her lips, dragging from her chest a long, low sigh of desire that stoked the barely-banked flames smoldering since their interlude in the library.

He broke the contact with a gasp and pressed his tongue and lips to the thrumming pulse in her throat. "You're sure?" he asked desperately as his eager hands ran along the soft skin of her arms, skipping her breasts and running down the ridges of her sides, bumping over the boning of her corset. Her shiver of desire spurred him on. "You're certain you want this, Lily?"

Please, he pleaded silently; *say yes...*

He kissed a fiery trail down her neck and over her collarbone. His lips hovered above the freckle on her breast. He thought he might die if she told him to stop. He would expire from unspent desire in a moment if she pushed him away and wisely admitted the disastrous mistake of it all. His hands had stalled at the graceful swell of her hips. Waiting.

Her nails bit into his scalp and tangled in his hair; he was amazed that he was able to hear the sound of her reply over the roar of blood in his ears.

"Yes," she whispered breathlessly. "Please..."

Chapter Nine

With a feral growl, Jeremy dug his fingers into Lily's hips and, with little effort, moved her skirts, lifted her, and set her to straddle his hips. She gave a breathless gasp when his tongue and lips explored her décolletage. He seemed to be lavishing particular attention upon a spot on the top of her left breast.

"You've no idea how long I've been waiting to kiss you here," he groaned, it seemed, more to himself than her, but she found it thrilling to experience him so undone. His tongue delved into the valley between her breasts, unleashing a rush of heat between her thighs. Lily lowered herself onto his lap in an unconscious effort to relieve that growing ache. Her eyes shot open at the unanticipated hardness she found there.

Not entirely unknowledgeable to what happened between a man and a woman—she'd spent much of her life on land where sheep were bred and raised, after all—she knew this meant Jeremy desired her. That didn't stop the shock of the sensation from giving Lily a moment's hesitation. There she was, straddling *Jem* in a carriage; and he *wanted her*. How many times had she barely dared to dream of such a thing? How many nights had she lain awake craving the knowledge of his fingers on her skin, the taste of his lips? And now, to learn that he'd been suffering the same questions and longing? It was nearly overwhelming.

Any nerves she felt were slowly burned away as Jeremy ran his fingertips from the base of her skull, counting each of her vertebrae until he reached her buttocks. Grasping her rear firmly with both of his large hands, he showed her how to give a testing rock of her hips. The motion brought her molten core into very intimate contact with the growing ridge in the front of his breeches.

She was delighted by the hissing breath Jeremy released between his teeth at the delicious friction.

"God, Lily…" He reached up and pulled her face to his in a bruising kiss. The action conveyed the same decade-or-so of desire Lily had felt and it nearly brought her to tears. All these years they could have been together and neither of them had spoken up.

One of his fingers hooked over the top of her bodice. She gasped when he made contact with her erect, sensitive nipple and then cupped the weight of her breast through her gown. He ran his thumb over the bud and, even through the layers of fabric, he was somehow working her higher to a heretofore unknown feverish height.

She began a tentative exploration of her own, admiring the impressive breadth of his shoulders with her palms, and the solid strength of his arms. The tightly coiled power she felt there. Lily knew how strong he was—she had seen him mend stone walls and repair broken carts with his tenants, control powerful stallions deemed unbreakable by lesser men—so she knew he was showing an impressive amount of restraint in his gentle treatment of her.

But the building heat pooling between her legs demanded more.

More force and less care.

She wrenched herself away from their kiss with panting breaths.

"More, Jeremy. I need—I don't know, I just need more." Lily should have known she needn't explain her yearnings to him. He gave her a wolfish grin the likes of which she'd never seen before and wrapped an arm about her waist. Rocking forward, he set her on the opposite seat once more. Fearing he was leaving her, she instinctively wrapped her legs around him.

"Don't worry," he laughed and disentangled himself. When next he spoke, he lowered his voice to a dangerous tone, sparking a thrill that traveled from the base of her skull to the tips of her fingers and toes; "We'll save that for another time."

She watched intently as he sat back as far as the space would permit. His eyes were locked on her face as he began to work her skirts and petticoats up to her legs and hips, revealing inch after inch of pristine, white silk stocking and lacey garter. She blushed and had to break connection with his gaze when he finally revealed the slit in her drawers.

"Look at me, Lily," he demanded, though his tone remained gentle. She did as he bid, though she feared her face might catch fire from the burning blush. "I've told you before how beautiful I find you. You," he said as he gently pressed her thighs open wider, "are stunning. Everywhere." His dark eyes flashed in the dim light of the carriage.

Lily's apprehensions fled when he ran his fingers up the pale, virgin skin of her inner thighs. *Yes, higher.* Her head fell back to the cushions when his palm finally made feather-light contact with her mound. He caressed her through the thin fabric before slipping a finger through the slit of her drawers, skimming the moist petals of her sex, making her jump in pleasure when he danced over the hidden pearl, testing her readiness. Dimly, she heard the rending of fabric as he widened the gap. She gasped and arched as he carefully, slowly slid the tip of a testing finger inside of her.

"You're so wet for me, love," Jeremy groaned; "I've dreamt about kissing you here, too." The naughtiness of the words tore a whimper from Lily's lips as an exciting, terrifyingly powerful wave of need crashed over her. He leaned forward and claimed her mouth once more, stroking her tongue with his as he began to move his finger in and out in slow increments. Her lungs struggled for air when the pad of his thumb found the sensitive bud at the crest of her sex. He stroked her, his fingers slick with her moisture, making her feel both weak and tightly strung at the same time.

Lily's pleasure mounted higher and higher the longer he continued his onslaught on her senses. His thumb working in tight circles, the thrust of his finger, the taste of him, all served to push her closer to the edge. Her hips undulated with his primal rhythm and her thighs trembled uncontrollably, but he used his body to hold her open and vulnerable to his machinations. She was suspended over a precipice; hanging and waiting in gasping anticipation for the fall to come.

Never had she dared to dream…

Never had she thought it possible such sensations could be wrung from her body.

"Jeremy," she whimpered and gasped against his mouth.

Sensing her climax was near in the fluttering of her sheath around his finger, Jeremy continued his rhythm. He ignored the painful throb in his breeches and focused instead on giving Lily pleasure.

He lapped up her sighs like a contented cat in cream. His ears devoured her tantalizing gasps and his body barely resisted the urge to take her, right then and there, with every one of her whimpering cries of delight and passion.

But this wasn't about him.

He wanted to give this to Lily. He longed to gift her with a memory—one of unfettered passion and honest affection—to carry forever.

Because this was certainly something Jeremy would never forget.

"That's it, love. Let go," he growled. "I need you to come for me. Give me this much." The desperate desire in his voice sent Lily beyond the point of coherent thought.

The strings snapped and Lily fell over that edge. A keening cry of disbelief and delight was torn from her by the overwhelming rush of her release, but Jeremy covered her mouth with his; swallowing her sighs and whimpers as if they could sustain him for the rest of his days.

After what felt like an hour of her body rocking from the force of her orgasm, Lily blinked and attempted to focus her cloudy vision as the last little waves of pleasure rippled through her. She found Jeremy smiling down at her. His dark hair was tousled from her fingers and the knot of his cravat was eschewed, but she'd never found him more attractive. It was a foolish thought, but his easy smile made her feel as if she'd done something worth praise.

"I didn't know it was possible, but you're even more beautiful now," he whispered huskily as he helped her right herself and adjust her many layers of skirts. Jeremy drank in the sight of the rosy flush of passion on her dewy skin, the glitter in her eyes, still dreamy and far away from her climax. He savored the sight before him.

Even more, he loved knowing he was the cause of it all.

She was adjusting her gloves and righting her bodice when she caught a glimpse of the unmistakable ridge still straining against the front of his trousers.

"What about you?" she asked, concerned. "Is there something— Can I...?"

"Don't worry about me," he replied as he straightened his jacket and cravat. "I've dealt with worse."

"You're certain?" Lily asked. Feeling emboldened by the waves of sensuality still coursing through her body, she began to reach for him. Jeremy swiftly caught her hands in his.

"While I appreciate the thought, we've nearly arrived at your townhouse." He pressed her fingertips to his lips in an achingly sweet gesture. "It wouldn't do to be caught in such a deliciously compromising situation."

Even Lily's inexperienced mind was able to come up with possibilities. Her cheeks warmed, but she was unsure if it was due to her last shred of modesty, or excitement.

"Am I set to rights?" she fretted as she attempted to shake out her skirts, hoping it wasn't as hopeless a task as it seemed.

"You look as if you've been ravished," Jeremy replied rather smugly.

"I'm sure our mothers would take that well, now wouldn't they? It's bad enough I need to tell my mother we've placed a rather large order of wildflowers on Townsend's tab, but now I've quite clearly had the most erotic experience of my life during the carriage ride home." She did her best to ignore her plummeting stomach at the mention of her fiancé's title and glanced up at Jeremy. His expression made her quirk a brow. "Do try not to look so pleased with yourself."

"I can't help it," he chuckled. "You're a pleasure to please."

Lily tried in vain to straighten her wide-brimmed bonnet and curls. It really was unfair that he needed only to run his fingers through his hair and give his cravat one swift tug to look more than presentable once more.

A glance out the window told her they'd turned onto her street and were only a few blocks away from her home.

"Where do we go from here?" she asked while she still had the chance—before the reality of other people infiltrated their heady cocoon. Jeremy shook his head slowly, seemingly in an effort to find his words.

"No matter how much I enjoyed that," he gestured between them as if to say, *us*; "we cannot allow it to happen again." His words obliterated any foggy bliss lingering in her brain. "You're engaged to marry another man, Lily. He'd be in his right to call me out for what just happened. Thank God I had some restraint and you'll still go to your marriage bed a virgin."

Lily couldn't believe his words; she didn't want to.

"You're going to let me go?"

"I have to," he said, pained. The warmth was beginning to drain from his chocolate eyes.

"Why, Jeremy? I thought you wanted me?"

"More than you know." His words were forceful, but his posture was one of defeat. "You're not mine to want, Lily. You never were."

"But I could have been!" she exclaimed, tears of frustration clogging the back of her throat. "I refuse to believe you can just walk away from me—from this. Surely you must have some feelings for me above desiring my body for one brief interlude in a carriage?"

The grim line of his mouth indicated she'd struck a nerve. His ardor had cooled and now she faced Jeremy, Baron Shefford; not Jemmy, her dearest friend. His eyes had hardened to dark chips of onyx.

"I have to stay away. It's what's best for you; I cannot give you what Townsend can. Breaking the engagement would be foolish and scandalous for your reputation—for your family."

"Don't tell me what's best for me, Jemmy!" she cried. "If you've taught me one thing, it's that what *I* want matters. If you're too afraid to take an account of what you want, then you're not as brave as I once believed. You're a coward." Her words were a knife to his chest.

They rolled to a stop in front of Stratford House and Lily leaped from the vehicle without waiting for a footman to hand her down. Jeremy released a great gust of pent-up air from his aching lungs; he thumped the back of his skull against the wall of the carriage a few times before dragging himself up and out of the vehicle.

If things had been bad before, now they were damn-near intolerable.

Chapter Ten

Not caring who in the street might witness her display, Lily flew up the stairs to the townhouse ahead of Jeremy. He watched helplessly as she floated away, the sound of slippers tapping furiously on the marble floor of the foyer. Having heard the clatter of the carriage, their mothers stepped from the parlor in time for Lily to narrowly miss a collision.

"Slow down, Lily! Stop dashing about like a little hellion," admonished her mother. "What is the matter?" she asked when she noticed the flush of her daughter's skin, though Lily did well hiding the glittering tears in her eyes beneath downcast lashes.

"Nothing, Mother. I—I am just overly fatigued. It was more work than I thought, deciding on the flowers for the wedding." Her emphasis on the last word was not lost on Jeremy. He commended his resistance to the desire to wince at the actual physical pain her derision caused him. He caught his mother eyeing him, but refused to acknowledge her attentions. She, of all people, would be able to read in his eyes that something had transpired. It would be draining enough to try to put her off when they returned home later.

"The Marquess of Townsend is here, dear," the countess added to Lily in a tone amounting to a stage whisper, halting her daughter when she would have turned to retreat upstairs. "Do you think you can muster up the energy to see him? He's only stopped by for a short time."

After a brief hesitation, Lily nodded once and their little party returned to the parlor. Jeremy followed after another second's contemplation; briefly torn between leaving without bidding the Stratfords goodbye (it was beyond the pale, but he trusted they would see his mother home safely) and desiring the sick pleasure of looking Townsend in the eye after having given his betrothed a shuddering orgasm not even a quarter-hour before.

He also wanted to show Lily he was no coward; he wasn't afraid to face the marquess, and he wasn't running from what he wanted, he simply needed to protect Lily by giving her the life and security she so rightly deserved.

Jeremy was forced to watch as Townsend's blond head bowed over Lily's gloved hand. The marquess was clothed in a smart hunter-green jacket with gold buttons and black breeches. It would seem as if Townsend was an impeccable dresser with a sense of style to rival even Sommerfeld's.

"How lovely you look today, Lady Stratford," the older man practically purred over Lily. Jeremy fought valiantly to club back his rising annoyance. Townsend turned to him and nodded a greeting. "Shefford." Was it Jeremy or had the other man's voice turned chilly? "I hear you accompanied my betrothed to pick out the wedding flowers. How...domestic of you."

Jeremy bit back his initial retort and tasted blood. Instead, he sketched a quick bow to the higher-ranked peer and ground out in as light a tone as he could manage, "As a lifelong friend of Lady Stratford, I can safely say I've been dragged to far less pleasurable outings."

He saw the vibrant green of Lily's eyes flash in his direction for a fraction of a second before she turned her attention back to the man who still held her hand in his.

"Indeed?" Townsend eyed Jeremy and Lily, looking for all the world to Jeremy like a rat; one wily enough to sniff out even the slightest crumb of falsehood.

Jeremy knew what he sensed.

This was now the second time Townsend had caught his betrothed in Jeremy's presence, accompanying her on outings in which no man without designs would normally partake.

Jeremy eyed the marquess, daring him to question the innocence of the outing. Jeremy knew in his soul that he would fight to the death to protect Lily's reputation. Townsend, perhaps sensing Jeremy's adamancy, moved on.

"Yes, well, I have come to offer to escort you to the Lucklows' ball this coming Saturday."

"That would be lovely."

Jeremy was torn between rolling his eyes at Lily's overly-cheery inflection and choking on the bile of molten jealousy forcing its way up into his chest.

"Will you be joining us, Shefford?" asked the countess, oblivious to the simmering testosterone in the room. She turned to the marquess and elaborated, "Shefford frequently joins us at these events, you see."

"Does he?" Townsend's sandy brows rose in feigned surprise. No doubt the bastard was fully aware that Jeremy did, indeed, attend those events and his name was always penciled on Lily's dance card for the first waltz of the evening. "Well? Will you be joining us this Saturday, Shefford?" Jeremy sensed the trap.

"I've not forwarded my response to the Lucklows yet," Jeremy replied smoothly; he had no desire for the marquess to believe he was overeager to tag along at every event to which the Stratfords attended.

He had to play this carefully.

This had become a dangerous game betwixt the two men, a wrong word or a misstep could cost Lily her future and create a scandal that would drag the Stratford name through the dirt enough that it could impact even the next generation. The *ton* loved scandal and didn't easily forget.

At that moment, Sommerfeld had the misfortune to step into the room after leaving his father's study. Looking back and forth from Jeremy to Townsend, Jeremy would have sworn he heard his friend curse, "Bugger," beneath his breath before pasting an easy smile upon his face.

"Townsend!" he greeted the marquess with a jaunty swing of that asinine cane. The older man glared at Jeremy for one moment more before twisting his face into some semblance of a grin and turning to Lily's brother.

"Sommerfeld," Townsend greeted him.

Jeremy experienced a twinge of relief when the marquess finally released Lily. She, however, still refused to acknowledge Jeremy's continued presence. He couldn't blame her—not after the way he'd touched her, defiled her, and pushed her away with a sorry excuse. She deserved better. Even if she told him that he was what she wanted, he needed to do the right thing. He had to regain his composure

and she would undoubtedly see that Townsend could give her everything he couldn't.

"I am meeting some friends at the club for dinner," the marquess
said to Lily's brother. "Why don't you join me?"

Sommerfeld accepted the invitation and, unexpectedly, the marquess turned to Jeremy. "You are welcome to join us, Shefford...un-
less you'd rather continue to pick posies?"

Jeremy felt that all-too-familiar urge to strike something; this time,
it was Townsend's even front teeth.

Recognizing the fury simmering just beneath her son's skin, Jeremy's mother smoothly interjected; "You'll have to excuse him, my
lord. He is my escort home."

"Nonsense," fluttered the countess. "The men may have their time.
You've hardly visited with Lily—and I'm sure she is so excited to tell
you of all of the planning we've been doing. If the hour grows too late
and they have not returned, then I will make sure you're properly escorted home."

"It's settled then," said Townsend, brooking no further argument.

Farewells were said—during which Jeremy had to endure
Townsend depositing another lingering kiss on Lily's hand—and the
coachman brought round the carriage of black and gold livery; the
Townsend colors. Sommerfeld and Jeremy stood on the steps while
Townsend discussed something with one of his footmen.

"This is going to be bloody miserable," grumbled Sommerfeld.

"You don't need to tell me that."

"I don't mean for *you*, you addle-brain; I mean for me. Sitting in a
small, enclosed space with the two of you is going to be like being
locked in a cage with a lion and a tiger, the way you two have been
eyeing one another tonight."

"I'll behave if he does," Jeremy ground out, attempting to affect the appearance of nonchalance.

"Like hell," his friend snorted. "When have you ever behaved?" Sommerfeld followed the marquess up into the vehicle.

You have no idea, Jeremy thought, recalling with striking vividness his most recent carriage ride.

The memory served to make his relaxed appearance and smile more genuine on the ride to the club—much to Townsend's confusion.

Jeremy had been content to allow Sommerfeld and Townsend to monopolize the conversation at dinner. He'd supplemented his smile in the carriage by picturing all the ways he'd like to ground the marquess's smug face into the dirt.

After spending a couple of hours in his presence, he'd come to learn quite a bit more about Lily's intended. The man was intelligent, Jeremy grudgingly had to concede that fact. Hearing him talk of his various business investments—machines for mills and weaponry production – was well and above Jeremy's head. The man had nearly a decade on Jeremy and Sommerfeld, and it was clear he'd used every one of those additional years to take the already grand Townsend inheritance and make it truly obscene. It was evident in his membership to this club—though the Stratford men were also members – in the gold buttons on his every jacket, the impeccable quality and shine of his boots; the perfect grooming of his sandy sideburns and pomaded hair. It was clear that Townsend saw himself as most peoples' better, and he'd be right a vast majority of the time.

Jeremy was, however, quickly noticing something else about the marquess: He loved to talk about himself. It didn't take a great deal of imagination for Jeremy to picture Lily being run over daily by this man's self-love. Not only would her voice never be heard, but—if his flippancy about the wedding planning had been any indication—she would forever be at the mercy of his dismissal of her needs and desires. It was more than a little disturbing. She'd be trading one oppressive situation for another.

With no small amount of effort, he pushed aside his discomfort. He told himself this was his jealousy rearing its green head once again. Surely Lily's future with this man wouldn't be as bad as he was beginning to believe it might be. She would be a marchioness, after all, and that was not to be taken lightly. The power and wealth which came with it could surely make up for a great deal of other shortcomings.

Following dinner, the trio went to smoke cigars and sip port in the billiard room. Jeremy didn't belong to one of these gentleman's clubs —he spent so little time in Town and he didn't feel the need to make false friends—but that didn't stop him from admiring the fineness of the paintings of hunting scenes, the quality of the port and tobacco, the gilt trim on the sconces, the heavy draperies in exceptional fabrics, and rich cherrywood paneled walls. The billiard tables, themselves, were covered in perfect swaths of cobalt cloth and boasted beautifully carved legs and intricately woven leather pouches. The billiard balls were polished fair to gleaming.

The extravagance was almost too much for him to take in all in one evening.

"Top-notch club, isn't it?" Townsend asked smugly, clearly having caught Jeremy admiring his surroundings.

"Indeed." Jeremy couldn't lie about that; it would have been too obvious since there was nothing unrefined about it.

Reining in his pride, Jeremy thought to try his hand at small talk. He benignly commented that he might inquire about membership and he was rewarded with more derision from the marquess.

Townsend laughed as he strode over to the nearby unoccupied billiard table. "One does not simply become a member. You require a sponsor."

"I've offered to sponsor Shefford numerous times," Sommerfeld chimed in, unwilling to watch Jeremy be trodden upon.

"Even then," Townsend replied as he eyed the shaft of a queue for straightness, "they do not allow just anyone to be a member." Despite Townsend's relatively light tone, this was inching dangerously close to an affront to Jeremy's honor. Sommerfeld sensed the impending danger in the tension gathering across his friend's broad shoulders.

"The Shefford barony is extremely old and well-respected. They would do well to have a member with such a pedigree."

Ignoring the comment, Townsend eyed the two younger men from across the table. "Are we going to play or not?" He shot a look at another man across the room and waved him over to be their fourth with an imperious crook of his wrist.

Jeremy and Sommerfeld glanced at one another briefly before setting down their drinks and selecting their queues. Sommerfeld's stiff movements belied his discomfort at the situation. Likely, loyalty to both his family and Jeremy were at war within him, and he was struggling to toe the fine line between politeness and anxiously steering these men away from a bout of fisticuffs over his sister.

Heaving a sympathetic sigh, Jeremy resolved to do his best to make the remainder of the evening as painless as possible for Sommerfeld. It wasn't his fault Jeremy had mucked up the entire situation—perhaps even the balance of his own life. He'd already resolved to move forward; now he had to come to terms with the fact that he'd be forced to interact with Townsend on occasion if he hoped to remain close with the Stratford family.

He genially clapped Sommerfeld on the back and gestured for Townsend to begin.

Several games later, the drinks had turned from port to warmed brandy. The tensions grew looser—at least they did for Jeremy—as he and George played and subsequently beat Townsend and his partner, Viscount Morley. He imagined himself showing Townsend a modicum of humility with each ball he sent sailing into the pockets with a satisfying click. Townsend may have been more adept at business dealings, but Jeremy was good with his hands.

Very good.

Despite his size and penchant for manual labor, he could be quite adept with details and finesse. Billiards was one such area in which he'd always excelled.

Jeremy sank the final ball into a leather pocket and tried not to look too triumphant. Townsend's response to the fourth loss of the evening was to give a brusque wave to a servant, signaling the purchase of yet another round of drinks on his seemingly bottomless tab. Sommerfeld excused himself for a piss, leaving Jeremy alone with the marquess and unfamiliar viscount.

"So, Townsend," said Morley as he leaned on his pool queue, "the wedding is fast approaching, is it not?" The heavyset man's already ruddy complexion was made more so by glass after glass of spirits. The broken capillaries of his face spoke of someone who was quite the elbow-crooker, perhaps even more so when he wasn't the one footing the bill.

"That it is," replied Townsend before taking a swig of brandy. "Nigh on five weeks. The first of the banns are to be read this coming Sunday."

Jeremy saw Morley's gaze flick to him before returning to Townsend. Ah, so Sommerfeld had been right. His "relationship" with

Lily had been a topic of curiosity here at the club. No doubt the viscount had asked such a question in Jeremy's presence to see whether or not he'd get a rise out of him. Jeremy refused to give him the satisfaction. Instead, he feigned interest in the hunting scene hung upon a nearby wall and leaned more heavily on his cue than was necessary; calculating that the appearance of a greater level of inebriation would free him from having to take part in this goading.

"You're a lucky man. Lady Lily Stratford has been one of the gems of the marriage mart for quite some time." Jeremy could feel Morely's watery eyes on him and it made his skin crawl with ire. "It's a wonder she didn't accept an offer before now," Morley added with a sound caught somewhere between a hiccup and a chuckle.

"Indeed. She'll make a pretty little marchioness, will she not?" Townsend replied, velvet smugness coating his voice like slime.

Jeremy's grip tightened on the polished wooden stick in his hand. He willed himself to not use it as a club, breathing measured inhalations through his nose.

"We won't be seeing as much of you around here with a chit like that at home, now will we?" Morley guffawed.

"We're going to do a bit of traveling for the honeymoon, during which I fully intend to get an heir upon her." Jeremy felt a wave of nausea. "I'll deposit her in one of my country houses; keep her busy with a new babe each year. She'll be content on her own and I'll be content here in Town, living life and doing my business as I always have."

A brood mare, Jeremy seethed, *He sees Lily as naught more than a broodmare to be kept, ridden at will, and only really good for furthering a healthy bloodline.*

"She's pretty enough," Townsend added; "I'll bring her to Town for events when she happens to not be in confinement."

Morely jabbed the marquess in the ribs with a conspiratorial elbow. "If I had a comely young wife like her, that wouldn't be very often," he snorted gleefully.

Jeremy didn't doubt that Lily would far prefer a life in the country than London, but what disturbed him was Townsend's seeming lack of interest in getting to know Lily. He *assumed* she would want to live in the country; he *assumed* she would want this life as a broodmare; he *assumed* she would want to live separately from her husband – that she wouldn't mind the implication of infidelity, even though it was more the norm than the exception in *ton* marriages of convenience.

Jeremy ached, knowing Lily would likely wither away in the country with little to no acknowledgment from this prig who felt the match was convenient in the sense that he could get his legitimate heirs on her and continue living the life of a bachelor. Meanwhile, Lily would be shuttered away in some far-off estate—away from all that she knew and loved. All the horses, flowers, and open air in the world couldn't cure loneliness. And Lily deserved more...so much more. She deserved to be cherished. She was made to be a companion—to be appreciated for the enrichment she would bring to a marriage, loved for her bright laughter, and adored for her quick wit.

Morley was soon pulled into conversation with another acquaintance, leaving just Jeremy and Townsend. He caught Jeremy's gaze; his ice-blue eyes narrowed into slits. Townsend tossed back the last of his drink and sauntered over to him. Jeremy's body tense reflexively. The rat smelled blood, either in Jeremy's silence or his poorly-disguised edgy demeanor. Townsend rested his hip against the bullnose edge of the billiard table.

"Care to play one-on-one while we await our errant companions?" he asked silkily.

"My start." Jeremy forced his voice to remain even.

Townsend retrieved a white cue ball and held it out to him. Before Jeremy could take it, however, the marquess snatched it back.

"Don't think me a fool, Shefford." Townsend inclined his head so close that Jeremy could smell the brandy on his moist breath, and proceeded to speak in a dangerously low tone. "I'm not deaf to the rumors around here that you were eyeing Lily Stratford for yourself. She's not for you; not anymore." Jeremy did his best to remain impassive. "I'll not be made a cuckold by the likes of you," he spat, happily ignoring his hypocrisy; "I'll not be mocked for allowing another man to escort her about Town.

"Be advised now that I'll see the two of you ruined and ensure her reputation is so tattered that she'll never make another match if you don't step away. Immediately. I'm the best option she will ever have."

Jeremy leveled his best glare at Townsend, but it was pointless. The marquess had correctly surmised that Jeremy would sacrifice anything to keep Lily safe. Any denial would have played right into Townsend's hands, so Jeremy remained steely and silent.

"Do we have an understanding, then?" Townsend asked in a much lighter tone, even having the gall to smile as if they were friends discussing nothing of more consequence than a wager on horseflesh.

Not trusting himself to speak, Jeremy had no choice but to give a single, slow inclination of his head in assent.

"Lovely." Townsend held out the cue ball again, but, before Jeremy could take it, he let it tumble from his fingers. The polished stone landed with an unforgiving thud on the toe of Jeremy's boot. The stiff leather was likely the only thing saving Jeremy from a broken foot. He couldn't halt the small grunt of surprised pain in his throat. Townsend's mouth tilted in twisted satisfaction when Jeremy reached to steady himself with a white-knuckled grip on the edge of the billiard table. Sommerfeld chose that moment to return.

"Have I missed anything?" he asked cheerfully, but Jeremy recognized his friend's inflection well enough to realize he was approaching the situation as one would a wild animal.

"Smashing!" Townsend said as he turned to Sommerfeld. "Shefford here was just congratulating me on managing to snag your angel of a sister."

"Oh, was he, now?" Jeremy could feel Sommerfeld's eyes on him over Townsend's shoulder. No longer under the scrutinizing gaze of the marquess, Jeremy leaned both palms flat on the tabletop and forced himself to breathe. The fierce throb in his foot took the air from his lungs. Jeremy swore he'd gut Townsend if fortune ever provided the opportunity.

The desire came not from the slights against him, but from how the man had spoken about Lily. Torture, Jeremy could take – and he was now, more than ever, aware that he would have to resign himself to a future filled with it—but threatening Lily nearly blinded him with rage.

Suddenly sensing how thin his friend's restraint had run, Sommerfeld began to make hasty excuses. "I hate to run out like this, but I've presently remembered a bit of business I must handle. My solicitors will be expecting my reply first thing in the morning." It was a brilliant excuse because the business-minded Townsend wouldn't think to question it.

"Duty calls," Townsend said and clapped Jeremy on the back harder than was necessary. "It's been a pleasure having you gentlemen join me. We must do it again soon."

Sommerfeld was able to rush his hobbling friend out of the club without further incident. He procured a hackney with ease and they were quickly on their way back to the Stratford townhouse.

"What in the hell was that about? Why are you limping?" Sommerfeld demanded when he was sure their voices would be drowned out by the clatter of hooves and wheels, the jangle of tack. Jeremy took the opportunity to stretch out and propped his aching foot on the opposite seat beside his friend. "You look like you could benefit from borrowing my cane," Sommerfeld observed, eyeing Jeremy's boot.

"I don't need your sodding cane," snapped Jeremy. He closed his eyes and inhaled deeply, allowing the rocking motion of the carriage to calm him as best it could.

"What happened while I was gone?" Sommerfeld's growing concern was evident in his voice.

"Don't worry, I have not mucked up anything between your family and Townsend."

At least, not yet; not past the point of being irreparable.

Not if he walked away now.

"At this moment, I'm more concerned about you. You must have had an apoplectic fit in there—that's the only logical explanation I can think of for you congratulating Townsend." A wry smile flitted across Jeremy's lips, but he didn't refute Townsend's statement. Several minutes passed in thoughtful silence before Sommerfeld spoke again.

"I miss my friend, Jem. I miss laughing with you. Seeing you this way over the past week has been hell for me; I can only imagine how it must be for you... It will get better. Over time, I'm sure it will have to get better."

"I'm returning to Kent tomorrow," Jeremy spoke decisively, effectively halting his friend's string of optimism which had only been serving to increase Jeremy's frustration.

"What about helping Lily with the wedding?"

"She has both of our mothers now; I'm sure she has more than enough help. You were right, besides. It was a mistake to offer my assistance."

Sommerfeld waited a few moments before gently asking, "What shall I say to Lily?"

"Nothing," Jeremy replied. "She shan't miss me. I've made sure of that."

"I'm sure she will—"

"She shan't," he cut Sommerfeld off and turned unseeing eyes toward the passing scenery. "It's for the best anyway." To that, Sommerfeld was unable to argue.

They rode the rest of the way back to the Stratford townhouse in silence. Sommerfeld solemnly shook his friend's hand in farewell and, while Jeremy waited in the vehicle, he went inside and informed Lady Shefford that her son had procured a hackney and was waiting to escort her home. If she noticed her son's odd behavior, Abigail did not mention it; nor did she bring it up during the uncomfortable ride back home.

She grew more concerned when she saw Jeremy's slight limp but still did not comment. He would explain if he wanted to and, clearly, his priority was getting into the house and locking himself away. On his slightly-halting climb of the stairway, she heard him give terse instructions to have his horse ready at daybreak and a trunk prepared and sent after him to Rosehall. The resounding slam of his door made her cringe, but none so much as the muffled string of curses she heard even from below-stairs.

Chapter Eleven

Saturday afternoon was filled with preparations for that evening's ball at the Lucklow townhouse. Lily was prodded, curled, pinned, tugged, yanked, and squeezed, all in the name of conventional beauty expectations. As always, none of it made any difference to the usual sense of dread that arose whenever she imagined being thrust into yet another crowded room. All the beauty regimens in the world did nothing for this. Still, she supposed it must have done something to her physical appearance, at least, because her mother couldn't seem to help repeating how beautiful the marquess was going to find her.

Lily remained unmoved.

There was only one man's eye she wanted to catch, and she didn't even know if he was going to show up. In any case, she'd chosen her best gown in rich, hunter-green silk trimmed in silver ribbon and lace. Jeremy had once told her the ensemble complimented her eyes, and, looking back on it, he'd seemed hard-pressed to stop staring. It was funny what one noticed when one was aware of unspoken emotions—

the admiring looks, the thoughtful gestures, the attentiveness. There was a fine line between affection and tenderness, and that line could so easily disappear.

When *had* it disappeared between the two of them, and why, oh *why*, had it taken her so long to notice?

She barely dared to hope that Jeremy would be there to see her in the gown he'd once admired. She'd had time to process everything that had transpired and Lily was convinced that Jeremy was doing what he'd always done: He was protecting her. She knew in her heart that he had more respect and genuine affection for her than to seduce her in a carriage and toss her to the wayside. He hadn't been making excuses after regretting his actions, he wasn't trying to take the easy way out; he'd been nothing but concerned for how she and her family would suffer a broken engagement to a powerful peer. He was willing to walk away from her forever—to break his own heart and ignore his own needs and desires—to protect her. The fact that she'd called him a coward for doing so nearly made Lily ill.

Her mother, noticing her wan pallor, patted Lily's hand. "Don't worry, dear. Townsend is going to think you're absolutely stunning. He couldn't have chosen a more beautiful woman as his bride." This did nothing to assuage Lily's anxieties; though her mother had been correct—almost to the word—about Townsend's compliments.

His lips had lingered on her knuckles and he gave her a charming smile that, no doubt, would have moved any woman to distraction. Any woman, that is, except for Lily. She politely accepted his compliments and felt a stab of guilt when he presented her with a brooch of sapphires and diamonds to wear that evening. Her mother pinned it for her in the center of her green bodice. It was an extravagant gift and not typical for a man to give to a woman to whom he was not yet wed, but, instead of feeling grateful, Lily could only hope Jeremy saw her and not the bauble affixed to her chest—the mark of another man.

The carriage ride with her mother, father, and betrothed was hazy at best. Later, Lily would recall the muffled conversation and could even remember Townsend had taken her hand in his as a show of his affection to her parents. She had looked at their joined hands and felt…nothing…as if she were watching another man and woman from afar. She'd turned and feigned modesty rather than join the conversation.

The queue to enter the townhouse of Lord and Lady Lucklow was where Lily's anxiety began in earnest. They exited the carriage and stepped in line amongst the rest of the guests. Cheerful talk and excited laughter surrounded them and, not for the first time, Lily wished she could partake in it with the same carelessness. The ease with which all of these other people interacted and looked forward to the crush of the ballroom was unfathomable to Lily.

The mere thought of all those bodies in an enclosed space; the air thick with unwashed flesh, cloying perfume, and candle smoke; all those prying eyes and judgmental whispers; were enough to cause an iron band of panic to wrap itself around her chest.

Townsend pulled her arm through the crook of his, letting his long, gloved fingers lay over his ring on her hand. This was their first public appearance since their engagement; it was natural that he would want to appear possessive and enamored of his bride-to-be. Practically every member of the *ton* was, after all, extremely concerned with appearances. The realization that everyone's eyes would be on them dawned on Lily with the weight of a boulder upon her heart. There was a crushing, sinking sensation that began to make her knees so weak she struggled to keep her footing when Townsend moved forward in the queue and all but dragged her along beside him.

Her heartbeat pounded in her ears; her hands went numb as they finally reached the top of the stairs to the ballroom. The announcement of their names was nearly drowned out by her frantic thoughts. Her chest heaved when she saw the collection of what had to be at least sixty couples crammed into the space. She barely resisted the urge to claw at Townsend's hands and free herself—she felt as if he were a ballast carrying her down to the suffocating depths of the Channel.

Unfortunately for Lily, there would be no quick retreat this time. She'd arrived on the arm of one of the most eligible bachelors of the *ton*. There were dozens of faces to greet, congratulations to accept, and compliments to receive. Lily attempted to step back from the crush, but Townsend held onto her arm in a bruising grip. He'd clearly felt her faltering all evening and he'd be damned if she was going to embarrass him now that they were in the throng. This was such a departure from the man she'd experienced thus far—he'd always been solicitous and polite. It was a harsh reminder of just how little she'd interacted with the man to whom she was to be married.

Lily's throat began to constrict painfully. The blurry faces around her were asking questions she didn't understand; worse, they expected her to answer. She smiled woodenly and hoped it would suffice.

When there was finally a break in the crowd before the next couple came up to greet them, Lily turned to Townsend and tried to sound as calm as possible when she requested a cup of punch.

"Please?" she asked as sweetly as she could manage. "I'm parched."

The croak from Lily's tight throat seemed convincing, even to her own ears. Though he didn't seem terribly pleased at the interruption to his mingling, Townsend placed a kiss on her knuckles and turned away to slip through a gap in the crowd. Lily immediately backed up until her spine met a pillar on the outskirts of the room. She turned and concealed herself behind a potted palm, gasping for breath, pressing her palms to her chest in an effort to stop her heart from crashing through her ribs.

No longer enclosed on all sides by people, Lily's thrumming pulse began to slow marginally. Her hearing latched onto another sound; this time, the plucks and trills of an orchestra preparing to begin the music for the evening.

"I believe the first dance is a waltz," Lily heard one be-plumed woman say to her companion as they strolled nearby. "After that, a country reel!"

Jeremy.

Lily's heart felt lighter. He had to come now that their waltz was about to take place. He could help her panic; only he knew how to comfort her and assuage her very real, if irrational, fears.

If she remained hidden, then Townsend would miss the opportunity to ask her for the dance—she didn't want to have to explain to him that this dance was claimed and had always belonged to another man.

Feeling for all the world like a girl sneaking out of bed to steal a glance at a ball, Lily peered through the stiff fronds of the potted palm and scanned the ballroom. Except for officers, all of the men were in black dress clothes. Several of them even had hair in a similar hue to Jeremy's, but not one of them matched his height or the breadth of his shoulders.

The instruments became more insistent.

Instead of beautiful, Lily found the screech of the violin only served to further shred her nerves.

Surely he'll come, Lily thought to herself, trying to ignore the rising tide of panic. *Surely he won't have forgotten.*

Lily's breath increased to short, quick pants. The stays of her corset felt as if they were tightening around her. The edges of her vision began fading to black. She screwed her eyes shut, willing herself to just breathe; breathe as Jeremy taught her. Thinking of him only backfired on Lily, however, intensifying her awareness that he was not present. For the first time in their lives, Jeremy Balfour was not there for her.

The orchestra paused.

And Lily felt something shatter deep inside of her as the first notes of a waltz swelled and washed over her.

Though no one was touching her, she experienced the overwhelming weight of the dozens of bodies as if they had all seated themselves upon her torso. The fingers of panic began closing around her throat, making each breath a struggle. She frantically searched for a way out of the ballroom. A balcony door stood slightly ajar in the middle of the far wall. Focusing on that point of freedom, Lily pushed her way through the crowd. Not caring whose dress she snagged or whose toes she crushed, Lily made frantic strides across the room. Outraged yelps and startled cries followed in her wake.

The door felt impossibly far away until, with one last lurch for freedom, Lily stumbled free. She heaved her weight against the door and sucked great gulps of the cool night air as she groped for a barely-visible bench in the shafts of golden light streaming from the ballroom. She sat roughly and pressed her hands to her stomach to control her breathing. When her vision failed to normalize, she bent forward as far as her gown and stays would allow, and attempted to hold her head between her knees.

The motion recalled how Jeremy had forced her into this position during a particularly violent panic as a teenager. Lily could still hear the frantic tone of his voice when she hadn't been able to catch her breath. He'd sat her down and held her like this, stroking her spine and the back of her head, murmuring soothing nonsense despite his obvious concern.

This time, however, Lily had only herself.

Several dark spots appeared on her skirts, evident even through her hazy vision. At first, she thought dimly that this was the beginning of a fainting spell...until the spots grew and multiplied as they were quickly joined by more tears.

It wasn't long before Lily's body was wracked with sobs. She clutched her sides, dug her nails into her ribs, and fought against the stiff boning of her corset. The torrent of frustration came pouring out of Lily in that darkened corner of the balcony. She fought the urge to scream and rage against her family's expectations of her as much as she did the constraints of her clothing. Never before had she felt such a keen stab of loss—no, it was a burning, searing sensation...a stab might heal, but a brand would forever linger.

She cried until her eyes felt swollen and her jaw ached from biting back anguished screams. Still, Lily sat alone in the night, rocking herself because she had too many torrid emotions to sit still.

The last strains of a waltz died in the air around her.

By the time the countess discovered her daughter huddled in the corner of the balcony—her cheeks stained with the salt of dried tears and her dress rumpled beyond repair—she was all too ready to accept Lily's half-hearted excuse that she felt unwell.

In a far-off tone, Lily had requested her mother take her home at once. Concerned just as much for Lily's wellbeing as she was for the whispers of the guests at the ball, her mother acquiesced.

Silently, Lily was led through another door off the balcony into a darkened salon—her mother didn't want her to have to face the eyes of the guests looking as bedraggled as she did. Word was sent to Townsend that Lily was poorly and that her parents would be escorting her home. He still hadn't made his appearance by the time their carriage was brought round to the front of the townhouse.

Lily thanked God for small favors; she didn't think she had the strength to concoct elaborate details of her sudden "illness" and Townsend's piercing eyes would surely see through anything she might say.

"Do you feel faint, dear?" her mother asked, removing her glove and pressing a cool, dry hand to the back of Lily's forehead.

She shook her head mutely and stared, unseeing, out the carriage window.

"Maybe she should have eaten something before we left home," Lily heard her father say in a helpful tone.

"I think it was simply all the excitement…"

Lily stopped listening to the rest of their discussion; thinking only of burrowing deeply into her bed and never stirring again.

Once back at their townhouse, she climbed the stairs wordlessly after refusing her father's offer of assistance. She'd assured her parents that she would go straight to bed and hope a good night's sleep would help. The lie felt hollow on her tongue. She doubted if anything would cure her sense of loss.

Mary helped remove her gown and petticoats. She was stripped down to her corset, chemise, and stockings when the girl loosened Lily's stays. The great whoosh of air that was subsequently permitted into Lily's lungs seemed to usher in a new, crushing wave of hurt and loss. The corset fell to the floor and she doubled over beneath the weight of the pain. Thinking that she'd somehow hurt Lily, the maid began apologizing profusely.

"I'm fine," Lily bit out between gasps. "Please just leave. Now." Her words sounded strangled to even her own ears. The maid dashed out, no doubt rushing to advise Lily's mother of the development in her mistress's condition. Lily dropped to her knees and held her face in her hands. Her tears began anew and the wracking sobs filled her newly-freed chest with a ferocity she'd been unable to achieve within the restraints of her corset.

She sobbed until the ache in her chest became an empty, echoing cavern. The void was not left simply because of what she knew would never be with Jeremy, but by the fact that she'd lost the one person – apart from her brothers – whom she considered her closest, dearest friend. Not only were the summers at Rosehall gone, but his smile and laughter, his teasing, and his kind heart. She'd lost her co-conspirator and confidant. She'd lost her best friend.

Hiccupping, Lily crawled into bed and buried herself beneath the sheets and coverlet, pulling the blankets above her head like a child. Shutting out the light of the candles she hadn't bothered to extinguish, she lay awake for many hours replaying her childhood with Jeremy and her brothers, carefully filing away all of the sunny, happy memories to serve her in the many years to come.

Sleep eluded Jeremy.

He paced the corridors of the Rosehall like a spectral ancestor, waif-like and silent—though with a gait slightly hampered by his injured foot. His white-and-tan hounds, Felix and Felicity, siblings born of the same litter, padded slowly after him. At first, they'd been overjoyed at their master's return, leaping and baying at his feet as he rode his mount to the stables around the side of the manor. The animals had become much more subdued, however, once they picked up on his morose agitation. Now, they followed him through the halls, their nails clicking softly upon the floors and whimpering occasionally to one another as if discussing what could possibly be done about their master. Jeremy, however, knew there was nothing to cure him.

The thought of drinking himself to sleep was unappealing, so, instead, he walked. He peered into the still, darkened rooms, not knowing what exactly he was looking for but realizing deep inside that he would never locate whatever it was. The house was filled with more ghosts than just he.

Lily was in the library, perched upon the arm of a chair and giving a dramatic reading from a collection of Shakespeare; she was in the kitchens, stealing freshly-baked buns and burning her fingertips; she followed him up the stairs only to challenge him to a race down the hallway. She dashed about the gardens, ducking into the hedge maze when the boys' teasing and chasing became too much, picking his mother's beloved hydrangea blooms despite numerous warnings. She was mounted atop her dappled mare, Posey, keeping pace with him and her brother despite their best efforts to run wild and free of her dogging – at least, that had been George's aim.

Was it really only two summers ago when Lily and his mother had packed a cart full of food and brought the refreshments out to Jeremy and his father? They'd been working through the heat of the day on a new footbridge to provide a shorter route for half of the tenants to reach the village of Wrothsborough. They and the tenants had been grateful for the respite. Jeremy, however, had been hardly able to drink or eat, so absorbed was he in the way Lily closed her eyes and turned her face to the sun, savoring the listless breeze.

Unbidden, Jeremy's feet brought him to the far chamber on the second floor—the one overlooking the gardens and thick copse of trees on the other side of the sheep fields. This room had always been designated as Lily's ever since they'd all graduated from the nursery on the third floor. Though Rosehall wasn't a far carriage ride from the Aldborough holdings, the room was available whenever the Stratfords might stay too late in the evening following a dinner party or inclement weather.

Jeremy carefully, slowly pushed open the door, as if afraid to wake someone sleeping inside of the room. The furniture was draped with white sheets and the curtains were drawn to protect the rug and furnishings from dust and sunlight while unoccupied. Jeremy shuffled over to the bed and sat on the edge of the mattress. The only sound was the creaking ropes of the bed frame beneath his substantial weight. Jeremy heaved a sigh and lay on his back. He fancied he caught a whiff of Lily, but it was impossible. Rationally, he knew the maids had done a thorough cleaning and stripped the bed after the last time Lily had been in residence, but it was a comforting thought, nonetheless. Felix nudged his nose beneath one of his palms while Felicity jumped onto the mattress, circled twice, and then flopped down to press her warm back to his side. Arms flung out as if in utter surrender, Jeremy closed his eyes and willed a benevolent, dreamless sleep to come and take him.

Chapter Twelve

The next week passed by in a haze for Lily. She felt like a wind-up dancer with her painted smile and automatic actions. She allowed her mother to guide her through the motions of wedding planning, presented an appropriate amount of gratitude when Townsend called to make sure she was feeling improved, feigned excitement at the first reading of the banns, and did her damnedest not to think of Jeremy.

At tea one day, Abigail happened to mention how Jeremy had retreated to Kent—something about business—though Lily knew the truth.

He was freeing himself of the Season in Town; freeing himself of her. The realization hit her like a knife being twisted in her gut.

She gradually learned to live with the hollow ache left behind by his absence from the Lucklows' ball; telling herself it was better to get used to it now while she was still in the comfort of her own home than while she was also trying to learn how to be a marchioness. Soon, she would be the lady of her own house with accounts to manage, staff to run, and various estates and homes to coordinate. Not to mention the parties…

Hosting Townsend's house parties, dinners, and balls would be some of her biggest responsibilities—as they were for all aristocratic wives. The other duties were daunting, but playing the role of a hostess was downright terrifying. Her limbs went numb at the thought of greeting all those people, of standing in a receiving line practically shackled to the floor by responsibility. Gone were her days of being able to duck into the background to catch her breath. As the wife of such a powerful and influential man, she would either be presiding over these events or be invited as an honored guest—a matron to whom all the debutantes would look for guidance in behavior and fashion so they might be so lucky as to land a husband as she had. There would be no escape…from her *own life*.

She'd tried for years to find a way to cope with large crowds in enclosed spaces, but nothing had worked. Forcing herself to breathe, telling herself she was being silly, only worked in so many situations. Begging, crying, and pleading with her mother to allow her to stay home had only worked so many times. Her insistence that this wasn't in her head had often created friction with her family – even earning her punishment on a few occasions.

The only true respite and respect for her circumstances she'd ever experienced had been with Jeremy.

Though she wasn't overly optimistic, Lily hoped to convince herself that, just maybe, Townsend could fill that void left behind by Jeremy's absence.

Eventually.

Her betrothed had visited only one time other than to make sure she hadn't expired after taking her abrupt leave from the ball, and he always made his presence brief under the pretense of some meeting or business matter. Lily didn't feel an ounce of warmth either for or from the man. He was pleasant enough to look at—certainly aristocratic in dress, manners, and refined features—but even his kisses on her hand left her feeling chilled. He smiled at her, but Lily noticed the glint in his gaze was not as kind as it should be. His ice-blue eyes sometimes appeared frozen, like ice upon a very deep lake. He treated their engagement as a business transaction and, while Lily was realistic and astute enough to realize this was exactly what it was, that didn't stop a part of her from longing for some tenderness, some congeniality between the two of them.

A couple of times she made overtures and attempts at getting to know him, but Townsend remained distant and, seemingly, uninterested. To be sure, he never asked her a single question about her interests. He certainly didn't ask her about her desires. He seemed content to keep Lily at arm's length, seeing her when it was convenient for his schedule, and leaving her to her own devices at other times. Most women might have found solace in such an arranged match: a husband who allowed her to go about her own business as he did his. Lily, however, was not like most women. She'd been raised in a loving (if sometimes overbearing) well-intentioned family, which had been extended to include the family of the old Baron Shefford. Lily had grown accustomed to the hope that she would find friendship and at least a modicum of warmth with the man whom she would marry— granted, the fanciful part of her had always imagined him with dark eyes and raven hair—but Lily knew now that this was not to be her reality.

She was contemplating as much when George walked into the library. She'd been staring unseeing at the striped wall papering, holding an open book in her lap.

"Didn't mean to disturb you," her elder brother apologized as she swung to face him, startled from her reverie.

"You didn't I was just…"

"Gathering wool?" he asked with a smile and a jaunty swing of that silly cane. He was carrying a book and brought it over to one of the shelves, to replace it amongst its companions. Lily closed the book she'd been pretending to read as he claimed the cushion beside her.

"You've been so quiet as of late, Lily," he gently observed. She opened her mouth to protest, but he cut her off. "I may not be around all the time and I know I can be a bit dense," Lily smiled at him; "but I am still observant enough to realize when something is troubling you." George's eyes searched hers. "What is the matter? You have not been the same since your…episode this past Saturday."

Lily averted her gaze and focused instead on her hands resting on the book in her lap. Townsend's diamonds glittered and flashed on her finger. Lily suddenly felt the desperate need to tell someone—even George—about her feelings for Jeremy. She no longer cared about the ridicule she might receive when he accused her of a girlish infatuation with his best friend. Lily was secure in the fact that Jeremy felt as she did, at least somewhat. She opened her mouth to speak, but was stopped by a rap at the door; Edwards slid into the room.

"A message has arrived for the countess," the butler advised. "She has gone for tea with Lady Lucklow, but the boy insisted it was of vital importance that it be read quickly."

"I can take it," Lily offered, holding out her hand for the missive. The butler retreated a respectful distance to await instructions if there was to be a response.

Lily's brow furrowed as she broke the unmarked, messily applied red wax seal. Her eyes danced across the short missive, widening as she read and re-read the words before her to be sure she understood what was in her hands. Her stomach felt as if it dropped through the floor and she shot to her feet

George immediately followed suit. "What's happened?" he questioned impatiently, watching the color drain from her face.

"Abigail has collapsed. She is ill. The note is from Mrs. Hallsworth —the housekeeper." Her heart pounded painfully against her ribcage. Her eyes darted back to Edwards. "Send word to my mother at the Lucklows' townhome," she commanded, the tremble in her voice mirroring that of her hand holding the note. "Let her know we've gone to the Shefford townhouse and to meet us there. Have the carriage brought 'round." The butler left with a swift nod, moving more quickly than she'd seen in years. Lily turned back to her brother. "Oh! We must make sure Jeremy knows. My God, what will he do if he loses his mother, too?" The note crumpled between her fingers as she clutched her throat.

George—while both fully aware of the gravity of the situation and rightly concerned for a woman he'd long considered a second mother—was still taken aback by the urgency in Lily's voice; her almost frantic concern for Jeremy.

"He will be devastated, George!" she continued and began to pace until he placed gentle, stilling hands on her shoulders.

"I'm sure Mrs. Hallsworth or the physician has already sent for him in Kent. Knowing Jem, he'll hop on the nearest horse and be here as soon as he can—daylight permitting. It'll be fine."

"You don't know that it will be fine!" she snapped, startling him with her sudden ferocity. "Everything is not 'fine.' It's not fine for Jeremy. Losing his father crushed him, but if his mother dies too and I…" Her words died in her throat as a bird might plummet from the sky.

"If you, what?" George asked gently, peering down into her face. "If you marry Townsend?"

The flicker of green fire in her eyes told him he'd guessed correctly.

Lily braced herself for the mockery, but it never came. Instead, George pulled her into a warm, gentle hug and rested his chin atop her head.

"You goose," he mumbled lightly and she could feel him shaking his head. She closed her eyes and let him comfort her, not knowing if he realized just how much she needed it. He spoke again just as she'd been about to relax into his embrace. "How long have you been in love with him?" Her eyes flew open at the question and she stepped back from his arms. It was difficult for her to believe, but there was no scorn in George's tone, nor derision in his eyes. If there was ever a time to confide in her brother…to admit to a secret she'd held so closely for so many years…this was it.

Now was the time for honesty.

"All my life."

"You certainly hid it better than he did," George chuckled. "I never guessed."

"I think you are simply less in tune with a woman's ways than you'd like to think."

"Now that," he shook his head, "is something I'll never fully comprehend. Why did you say nothing all these years?"

She cocked a brow at him as if the answer was quite obvious. "I have two brothers and I loved their oldest friend. I would have been an idiot to arm you with that sort of ammunition for my torture. My child's heart could never have borne it."

George shrugged, conceding the point. He knew as well as she the kind of torture young boys are capable of inflicting upon their female siblings.

Both her body and her mind suddenly froze as the weight of his earlier statement sunk in.

"Do you mean to say that Jeremy is in love with me as well?" Cared for her? She'd never doubted it. Desired her? Obviously. But *loved* her?

"Stubborn man won't vocalize it so bluntly, but I know he cares for you. Deeply. Enough to remove himself entirely to allow you to have a more advantageous marriage than he could ever provide."

"That's nonsense!" Lily shook her head vigorously. "Whatever gave him that idea?"

"It's true, though," George conceded. "Townsend can give you social standing and wealth that most women would lop off one of their fingers to have."

A thought occurred to her and her tone rose in indignation. "Surely *you* didn't tell him he was unworthy of marrying me?" Before Lily's anger could rage too high, George held up his hands in defense.

"You don't think me that shallow, do you? I'd have been thrilled with the match." As if reading her expression, he added, "Father didn't either. *Jem* believed you to be too good for him." Lily's heart gave a painful twinge. "He only wanted you to have what he could never give you – everything any woman would want."

"I am not most women, Georgie," she groaned exasperatedly. "I can't abide balls or grand dinner parties. I'm much more comfortable in the country surrounded by sheep and the open air. I'd rather be married in the parish at Wrothsborough than at a grand event at St. Margaret's with hundreds of eyes scrutinizing my every move. The very thought makes me nauseous."

"In other words," intoned George; "you'd far rather be marrying Jeremy in three weeks than Townsend."

"If he'd have me," she replied, feeling her cheeks warm. She'd never before spoken to her brother about matters of the heart and she found it awkward, to say the least. However, as her brother, heir to the earldom, and closest friend of Jeremy, he was her greatest ally if she was going to be freed from this betrothal in time. He heaved a sigh and raked a hand through his golden hair.

"Now if the damned fool had thought to say anything sooner, then this mess could have been avoided..."

"Will you help me, Georgie?" she poured every ounce of emotion she had left into her plea. "Please don't confine me to a loveless marriage. Don't make Jeremy suffer any more than he already has. I'll die inside and Jeremy might just fall apart if he continues at the rate at which he's been going."

George turned his gaze to the ceiling as if imploring a higher power for guidance. The heartbeats of silence weighed heavily upon Lily's shoulders. He could tell her no. He'd be within his rights to demand that she follow through with the marriage. The betrothal papers had been signed; her dowry had been set aside. It was a business transaction, after all. Townsend could sue their family for breach of agreement if she backed out; not to mention a dissolution of the engagement would no doubt destroy any future investment opportunities George could have had with Townsend as his brother-in-law. This decision did not affect only Lily and her future.

Finally, George met her eyes. While his mouth was stern, the glint in his eyes told her she'd won.

"I will see what I can do. Now go," he said, turning her toward the door with a nudge; "grab your gloves and be ready to leave. I'm going to take you to the Shefford townhouse. It wouldn't do to not be there when Mother arrives."

Lily's heart felt lighter than it had in days. With George on her side, she knew she had a better chance of being freed from a miserable future. If George was to be believed, then her next step would be to convince Jeremy that she wasn't deigning to be with him.

Ever efficient, Mary was already waiting in the entryway with Lily's gloves, pelisse, and bonnet.

Right.

She shook herself; the brief respite gave way to guilt. Jeremy's mother was ill and helpless at that very moment. She had to make sure Abigail was all right before anything else.

Then, and only then, could Lily contemplate her future.

Chapter Thirteen

Jeremy's horse was sloughing sweat and frothing at the mouth by the time he finally reined in before the door of his London townhouse. Not wanting to kill the animals in his reckless charge back to Town, he'd had to change horses several times on the journey. Still, he'd pushed them to the brink to get back to London as quickly as he could.

The message he'd received from Mrs. Hallsworth had already been a day old by the time Jeremy held it in his hands. The rider arrived at Rosehall just as the sun dipped beneath the horizon, so Jeremy was delayed further by the late hour. He knew even through his anxiety for his mother that he'd be of no use with a broken neck from a fall in the dark.

Mrs. Hallsworth—hearing the clatter of hooves in the street and correctly assuming it was Jeremy—sent out a footman to handle the reins of the agitated horse. Taking the steps three at a time, Jeremy burst into the house. He stripped off his greatcoat and tossed it on the small table in the entryway.

"How is she?" he panted, attempting to catch his breath from the cold ride. Though his lungs had frozen and fingers cramped from the journey, he could feel the heat rolling off of his body. Knowing the ride was going to be hard and fast, he'd donned only an old linen shirt beneath his greatcoat. The thin fabric was damp and plastered to the skin of his chest, back, and arms. He tugged at it in an effort to appear somewhat less beat-to-hell.

"She's resting now," his housekeeper replied, waiting for him at the bottom of the stairs. "The physician left an hour ago." She moved to collect his coat and he nodded his thanks, still unable to speak a sentence of any real length.

Jeremy vaulted up the stairs and headed straight for his mother's room. Even though he'd tried convincing her otherwise, she'd insisted on moving from the baroness's suite into a more modest chamber down the hall.

He knew he reeked of horseflesh and sweat, but Jeremy couldn't have cared less; he needed to see that his mother was all right and breathing. Placing his hand on the burnished brass knob, he took a deep breath and willed his racing heart and lungs to slow. He opened the door to find what, for a split second, he was certain was a benevolent angel sitting vigil at his mother's bedside.

He blinked his dry, weary eyes several times before reexamining the scene before him. Lily was sitting in a chair pulled up to the edge of the bed opposite the door. She'd been lying with her head atop her arms, resting or dozing, and lifted her golden head at the sound of the door being opened. She blinked at him, her eyes bleary with drowsiness, and he dimly wondered if she believed him to be an apparition, too.

"Jeremy?" Her husky voice sent unwelcome chills throughout his body. Recognition dawned fully and she sat up straight. The flickering firelight made her skin glow like molten silk. His mouth suddenly went dry. "I was just—"

"How does she fare?" he asked in as gentle a tone he could manage over his racing heart and strode over to the bed. He refused to allow himself to meet Lily's eyes and, instead, focused on his mother. She looked as small as a child in the bed, the blankets tucked up beneath her chin. Her chest rose in short, even breaths and he noted the vials of laudanum on the bedside table. The deep, healing sleep had relaxed some of the lines from around her mouth and eyes, somewhat returning her appearance to the youthful beauty he remembered from his childhood. Her dark hair, streaked with more silver than he'd noticed when it was pulled back and styled, was fanned out across the pillow like the dark, curling fingers of a river. The hollows beneath her eyes and the thinness of her face underscored her fragile condition.

"She's resting peacefully," he barely heard Lily as she gently reassured him. He couldn't help but reach out to touch his mother's cheek, assuring himself with its dry warmth that she was, indeed, still alive. "The physician said she hadn't been eating and hardly slept. She's been declining since your father's passing, but something…something caused her to take a turn."

Jeremy clenched his jaw at the wave of guilt. His mother had been wasting away and he'd hardly been present to notice. He should have pressed her to eat more, to take better care of herself. He'd been so caught up in his own ridiculous problems to fully realize the depth of his mother's suffering. Here, he'd been railing against the situation with Lily, when his mother had been evaporating in front of him. He knew she'd loved his father with her whole being and recognized that she suffered his absence every day, but this…this was something else.

As Lily said, something had caused this fall. And Jeremy felt the weight of that responsibility solely upon his shoulders.

As if reading his spiraling thoughts, Lily whispered, "There's nothing you could have done, Jeremy. She has to want to live."

He pulled his hand back and began to work his stiff, sore fingers. The knuckles of his right hand were nearly healed, but the gash on the palm of his other hand was taking longer—working out of doors in Kent and the frantic ride back to London hadn't helped matters. He really should have allowed them to stitch him up.

"The doctors assured us that sleep would help; exhaustion and hunger overtook her. They hope her disposition will improve as well with rest."

"Us?"

"M-my mother and I have been staying here taking turns sitting with her. I hope you don't mind."

Jeremy finally looked Lily in the eye and what he saw there gutted him all over again. The mixture of worry, pity, and—dare he say—affection caused him physical pain. He'd done all he could to purge her from his mind these past several days. He'd set off with every intention of following through with his vow, and yet here she'd landed in his bloody home. The proof was before him, gazing up at him from beside his mother's sickbed with wide, emerald eyes: He'd never be rid of Lily. She was as much a part of his life as the title he'd inherited, the soil his tenants tilled, and the sweat upon his brow as he labored to maintain and improve everything for which he was now responsible. He'd been trying to fool himself into believing he could move on without her, but the truth was plain to him now. Without her, he'd become as much a shell as his mother had in the months since his father's passing. It was never a fate that he'd imagined for himself, but it was now his reality…and it was bleak, indeed.

"Of course not," Jeremy choked out and then attempted to swallow past the massive lump in his throat. "I don't know how to thank you...for being here." He meant that in more ways than one. Now that he was forced to distance himself from the Stratfords, his mother was the only family he had left. It meant the world to him that, even after the way he'd had to push Lily away, she and her family were still there for them. For him.

He and Lily held gazes for a long while, attempting to convey with their eyes everything that had remained unsaid between them over the last week.

Lily finally opened her mouth to speak, but Jeremy, not believing he could take her well-deserved admonishments for his boorish behavior just then, cut her off.

"I need to bathe – I reek of sweaty beast."

"You've smelled worse," Lily said so matter-of-factly that he couldn't help but smile.

Jeremy's flicker of a grin was so brief that Lily almost believed it to be a trick of the light.

He was clearly exhausted in both mind and body. Even so, Lily found him dangerously handsome. He'd clearly ridden straight through from Kent. His wind-whipped hair clung to the sweat on his neck and stuck out at odd angles. The dark stubble on his jaw indicated he hadn't bothered to waste the time shaving before setting out. His soiled linen shirt clung to the hard planes of his chest and shoulders, its transparency hinting at his flat abdomen and the open neck revealing a light speckling of dark hair on his chest and disappearing lower. Lily wrenched her gaze up back to his eyes, hoping the shadowy room had concealed her wayward attentions.

"Jeremy, I should like to speak with you," she said softly.

"I need to bathe," he repeated and broke their eye contact once more. "Would you mind sitting with my mother until I'm done? Then I can relieve your watch and you may sleep."

Slightly taken aback by his brusque tone, she could only nod and watch as he turned and left the room, closing the door behind him. She watched the space where he'd been for several minutes afterward. The room somehow felt bigger without his broad shoulders and imposing frame within it.

She supposed it was unfair of her to want to speak to Jeremy about her conversation with George as soon as he'd arrived, but she'd been waiting days to discuss it. The physician had repeatedly assured them that Lady Shefford should recover after she'd received rest and good, proper food. While this should nourish her weary body, Lily only hoped that this meant her disposition would improve well. When he'd learned the extent of the situation, the physician had indicated all the physical cures in the world could not cure true heartsickness. Lily hoped maybe, when Abigail saw how concerned Jeremy was for her —how much he still needed her support in his life—she would find a new reason to care for herself and continue living.

Lily's mother had felt entirely guilty for not forcing her friend to take better care of herself. She'd seen the signs, she'd told Lily, yet she now realized she hadn't done enough. Abigail had continued to grow thinner, the dark circles beneath her eyes became even more pronounced, and her behavior shifted from quiet and contemplative to decidedly melancholy. Being the proper Englishwoman she was, her mother had avoided commenting on Abigail's appearance. Now, however, she regretted erring on the side of social niceties rather than speaking her mind.

It had disturbed Elizabeth enough that Lily had to step in and insist her mother calm herself. The last thing she needed was for her mother to suffer a nervous spell or succumb to her own fit of the blue-devils. Instead, she occupied the countess by giving her small tasks to give her a sense of purpose and helping. Of course, there was only so much responsibility she could assign to a woman who'd spent her entire life with the privilege of people doing everything for her—in fact, Lily couldn't recall a time her mother had taken care of *her* with her own hands. Still, the countess had been rather adept at coordinating the Shefford staff in the care of their mistress, readying rooms for herself and her daughter, and having necessities carried over from their town-house so she and Lily had changes of clothing and other items to sustain them until their presence was no longer required.

Perhaps the most moving moment had occurred the first night of their stay. Both Lily and her mother had been sitting at Abigail's bedside, watching the peaceful rise and fall of her chest beneath the blankets. As the physician had promised, the laudanum had carried her away into a restful sleep. Lily had nearly jumped when her mother's hand covered her own and squeezed it tightly. She couldn't recall a time when her mother had ever held her hand – even as a child. She'd stared disbelieving at their joined hands for several moments before looking up into her mother's face.

"Thank you for being so strong, Lily." Her mother's voice had been barely above a whisper as she gave her a watery smile. "I'd no idea you could be so steady and composed." Lily chose to take it for the compliment it was intended to be and squeezed her mother's fingers back.

"She'll be fine," Lily replied. Her mother's face had nearly crumpled with worry, but she nodded. She had to believe it. They both did.

And, now that Jeremy had returned, Lily had to believe that it would provide more incentive for Abigail to regain her strength and will to live.

Lily stood and adjusted the coverlet, making sure the older woman was not overly warm. She quietly padded over to the vanity and glanced at the dowager baroness's small trinket watch. It was nearly midnight, which would explain her fatigue. She stretched her sore back and picked up the book she'd left on the reclining sofa near the fire, kicking off her slippers and tucking her legs up beneath her pale pink skirts.

Reading, however, only seemed to worsen her tiredness; Lily managed only a handful of pages before sleep claimed her.

She awoke with a start when her book hit the floor. It took her a second to regain her bearings before she looked over to the bed to see that Jeremy's mother was still sleeping soundly, her chest rising and falling in a smooth rhythm. Lily retrieved her book from the rug and set it on the vanity. She was startled to notice that more than two hours had passed and Jeremy had not returned.

She checked on Lady Shefford and, after a minute's hesitation, she rang for a maid. What could have caused Jeremy's lengthy delay?

Lily asked the sleepy girl to sit with Jeremy's mother for a bit. Closing the door behind her, Lily peered up and down the hallway. Knowing the baron's quarters to be down the hall to her right, she soundlessly crept past her mother's room, another guest room—the one she'd been occupying—and then reached the large double oaken doors. She held her breath and listened for any sign of life. Surely Jeremy wouldn't have asked her to stay with his mother, telling her he would return shortly, and then went to bed instead? Was he so afraid of being around her that he was now concocting lies?

Growing more indignant by the second, Lily placed her hand on the knob and swung the door open without knocking, believing she would find Jeremy asleep in the bed. Instead, she was admitted to a small, well-appointed antechamber. The fire in the hearth was still burning fiercely, heating the enclosed space to a cozy climate. A dreamy oil painting of the chalky cliffs at Dover was hung in a prominent place on the far wall. Papered in the uniquely unisex color of burgundy and draped with ink-blue curtains, the dressing room was tasteful without being opulent.

Jeremy's boots lay near the doorway, his shirt was flung carelessly over a nearby armchair, and his buckskin riding breeches lay in a heap on the ground where he'd peeled them off and discarded them. However, none of this was what held Lily's rapt attention.

An oversized polished brass tub sat near the hearth. It had been positioned so the bather faced the hearth, but there was no mistaking the back of Jeremy's dark head leaning against the lip of the tub. Each of his bare arms rested on the tub's rim, spread wide as he reclined. He must not have heard her enter, because he didn't turn to see who had interrupted his bath.

Heart pounding, in her throat, Lily made to back out of the room, but then the most curious thing happened: Jeremy let out a light snore.

Lily clapped her hand over her mouth to stifle her surprised giggle. The poor man had been so exhausted with worry and from his hard ride from Kent that he'd fallen asleep in the middle of bathing. He'd likely slept even less than she these past thirty-or-so hours and his poor body had succumbed to the steaming water and obvious relief at seeing that his mother remained alive.

She worried her lower lip between her teeth, torn between calling for Jeremy's valet to wake him, and pretending she hadn't seen Jeremy. Finally, Lily decided they'd had enough timidity in their relationship to last a lifetime. She took a bracing breath, stepped into the room, and closed the door behind her with a soft click.

She carefully made her way over to the tub, her footsteps dampened by the thick rug covering the floor. Jeremy let out another soft, growling snore and she had to bite her lip harder to keep from laughing again. She stood behind his head when she reached the tub, savoring the opportunity for unabashed appreciation afforded by his unconscious state.

His dark hair had been washed and slicked back from his forehead, already partially dry from the heat in the room. His charcoal-colored, impossibly long lashes fanned out on his cheeks and she was struck by how young he looked in sleep. His softened appearance reminded her of the young boy she'd once known—except for the day's growth of beard coating his chin, that was. Her eyes drifted lower of their own accord to his tanned neck and the sculpted lines of his arms and shoulders as they melded into the defined muscles of his chest. She saw that the short, wiry hair she'd glimpsed earlier covered most of his chest and then narrowed into a line that disappeared beneath the opaque water of the tub. The oils his valet had added to the water and the soap with which Jeremy had washed had turned the bath an almost milky white, obscuring any further investigation her errant eyes might have performed.

She felt certain, however, that the rest of him was as well-muscled as his torso from long hours spent riding and working with his tenants. Most lords did not partake in this much physical activity, so he was undoubtedly a rare specimen indeed, her Jeremy.

Lily carefully gathered up her skirts and knelt beside the tub, hesitating another moment before reaching out and gently stroking his hair, just as she'd longed to do for more years than she could remember. The black silk was softer than she'd ever imagined—she didn't believe she'd ever grow tired of twining the strands about her fingers. Those fingers began to stray of their own volition, the back of her hand softly caressed his temple and relished the scrape of the beginnings of his beard on her skin. It was so pleasantly rough, so different from her own body.

Jeremy inhaled deeply, like a hound catching wind of a vixen.

"Mmm…Lily," he groaned her name, sending chills down her spine. Eyes half open, he turned his cheek into her palm and inhaled once more before he seemed to suddenly grasp the reality of her touch. He blinked the sleep from his eyes several times before registering that she was, indeed, in his rooms.

"Lily?" Jeremy started and sloshed tepid water onto the floor and Lily's skirts. She yelped in surprise and tipped backward onto her backside. "What the devil are you doing in here?" he demanded; his voice rough from sleep and exhaustion.

Lily picked up her saturated skirts in vain. "I was waiting for you to come to your mother's bedside, but you never came. You fell asleep." She gestured lamely at the tub from her undignified position.

Jeremy registered his state of undress for the first time and sank lower into the tub until only his face was visible above the brass lip. She might have laughed had he not been so serious. "You shouldn't be here. You need to leave."

Her reply came to her in a lightning bolt of clarity.

Lily smiled up at him from her puddle on the floor and gave him a very sweet, "No."

Chapter Fourteen

Jeremy had known Lily her entire life and, in those years, he'd learned a great deal about her. She could be stubborn and contrary, but Jeremy had never known her to be stupid. He supposed there was a first time for everything...because what woman in her right mind would refuse to leave the presence of a naked man—a man *not* her betrothed; a man who desired her beyond measure?

"No?" he asked in a long, drawn-out syllable, unsure if he'd heard her correctly.

"No," Lily repeated herself, still smiling.

"It's not proper—"

"To hell with propriety," Lily laughed incredulously. "Propriety has gotten me—us—into this ridiculous mess with my farce of an engagement. I'll be damned if I'm going to let it continue to have its way with us." Her blunt speech was proof of just what terrible influences he and her brother had been in their youth.

Lily curled her hands around the lip of the tub and hauled herself up. Her sodden dress clung to her shapely legs and hips, doing nothing to disguise them from his wandering eyes.

Jeremy swallowed hard.

"Lily...this isn't some opportunity to kick up a lark..." he choked out, but his protests died on his tongue when she placed her dainty hands on his shoulders and pushed him back to recline against the edge of the tub once more.

"Shut up, Jeremy," she whispered firmly, an unfamiliar wicked glint in her green eyes. He narrowed his eyes but did as he was bid.

Lily spread her fingers through the damp, dark curls on his chest; he nearly groaned at the sensation of her nails on his flesh. His resolve was rapidly weakening.

"Lily, what are you—"

She shushed him and planted a tender kiss on the sensitive bit of skin beneath his ear.

"I'm finally brave enough to take what I want." Jeremy heard the smile in her voice. A rush of heat swelled in his groin despite the tepid bathwater. It wouldn't surprise him in the least if the air around him began to steam. Her light breath tickled his ear when she spoke again. "Haven't you wanted this too, Jeremy?"

As if struck by a physical blow, he closed his eyes and let his head thunk back onto the rim of the tub. "More than you know," he groaned as she continued to explore his chest. How many nights – how many years – had he dreamt of her hands on him...her mouth...?

"I think I have some idea," her voice trembled—with need or nerves, perhaps a combination of both—sending ripples of awareness throughout his body.

A feather-light touch against his lips, and then Lily was kissing him. Gently. Carefully. He let her explore and taste, kissing her back with the same exploratory tenderness. He fought to restrain his lust until it snapped with a tentative flick of her tongue against his lips.

Jeremy's dripping hands shot up and tangled in the hair on the back of Lily's skull, crushing her lips against his. He kissed her deeply, stroking her tongue with his while she bent over him and gave a little moan of desire as their mouths met in a furious mating.

"You're sure?" he asked against her lips—a brief appearance of his last shred of sanity. "What about—"

"Don't say his name," Lily pleaded and moved her hands down his chest to graze the hard ridges of his abdomen. The muscles flexed involuntarily against her palms. "George is helping...will break betrothal..." She was barely able to mumble a fragmented sentence as he continued his onslaught.

Jeremy froze and loosened his grip on Lily's golden hair.

"Break the betrothal?" Her eyes were hooded with desire and she seemed only able to nod in assent. His heart's pace redoubled. "Do you...do you expect to marry me, then? You'd give up being a marchioness to have me?" She smiled down at him and cupped his cheek.

"You silly man," she said, as if the answer were truly obvious.

Jeremy hauled himself up and, facing Lily, stood in the tub. He watched with masculine pride and pleasure as her face flushed at his nakedness. Her eyes refused to leave his at first, but then they inevitably darted along his dripping flesh.

In the dancing firelight, Lily thought he looked hewn of polished, golden marble. Every glistening inch of him. His broad shoulders tapered to a narrow waist and flat, sculpted stomach; he stood like a statue of a Greek god, strong legs braced apart in unabashed confidence. Lily swallowed hard at the sight of his thick, erect manhood jutting proudly from a nest of dark curls. Her suspicions had been verified; the tapering line of hair from his chest did, indeed, lead to that mysterious…impressive part of his body.

Fearing she was staring too long like the green girl she was, she tore her eyes away and back up to Jeremy's face. He had the audacity to give her a cheeky grin and wink; knowing full well that this was her first look at a naked man. Her cheeks grew unbearably hot, but Lily forced herself to remain composed. She'd asked for this. She wanted this with her mind, heart, and every aching inch of her body. She couldn't, wouldn't back out now.

Jeremy jerked his chin over to the nearby chair. "Would you please grab a sheet for me?" Lily spied the bath cloths and used the edge of the tub to stand. Her knees felt weak – even more so when she could feel Jeremy's eyes boring into her as she moved; eyeing the way her sodden skirts clung to her body.

She handed him the length of soft linen without touching him, watching as he toweled off his head, arms, and the remainder of his body with brisk efficiency. He stepped from the tub and tossed the cloth aside. He didn't approach her or intimidate her with his nakedness. Instead, he held his hand out to her as if they were in no less state of dress and dishevelment than they would be at a country dance.

Lily settled her tiny hand in Jeremy's and he gently pulled her closer to him, stopping just short of the point where their bodies would touch. The heat rolled off of him as if she'd moved too close to a roaring flame.

"Don't be afraid," he breathed softly. "I won't do anything you don't want me to." She knew he was trying to be reassuring, but that darker timbre of his voice didn't fail to send chills racing up and down her spine.

A shiver traipsed across her skin, but she was far from cold beneath her damp clothing. Lily didn't think she could have felt a chill had she been naked in the snow—not with the heat of her flush and the swelling, liquid fire that pooled between her legs when Jeremy's sinfully dark eyes met hers.

She saw a hunger burning there.

A primal hunger for *her*.

"You should get out of that wet dress before you catch a chill," Jeremy observed and then proceeded to lead Lily through one of the doors off of the antechamber. He showed her to the baron's chambers and he pressed the door shut behind them. Turning back to Lily, he was struck by how small and fragile she appeared. All of the brazen desire he'd witnessed in the other room had seemed to cool and was replaced by demure uncertainty. He reached out and gently bracketed her face in his palms, running his thumb along her full lower lip.

"Do you know," he began as a fresh wave of desire rolled through him, "that you sometimes move your lips when you read?"

She smiled beneath his touch.

"Do I?" She frowned good-naturedly.

Jeremy nodded. "It's adorable." His fingertips trailed down to the neckline of her gown. "And this," he added as he traced the freckle on the top of her breast, "is perhaps one of the most erotic little marks I've ever beheld."

"You can't be serious?" This time, she laughed aloud.

"Truly," he replied, unable to tear his eyes away from her petal-soft breasts and the shadowy, inviting valley between them. He could make out the perfect buds of her pert nipples against the damp fabric. She gasped when he cupped her breast, testing its weight. "And these…have been the object of many a fantasy of mine." His cock gave a powerful throb at the sharp intake of her breath.

Unable to control himself, Jeremy covered her mouth with his once more. "Tell me you want me, Lily," he groaned and held her against the length of his body, letting her feel the stiff evidence of his need against her belly. Grasping the mounds of her rear in his hands, he ground himself against her. Lily gasped and threw her arms around his neck.

"Yes. Yes, I want you," she hissed. Jeremy fisted her skirts in his hands and hiked her up. She wrapped her legs around his waist, positioning her right above the part of him that longed to feel her the most. He carried her and backed her toward the big four-posted bed against the far wall.

He laid her down with infinite care and ended their kiss, peering down into her soft, angelic face and holding the weight of his body to hover above her.

"Say you want *me*," he repeated, pleading with his eyes for her to understand his meaning.

"I want *you*, Jeremy," she breathed, intertwining her fingers in the soft curls at the nape of his neck. Reaching back, he slowly lifted her skirts past her knees and hips. His hand dipped between them, deftly locating the slit in her drawers. A soft moan escaped her throat when he found her molten core ready for him. Unable to resist, he slid a finger deep inside, savoring the pull and grip of her feminine muscles around him. She was so tight that it was entirely possible she would kill him with pleasure.

Withdrawing his finger, he traced her dampness up and around the sensitive bud at the apex of her sex. She gasped and panted, rocking her hips against his hand—seeking her pleasure upon instinct. Her damp skirts clung and tangled between them, concealing Jeremy's view. He desperately needed to see her, all of her. She whimpered when he pulled back.

"Let's get you out of that dress, love," he explained restlessly.

Lily allowed him to pull her to her feet and turned to let him undo the laces of her gown. Jeremy's hands were trembling too badly with lust and excitement that they were rendered useless. He spent a few minutes fumbling before frustration took over; he gripped the edges of her gown in his hands and popped the seams with one great grunt. The garment fell away into a pale pink puddle on the floor. She stood before him in only her shift and stays, rendered sheer by the dampness. Another few tugs and she was free of those as well; standing only in her stockings.

He placed gentle hands on her shoulders and turned her to face him. Her hands flew to her breasts, but Jeremy caught them.

"What did I tell you about hiding from me?" he asked, his voice vibrating the very air around them as she recalled their interlude in the carriage. She hesitated only a moment longer before raising her head proudly and dropping her arms to her side.

As vivid as Jeremy's imagination had been, it hadn't come close to the real Lily standing before him. She had full, pert breasts and tempting nipples the color of strawberries and cream; gracefully rounded hips, and smooth, flat abdomen. She was soft. She was perfection.

To him, she was *home*.

"You've slain me, Lily," he whispered.

Her gentle laughter lit up her face. "And you're attempting to turn me up sweet," she admonished lightly. Her blush, however, belied her pleasure.

"Sincerely," Jeremy said and brought her palm to his chest, placing it flat against the spot he knew she would be able to feel the frantic pounding of his heart. Just as he'd anticipated, she realized the truth of his statement. He watched raptly as she pulled her lower lip between her teeth.

"Touch me," he ground out. He knew she'd be more comfortable once she was more familiar with him. With his body.

Lily—seemingly grateful for the invitation—placed both palms flat upon his chest. His pulse quickened, increasing the throbbing thrum in his throat. Slowly, she smoothed her light touch down his torso, tracing the flexing muscles of his abdomen, and the carved lines of his pelvis, which inevitably led her to the part of him straining for her touch.

Unsure how to proceed, Lily halted her perusal of Jeremy's flesh. Jeremy noted her hesitancy and gently took her hands in his. "It's all right," he said softly. "You can touch me." He guided her hands to his member, but stopped short of forcing her to take him in her hands.

Emboldened by his encouragement, Lily tentatively wrapped her fingers around his length. Jeremy's chest heaved in a great exhalation—as if he'd been holding his breath for years on end—and she yanked her hand back, concerned she'd hurt him.

"It's all right," he repeated shakily. "That felt good."

Lily cradled the weight of his turgid length in her palm, surprised at how soft and delicate the flesh was; how heavy he lay in her grasp. She nearly jumped when he throbbed in her hand as she wrapped her fingers around his girth. She had no prior experience with the male body, but even she knew Jeremy's size had to be what the other women had tittered about speculatively in those powder rooms—given his general height and imposing bulk. (It was amazing what some women would gossip about when they'd had a few too many glasses of claret.)

Growing more curious, Lily used her other hand to cradle the soft sac beneath his length, caressing the weight with the pad of her thumb. She took Jeremy's guttural groan as encouragement. Tracing a fingertip along the dusky head of his member, she gave an experimental stroke of her hand.

Jeremy's eyes slid closed and his head fell back, reveling in Lily's gentle assault on his senses. He thought he might spill right then and there when she figured out how to stroke him.

"That's enough." He gave a shaky breath and closed his hand over hers. "I've been waiting for you too long to tolerate much more."

Claiming her mouth with a feral growl, Jeremy backed Lily onto the bed once more; prowling after her as she blindly found the center of the mattress. He kissed and licked his way down her throat, savoring the frantic pulse in the hollow of her throat against his tongue. He tasted the sensitive underside of her left breast, cradling the other in his palm. He nibbled shrinking circles around the tender flesh, until she was all but whimpering beneath him when he finally claimed her nipple. He suckled the sensitive bud, holding it between his teeth and laving it with his tongue. Her fingers tangled in his hair, pressing him closer to her breast. By the time he'd finished lavishing similar attentions upon her other breast, Lily was panting with need beneath him. Her fathomless green eyes were glazed over with desire and, indeed, that flush of pleasure did spread down her throat to the puckered rosebud tips of her breasts.

He gently disentangled her hands from his hair and tasted the petal-soft skin of the underside of her wrists. The glint of diamonds on her finger in the flickering light caught his attention.

That wouldn't do.

Jeremy kissed her fingertips and used his teeth to slowly, sensuously remove the gold ring from her finger. She gave a little moan at the sensation, stoking the growing fire inside of him. He dropped the ring to the floor and, with it, he imagined the connection between Lily and any other man.

She was his.

She always had been.

And a deep, secret part of him hoped she always would be.

Still craving more, Jeremy caressed and kissed a line down between her breasts as he retreated off the edge of the bed. Slowly, he rolled down each of her stockings, pressing his lips to the quivering, sensitive flesh of her inner thighs as he went. Discarding the last of her garments, he looked up her body, watching her reaction as his lips and tongue worked ever closer to the apex of her thighs. Hooking her knees over his shoulders, Jeremy flattened his palms against her pelvis. He pressed his mouth to her, causing her to give a little yelp and buck her hips in surprise. She lifted her head, gazing down the length of her body at him.

"I did say I wanted to taste you here, did I not?" He flashed Lily a wicked grin and bent his head to sip deeply. Her shock quickly melted into a pool of pleasure. His tongue stroked her higher, flicking and caressing her most sensitive of places. She tasted of sunshine and sugar—sweet and warm—drugging his senses; her panting breaths as she rocked her hips against his mouth drove Jeremy closer to breaking his fine thread of control.

He noticed the change in her—that point where her pleasure climbed inexorably higher. Releasing one of her legs, Jeremy slid one finger, and then another, inside her tight sheath; not once stopping the erotic patterns he was tracing with his tongue.

Lily whimpered his name the moment her climax crashed and broke over her. Her body convulsed and tightened around him; her intimate muscles clenching him, pulling his fingers deeper into her slick heat. As the last ripples of her orgasm left her quivering, Jeremy climbed his way back up her body. She was still trembling with pleasure when he kissed her deeply, letting her taste herself on his tongue.

He nestled the weight of his erection in the natural cradle of her sex. Giving a few testing thrusts with his hips, he slid easily through the moisture left by her orgasm and teased her swollen, sensitive petals. Reaching between them, he took himself into his hand and rubbed the thick, broad head of his shaft along her slick flesh. She moaned and gasped in disbelief as he began to stroke her toward another high.

Jeremy peered down into her face. "Say you want my cock, Lily. Say you want it inside of you."

Her passion-hazed eyes widened at his vulgar language. His coaxing rang of their childhood—when he and George had been terrible influences upon this incorrigible little girl who followed them everywhere—and she'd learned colorful curses the boys had picked up at school. Her face warmed, but she did as she was bid, surprised at how much she enjoyed the power of the words as they rolled off her tongue, seeming to weaken this enormous man above her.

"I want your cock, Jeremy. I want your cock inside of me," she answered breathlessly.

"God, yes," Jeremy groaned and closed his eyes. Positioning himself at her entrance, he was poised to possess her. The last shred of his sanity kept him from thrusting into her in one hard motion.

"It'll only hurt for a moment, love. I'll try to go slow." He was still coherent enough to realize "try" was the operative word in that statement. Jeremy's lust and desire had been leashed tightly for many years. Now, with Lily more than willing beneath him in his bed, he didn't know how much self-control remained.

Lily nodded silently, but the trust conveyed in her emerald eyes nearly broke his heart. She was giving him everything—not just her body, but her reputation, and every ounce of trust she had. He did not take that lightly.

He braced his forearms on either side of Lily's head and placed an achingly sweet kiss on her forehead as he flexed his hips and entered her. He felt Lily tense beneath him and he retreated slightly. Her hands clutched at his flexing biceps, her nails biting into the flesh on the backs of his arms, but he did not flinch. Knowing it would only be made worse if he stopped altogether, he pressed forward again, deeper this time. He continued this pattern of attack and retreat until Lily grew accustomed to his girth. Her legs relaxed and fell wider, opening her up to accommodate more of him.

Her inner muscles gripped and caressed Jeremy's rigid length as he moved, stroking both of them closer to the edge. His breath became ragged and desperate and he increased his pace.

The room filled with the heavy sounds of panting breaths and the slick rhythm of flesh-on-flesh as Jeremy took his pleasure, finally claiming Lily as his own.

The realization that, after all this time, Lily was finally *his* drove Jeremy over the edge of his control.

"Wrap your legs around me," he demanded.

Lily, barely hearing him through the thick fog of her pleasure, did as she was told. She angled her hips and took him even deeper, hooking her ankles around his thrusting hips and wrapping her arms around his neck. She clung to him as her climax broke once more. Jeremy swallowed her sobs of joy with a kiss just before his own time came. The steadily growing heat broke through the dam and he spilled himself deep inside Lily with a low, guttural roar.

The last shocks of Jeremy's orgasm left his body and he collapsed over Lily. She relished the feeling of his weight atop her, the contrast where his hardness met her softness, the sensation of his solid thickness still throbbing hotly inside of her. His lips pressed against her neck while he inhaled deeply—whether to catch his breath or savor her scent, she wasn't sure—while she traced lazy patterns on the sweat-slick planes of his back.

When he'd finally regained some of his composure, Jeremy slid from her body and rolled, pulling her with him and nestling her to his side, her head cradled against his chest.

"Is it always like that?" Lily asked when she was finally able to remember how to speak.

Jeremy's chuckle vibrated against her cheek, humming pleasantly inside her skull. "No, it's not. It can be rather unfortunate if one is not with the right person."

Lily hooked one leg over Jeremy's thigh, loving the way his solid limb felt beneath her; how the rough hair on his leg tickled her sensitive inner thigh.

"I like knowing that we're compatible," Lily said with a yawn. The lazy circles Jeremy was tracing on her bare shoulder along with the afterglow of her climaxes were beginning to lull her into a sense of peace.

"Me, too." She heard the smile in his voice.

"Who'd have thought the boy who pushed me in the river and dropped grasshoppers in my hair would be 'the right person?'" Lily laughed. He shifted to look down into her face.

"And what about you? I seem to recall a rather annoying chit who followed us everywhere, climbing trees, riding her horse astride, and carrying lambs like kittens."

"At least I didn't attempt to do all those things at once," she retorted with a smile, her voice growing heavy with exhaustion. Jeremy listened while her light breathing grew slow and even as sleep overcame her.

He lay there for a long, uncertain amount of time just holding her softness against him and listening to her breathe. He was loath to move, half of him irrationally afraid that she would dissolve and slip through his fingers like so many grains of sand. He'd hardly dared to dream of holding her in his arms like this one day—he'd always told himself that he was not good enough, refined enough, wealthy enough for a woman with her breeding, grace, and heart. And here she was lying with him in his bed, and she'd given him her maidenhead, a woman's most closely-guarded treasure.

Still, called a niggling voice from the depths of Jeremy's mind, *she didn't promise you her heart.* And a selfish part of him desired that as well; to possess her heart just as he'd claimed her body, branded her as his own.

He was sure she craved him, desired his body—he knew Lily well enough that she wouldn't have allowed it to happen had she not wanted it to—but her cryptic answer when he'd tested the waters of marriage left him confused.

Jeremy had never allowed himself to consider spending the rest of his life with Lily, raising a family with her as his baroness. He'd had more than his share of sexual musings, but he was not a man prone to matrimonial fantasies. Lily had made it clear that George was going to help her break her betrothal to Townsend, but that didn't necessarily mean she wanted to jump right into another engagement—not to mention the scandal it would cause for her family. Jeremy cared for the Stratfords far too much to allow such a thing to happen.

He lay awake for much of that night pondering the situation he and Lily had gotten themselves into by daring to act upon their desires.

Chapter Fifteen

Lily awoke the next morning in a strange room and unfamiliar bed. It took her a moment to realize where she was and how she'd gotten there. The previous night's activities brought a warm flush back to Lily's cheeks and she buried her face in the pillow.

She'd dozed until Jeremy had woken her again with tender, but insistent, kisses and caresses. The fire had died low and the room had gone dark; his hands had been over every inch of her body—like a blind man learning her every contour by touch, committing it to his mind as a precious memory. His skilled fingers and mouth brought her to another shattering climax before he sought his pleasure. She could feel his power and restraint in his every movement; it excited her that this big, commanding man was held at bay by his affection for her. The thought and tenderness with which he handled her nearly brought Lily to tears, and she was grateful for the darkness. The last thing she wanted to do was make a fool of herself.

Rolling over, Lily discovered she was alone in the chamber. Sunlight glowed behind the heavy curtains, curling its fingers around the edges of the drapery. She didn't know what time it was or when Jeremy had left her, but it didn't bother her. Instead, she stretched languorously, savoring the sweet soreness and tender ache left behind by their lovemaking.

She hadn't known what to expect from a naked man, but he'd certainly been even more beautiful than she could have imagined—all chiseled lines and hewn silk. Jeremy had most certainly become a *man* over the years. And Lily liked to think he appreciated her as a woman. If any of his whispered endearments had been any indication, then he found her pleasing, indeed.

Lily rose from the bed and pulled the green coverlet around her shoulders; its enormous volume followed her like a train as she moved about the room and took her opportunity to examine a more private side of Jeremy than even she'd been privy. Similar to the antechamber dressing room, the room had dark, heavy drapes and elegantly patterned wallpaper in alternating masculine shades of green, matching the hunter-colored coverlet she currently held draped around her shoulders. A small mahogany desk sat in the far corner; writing implements and a neat stack of paper were all laid out, ready for use in case their owner might be struck by a thought in the middle of the night.

As comfortable as the room was, it felt impersonal. It could have belonged to any number of lords. Noting the subtle fade in the papering and lightly worn path in the once brightly-dyed rug, Lily doubted Jeremy had updated or changed anything since his father's death—perhaps, even since his grandfather's time as Baron Shefford. She pondered how odd it must have been for him to be thrust into the role of Baron Shefford and all that it entailed. He'd been forced to take over estates and tenants, accounts and business, all while grieving for the father he'd lost so suddenly and so young. She was struck by a deep pang of sadness at the realization that, perhaps, Jeremy didn't even feel as if this home—this room—actually belonged to him.

It was gauche to discuss money, but even Lily was aware that the Shefford Barony had suffered losses in the past. Still, Jeremy and his father had worked hard to return Rosehall to its former glory, to make the estate profitable and ensure the happiness of the tenants. Surely there was enough in the coffers to do some simple redecorating of a single room…if only to help Jeremy feel more at home in his role.

Lost in her thoughts, Lily was startled by the click of the oak door opening. She whirled on the sound, nearly losing her coverlet in the process, and was mortified to come face-to-face with Jeremy's house-keeper, Mrs. Hallsworth. Lily had known the older woman since she'd been but a girl terrorizing the hallways of Rosehall with Jeremy and her brothers. That familiarity, however, only seemed to worsen Lily's mortification at having been discovered in so obvious a state of ruination.

The housekeeper, on the other hand, didn't so much as bat an eye. She gave Lily a friendly, reassuring smile and bobbed a curtsey.

"I've taken the liberty of retrieving a gown for you m'lady," she said, walking over to the hopelessly rumpled bed, straightening the sheets with an expert flick, and carefully laying out a sunny yellow muslin morning dress edged in little blue forget-me-nots, along with a clean shift and set of petticoats.

"I—thank you," was all Lily managed to squeak out. The woman's nonchalance had thrown her off-balance; not to mention the fore-thought she'd had to bring Lily a change of dress. It was as if she'd known exactly what had transpired.

A fresh flush crept up the back of Lily's neck. She loved Jeremy, but that didn't mean she wanted everyone and their aunt to know what went on behind closed doors.

Before Lily could say anything else, the woman retreated to the dressing room and returned with a large bowl of warm, scented water and some linen. "I thought you might like to freshen up," she said kindly, setting the bowl on the desk. "You help yourself while I tidy up out there—Lord only knows how that man always seems to leave a trail of clothes in his wake, and now a small lake around the tub to boot—and I'll be back in a trice to help you dress."

The housekeeper breezed from the room, leaving Lily to compose herself. She was torn between melting into a puddle of mortification and doing as she was told. The warm water looked so inviting...and she caught the scent of lavender oil—her favorite...

Knowing Mrs. Hallsworth would return shortly, Lily released the coverlet and, gratefully, took her advice and washed. She wiped the sweat from her neck, arms, and between her breasts, then took a clean linen soaked in the lightly scented water and pressed the warm compress to the ache between her thighs. A sigh of pleasure escaped her lips.

Lily dropped the linens into the bowl when she was done and began to dress as best as she could on her own. As she slipped her shift over her head, however, a sickening idea struck her and she froze.

What if Mrs. Hallsworth's easy demeanor was because she was used to finding women in Jeremy's bed – what if her presence in his chambers was no more inconsequential a mess for her to tidy up than the clothes and bathwater out in the antechamber? Lily swallowed in a vain effort to remove her heart from her throat.

She'd known Jeremy was no virgin—his obvious experience and intimate knowledge told her he was well-versed in the subject of intercourse—but that didn't stop the pain she felt at the picture of another woman in his arms and his bed. Lily pressed her palm to her roiling stomach and tried to convince herself that she was more to Jeremy than another good tup. George had told her Jeremy cared for her, deeply, for many years. Surely he wouldn't just use her if that were the case?

Mrs. Hallsworth slipped back into the room and smiled at her again; unaware of the storm brewing in Lily's mind. Beyond the door, two maids were busy mopping the spilled bathwater and taking the clothing to be washed. Lily could hear the sounds of their pleasant chatter as they worked until the housekeeper closed the door to the bedchamber.

"There now," she smiled gently, "doesn't that feel better?" Lily nodded and stood, allowing Mrs. Hallsworth to play at lady's maid as she helped Lily slip into her stays she'd recovered from the floor, and the yellow morning dress. Lily gripped the thick bedpost with both hands to steady herself while Mrs. Hallsworth tugged and tied Lily into her clothing. Finally, when Lily could take the silence no more, she blurted out the words which had been burning on the tip of her tongue like an ember.

"You do not seem surprised to see me in here, Mrs. Hallsworth." Lily paused to catch her breath as another string was pulled. "You seemed rather to be expecting me. Why is that?"

"His Lordship rang for me earlier and said you'd need tending to," she replied matter-of-factly. This, however, only played into Lily's anxieties.

"So…this happens often then? You being sent to clean up Shefford's leavings?" She winced when the older woman laughed, expecting to be told she was a silly girl for ever thinking otherwise.

"Heavens, no! Boots, cloaks, and waistcoats, to be sure—his poor valet is about at wit's end—but you are the first woman I've 'cleaned up;' and you, Lady Lily, are far from what I'd consider a 'leaving.'"

Lily couldn't have stopped her hopeful heart from soaring had she tried. She chided herself for believing any less of Jeremy. Not only was she not the latest in a slew of conquests, but he—being his usual, caring self—had thought to have his discreet, long-time housekeeper see to her needs.

"If I may be quite blunt," Mrs. Hallsworth continued; "I've watched the two of you for your entire lives and I couldn't help but feel a sense of relief that you both finally came to your senses. Too caught up in your insecurities, the lot of you."

Lily released a bubble of laughter. She didn't know if it was amusing or annoying that everyone seemed to know more about their relationship than they did.

Mrs. Hallsworth finished tying her gown and gently turned Lily to face her. The humor in the older woman's eyes was evident despite the stern set of her mouth. "Now don't you let him go and take what he's been pining after without compensation. Bring the man up to snuff." She punctuated her words with wags of her stubby finger.

Grinning, Lily took the lady's admonishing hand in both of hers. The overfamiliarity was born of a lifelong acquaintance. "I'll do what I can, but I'm sure you are very aware of just how obstinate he can be."

"It's not about forcing the man, dear; it's about making him admit to himself that he's allowed to be happy, and to admit to you that he hopes you feel a fraction of what he feels for you."

Lily, touched by the housekeeper's words, squeezed her hands in gratitude for bolstering her fortitude before she left the chambers in search of Jeremy.

Lily found him in the very first place she looked; however, the scene she happened upon was not quite what she had been expecting.

Jeremy was sitting at the head of his mother's bed in the chair Lily had occupied the prior evening. He was dressed for comfort in breeches and an open-necked linen shirt. His hair was clean, if unkempt, and it curled into his face and shone with flairs of blue in the warm sunlight streaming through the open windows, the curtains having been thrown wide to admit the morning light. He'd also somehow found the time to shave, his angular jaw now smooth and free of the dark stubble which had tickled her skin and chafed her inner thighs the previous evening.

To Lily's delight, Jeremy's mother was awake and alert. She was propped up amongst a sea of pillows, allowing her grown son to spoon-feed her weak beef broth and serve her sips of barley water. Lily had entered the room without knocking and felt suddenly terrible for interrupting the intimate scene between mother and son.

"I'm sorry for intruding," Lily stammered an apology and began backing from the room.

Jeremy looked up from his task; his dark eyes smoldered like coals, causing chills of awareness to dance across her skin. His mouth tilted in a self-sure smile as if he knew the effect his presence had on her here in the daylight, where there was no hiding from what they'd done. Lily's eyes darted to his lips and she instantly regretted it; recalling just *where* he'd put those lips the prior night. She felt her knees grow weak and she gripped the doorknob for support; her breath quickened in her chest.

"You're not intruding, dear," Jeremy's mother assured her weakly. Her voice was slightly hoarse from disuse over the last several days. "I am done eating anyway."

"No, Mother, you're not," Jeremy insisted, turning back to Abigail and breaking the sizzling contact of their eyes. "The physician insists you need to eat."

"He also said I need to rest." She rubbed at her temple with slender fingers.

"Perhaps you should at least finish your broth," Lily interjected before an argument could take place. Both mother and son turned to look at her. Suddenly nervous that she'd crossed a boundary, Lily carefully added, "For Jeremy."

Jeremy stared at her, spoon forgotten in his hand, still poised above the bowl of broth in his lap.

"If you don't eat for yourself," Lily said softly, hesitantly; "then do it for Jeremy." She could feel his eyes upon her, boring into her. Abigail looked back and forth between her son and Lily. She may have been weak from incapacitation, but she was not so dense as to notice the crackling tension between the two of them. Privy to her son's feelings for the young lady, she decided that something either very bad or very good had happened between the two of them. Whatever it was, she knew they needed ample time to work through it. Standing in her bedchamber was certainly not conducive to an open, honest conversation.

"Very well," Abbigail said lightly, reaching to take the spoon and bowl from her son. "I will finish this and the two of you go break your fast. I can manage some broth on my own." Jeremy opened his mouth to protest, but she silenced him with a practiced glance. "How can you expect me to get stronger if you continue to treat me like an invalid? I promise to eat all of it." He reluctantly handed her the bowl, made sure her pillows accommodated her seated position, and walked around the bed to stand near Lily.

"I'll return when I've finished eating," he warned his mother.

"Don't rush," Abigail said and waved him off. "I'll probably take a nap after eating. Enjoy your day. Send a maid to check on me if you so desire, but I don't need my grown son playing nursemaid. You've far more important things to attend to."

The young couple turned to leave the room and the distance they kept from one another—the careful way in which they avoided all contact in her presence—confirmed Abigail's suspicions: Something very good had happened, indeed. She couldn't help but smile as she sipped her broth and noticed for the first time in months that the food did not taste entirely of sawdust.

As soon as they were alone in the hallway, Jeremy placed his hand on the small of Lily's back and bent his head to speak to her in a gentle tone.

"How are you this morning?" he inquired, his voice low enough for only her hearing.

"Fine, thank you," Lily replied, slightly distracted by the delicious warmth of his large palm through her dress. "I appreciate you sending Mrs. Hallsworth to bring me a change of dress."

"We couldn't very well have you dashing through the halls naked —no matter how enticing a picture that would have made." Jeremy gave her a devilish grin, warming Lily's cheeks and quickening her pulse.

"You did destroy one of my most comfortable dresses," Lily feigned admonishment, enjoying the ease with which they still interacted. She didn't know how illicit lovers treated one another in daylight, but it would seem that she and Jeremy had enough of a foundation to their relationship that there was no awkwardness. Rather, everything he did seemed to heighten her sexual awareness of him. For a man of his stature and build, Lily was now appreciating the smoothness of his gait, the elegance and tenderness with which he guided her. He displayed a remarkable amount of restraint, but she knew the strength and power, the passion which lay beneath.

It was thrilling.

And it was all hers.

If Jeremy had believed Lily beautiful before, he found her stunning that morning. She looked pleased and content—dare he say, well-loved. Jeremy's pride swelled with the knowledge that he had gifted her with that; as well as the fact that she had given him the same. And he was hard-pressed to stay away.

He couldn't recall a morning that had been as pleasant as this. He'd spent hours the night before just holding Lily's sleeping body against him. When he was sure she would not wake, he slipped from the bed and dressed in breeches and a loose shirt to look in on his mother.

The young maid Lily had left at her bedside startled at his entrance, nearly dropping her mending. Jeremy had gestured for her to remain silent and motioned for her to take her leave to return to bed. He made a mental note to advise Mrs. Hallsworth to give the girl several extra hours of rest to make up for her late-night vigil.

He assumed the seat recently vacated by the maid and made himself as comfortable as one could be when confronted with a parent's mortality.

Where his father had succumbed to a sudden death, his mother had been wasting away before his very eyes in a slow, steady deterioration. He'd known she was lost. He'd recognized the emotional and physical manifestations of her grief. But he'd foolishly believed she was improving when he'd convinced her to start leaving the house. How could he not have seen how bad it had gotten?

Cursing himself, Jeremy placed his hand atop his mother's where it lay beneath the coverlet. He silently willed her to open her eyes. He needed to tell her where things with Lily stood—well, perhaps not the *exact* details...but enough to show her that there was hope. For the first time in a very, very long time, Jeremy had hope for the future. Now, if only his mother would wake up and see it with him.

It was sometime after dawn when his mother did, finally, shift on her pillow toward the sound of his voice where he read in a low, steady tone. He'd quickly set down the book on the side of the bed and leaned closer when he saw her attempt to drag open her leaden eyelids.

The rush of relief he felt when her eyes finally met his was overwhelming. Of course, he'd been sick with concern, but he hadn't allowed himself to fully comprehend the depth of his worry until he faced his mother's gaze. She was drowsy and confused, but Jeremy spoke past the lump in his throat to explain what had happened – that she'd collapsed and would likely be sore from the fall, that the physician had come to treat her and prescribed rest and healthful food, how Lily and her mother had been caring for her until he could arrive. Weakly, she worked her hand from beneath the covers and cupped Jeremy's cheek. His eyes were suspiciously moist as he covered her frail hand with his own.

"Please..." he choked out, but even he was unsure of what he was trying to say. Please recover from this? Please forgive me for not being here? Please forgive me for not doing more? Please don't leave me, too?

Like most mothers, Abigail didn't need her son to finish his sentence. She gave one nod and a wobbly tilt of her lips before she drifted off into a comfortable sleep once more. The next time she awoke,

Jeremy was able to convince her to drink and eat some. It wasn't nearly enough as far as he was concerned, but it was a start.

The true miracle had transpired when Lily had walked into the room, as mouth-watering and refreshing as lemon ice in her yellow morning dress. Somehow, she convinced his stubborn mother to promise to continue to eat. And he loved Lily all the more for it. She understood how much his mother meant to him and how now, with his father gone, she was all he had.

As Jeremy escorted Lily down the stairs and into the small dining room, a part of him glowed with the hope that maybe now he'd have Lily as well.

The pair was immediately welcomed by the irresistible scents of a full breakfast. No doubt it was Mrs. Hallsworth who had anticipated their ravenous hunger and instructed the staff to prepare it all. Like any good housekeeper, she'd remembered Lily's penchant for taking tea and bread with preserves to break her fast. Jeremy, on the other hand, always opted for hardier fare—sausage and eggs; soft-boiled or prepared otherwise, he always consumed at least five each morning. A man couldn't be expected to tend to his estate without proper sustenance.

He showed Lily to her chair, indicating that he would fill plates for the both of them at the sideboard. A footman served them strong breakfast tea, which Lily sipped as she admired the breadth of Jeremy's shoulders. Her hands flexed with the memory of how those shoulders felt slick with salty sweat beneath her fingertips.

Jeremy turned back to Lily and found her eyes watching him with rapt attention. She'd pulled her lower lip between her teeth. He wondered if, perhaps, she was replaying their lovemaking as he had done for the remainder of the night. His breeches suddenly became tighter at the memories. Had he been certain they wouldn't be discovered, he'd have liked to swipe everything from the table, set her atop it, and take her right then and there. He cleared his throat, breaking Lily's contemplation, and carried the plates back to the table.

He placed Lily's plate in front of her and, foregoing the traditional seating, he took the place beside her instead of across and down the table. The footman swooped in and moved his teacup and saucer in front of him before silently returning to his post on the perimeter of the room. Knowing she'd been caught gawking, Lily lowered her eyes and quietly thanked him for the plate.

Jeremy sawed into his sausage. Taking a bite, he sat back in his chair and was struck by the comfortable intimacy of the scene. They could have been any husband and wife sitting down for a meal alone together in the comfort and privacy of their home. The thought caused a pang of something—longing, perhaps—deep within Jeremy's chest. Swallowing his food, he set down his utensils and leaned forward on his elbows. Jeremy watched in fascination as Lily innocently, efficiently spread strawberry preserves on her toast. The red jam stopped very precisely at the edge of the toast and she finished spreading with a flourish as he'd seen her do a thousand times—as he imagined her doing a thousand times more. She took a small bite of the toast and caught him watching her.

"What is it? Do I have strawberry on my face?" she asked, swiping ineffectually at her mouth with a napkin.

Jeremy shook his head and leaned back again.

"I was just thinking."

"About what?" Lily broke off a bite of toast and popped it into her mouth like a sweet.

"You said your brother was going to help you break the betrothal with Townsend."

Her chewing slowed and she set down the toast. He watched her swallow and take a sip of tea. "Yes. He said he would help."

"When?"

Lily shook her head. "I'm not certain when or how, but it does have to be soon, doesn't it?" She lifted her teacup to her lips for another sip. When he spoke next, his tone was low enough to escape the nearby footman's notice.

"Especially because you could already be carrying my child," Jeremy added matter-of-factly; though Lily's reaction was anything but. For the second time in nearly as many weeks, she practically choked on her breakfast. The men in her life really did need to find better times to say such things to her.

She regained her composure and was finally able to reply. "I—I suppose that is possible." Lily resisted the urge to place her hand on her lower abdomen. She was nearly blinded with joy at the image of a tiny, cooing infant with a shock of dark hair and eyes like melted chocolate. The thought filled her with an immense amount of pleasure.

Jeremy thought he spied a flicker of a smile on Lily's lips; however, it withered away rather quickly with his next pronouncement.

"We'll have to be married, you know. Soon. As soon as we are able after the scandal of the broken betrothal with Townsend has blown over."

"'We'll *have* to be married'?" Lily echoed. "Was that supposed to be some sort of proposal, Jeremy Balfour?"

The image of Lily floating up the aisle, draped in wildflowers, at the tiny parish in Wrothsborough was nearly enough to make Jeremy spring from the chair, fall to his knees, and place his head in her lap like one of her little lambs. It was something he'd never allowed himself to consider—let alone hope for. And now, it would be his reality. She was *his* Lily—his sweet, benevolent, delicate flower.

"I suppose it was, wasn't it?" he said, affecting a nonchalance his racing heart did not feel.

Lily's face scrunched in an unexpected frown and she opened her mouth to speak but stalled as her mother breezed into the room. Jeremy's manners took over and he stood in greeting.

"Oh, Jeremy! Your mother said you'd be down here." The countess planted a kiss on Lily's cheek. "I left after settling her in for a rest. She seems to be doing much better now that you're home. She finished all of her broth!" she rambled excitedly as she waved Jeremy to his seat and began selecting morsels for herself from the sideboard.

Jeremy sat back down and, as he did so, the length of his lower leg met with Lily's. She moved to pull away, but he wrapped a hand around her thigh, keeping her still. The glare she shot him from beneath her long, golden lashes was meant to chide him, but it only served to inflame Jeremy's ardor once more.

He left a slow trail with his fingertips as he removed his hand. This time, she did not move. She turned her attention back to her plate while her mother happily prattled on about Abigail's improvement, the weather, etcetera, etcetera.

Jeremy watched as Lily focused her attention on her piece of toast and strawberry preserves. She took another dainty bite and, realizing some of the sweet jelly had stuck to her lip, her tongue darted out to reclaim it. That little glimpse of her perfect pink tongue on her lips kindled the flame low in Jeremy's belly. He nearly groaned aloud when she did it again.

"You know," he whispered low enough that the countess couldn't hear him over her own voice, "you taste like strawberry preserves." He saw a pink tint rush to her cheeks when she realized his meaning.

He lowered his voice another octave and, for good measure, added, "Everywhere."

The piece of toast fell to her plate, jam-side down, as toast was wont to do. He watched in pleasure as her face deepened another several shades; no doubt she was recalling exactly where he'd tasted her, just as he was contemplating ways to do it again.

"You're wicked," Lily hissed just before her mother turned back from the sideboard and took the chair across from Jeremy. He gave a guilty shrug and turned back to his breakfast, subtly readjusting the falls of his trousers beneath the table.

"You look a bit piqued, Lily, dear. Are you coming down with something?"

Jeremy tried not to smile when her mother took note of Lily's flushed skin.

"No, Mother." Lily was saved from having to concoct an excuse by the clatter of silverware.

The countess dropped her fork to the china plate and exclaimed, "Lily! Your ring!"

Lily glanced down at her hand and, for the first time that morning, realized the weight of the marquess's diamonds was missing. The memory of Jeremy's teeth on her finger caused her to release a nearly imperceptible shiver. Luckily, her mother was too distraught over the missing bauble to notice her reaction.

"What did you do? Where do you last remember having it?"

Lily's eyes darted to Jeremy. He raised his dark brows at her, waiting to see what she would say to get herself out of this mess. The ring had likely been kicked beneath the bed or, hopefully, Mrs. Hallsworth or a maid had found it while tidying up Jeremy's chamber and would return it shortly without asking too many questions.

"I got it dirty and had it sent for cleaning," Lily blurted out, hoping it would suffice.

Her mother, in her anxious state, was willing to grasp onto the logic of her excuse and melted back into her chair in an uncharacteristic slump.

"Oh, thank goodness. I don't know how we would have explained *that* to the marquess."

"Indeed," Jeremy intoned smugly around a bite of sausage and eggs.

Chapter Sixteen

After breakfast, Lily feigned weariness—taking advantage of the flush Jeremy had forced upon her—and ducked away upstairs to her bedchamber. She checked the dressing table, but there was no sign of Townsend's ring. Either it hadn't been located yet or Mrs. Hallsworth hadn't had a chance to return it without anyone noticing. Lily experienced a brief moment of panic.

That ring was worth a small fortune and she had to be sure to return it when she was finally free of this betrothal.

The last thing she wanted was to give Townsend any further opportunity to take legal action against her family. He'd already have enough fodder to do so once the betrothal was dissolved.

There was a small scratch at her door and her heart leaped. Perhaps Mrs. Hallsworth had simply been waiting until she could discreetly pass along the jewelry? When Lily opened the door, however, it was not the kind round face and graying hair of the housekeeper she encountered, but the broad chest and shoulders of Jeremy Balfour.

She took an involuntary step back as his breadth filled the doorway. Leaning one cocky shoulder on the doorframe, he held up his left hand. There, twinkling on the tip of his smallest finger was her gold-and-diamond ring.

"I had the misfortune of finding this in the pile of my chamber rug."

Lily shushed him, hoping no one was near enough to hear. "Thank you, Jemmy." She reached to take the ring, but he tossed it in the air and snatched it back.

"I don't want to see this ring on your finger again. Ever." His dark, dangerous tone and stormy eyes both chilled and excited her. "As of last night, you're mine, Lily." His eyes began to smolder.

Lily swallowed convulsively and held out her hand for the ring, willing her fingers to remain steady. If she hadn't known his true feelings, she likely wouldn't have found his adamant possessiveness as electrifying, thrilling. But this was Jeremy.

How long had she waited to hear such things from him?

How foolish had she felt when she'd wished he would rescue her from a loveless engagement?

Still, that didn't absolve him of his sorry excuse for a proposal down at the breakfast table. Lily's stomach had flipped when he'd essentially told her what *would* be done rather than asking her what she would prefer. She loved him, really she did and had for a long time, but that didn't give him leave to go against his own advice and attempt to dictate to her what her life would be without so much as consulting her. She was about to break an engagement to a marquess, and she'd be damned if she walked into another arrangement where everyone thought they knew what was best for her – even if that person was Jeremy.

"Thank you for returning the ring," Lily said evenly as he finally dropped the jewelry into her open palm. The ring felt even heavier than she remembered.

Jeremy cocked his head and narrowed his eyes at her. "What is bothering you?" he asked. Lily should have known he'd be able to tell she was upset. "You're not rethinking breaking your betrothal, are you?" She saw him begin to bristle in disbelief and held out a hand to calm him down.

"No, it's not that," Lily reassured him. Poking her head around his shoulders, she made sure the hallway was clear and gestured for him to come into her bedchamber—she couldn't be any more ruined than she already was; Jeremy had made sure of that—but she didn't want to have to explain her newfound physical relationship with Jeremy to her mother.

"Your proposal downstairs…"

"What of it?"

"It's logical, given what transpired—"

"Precisely. I'll speak with your brother and your father as soon as I can; though I don't think George will take too kindly to the thought of me defiling his little sister."

"Jeremy, stop!" Lily exclaimed, horrified. "No one is telling anyone about any 'defiling' that may or may not have occurred."

"Oh, but it did," Jeremy said with a smirk. "I remember it quite vividly." He began to reach for her, but Lily retreated several steps and put out her hand to hold him off.

"Would you just let me speak?" she demanded. Realizing he'd truly upset her, Jeremy inclined his head and gestured for her to continue. "Thank you." Lily took a bracing breath. "Wasn't it you who said

my desires matter? You once told me that I needed to take my preferences into account – that no one is allowed to tell me my opinions do
not matter." Jeremy frowned. The poor man was clearly confused and
had no idea he'd even been treating her like her well-meaning, yet
pushy, family. "You expect me to leave one betrothal and launch myself into another without so much as asking me if that is what I care to
do."

A muscle in Jeremy's jaw twitched. How could he have forgotten
that this flower had thorns?

"So, you're saying that you do *not* wish to marry me?" he asked
coolly, evenly.

"I don't—" Lily broke off with a rough sigh; "I'm not explaining
this correctly. I simply want you to respect your advice and give me a
choice instead of demanding that we wed as soon as possible."

"And if you're with child?"

This time, Lily couldn't stop herself from pressing her palm to her
abdomen.

"Then we shall cross that bridge as we come to it."

Jeremy shook his head slowly. "I do not understand. Last night you
said you wanted me." He was beginning to witness the happy picture
he'd dared erect in his mind's eye peel and crumble.

"I do, Jemmy," her green eyes were pleading with him, but he had
no interest in their pity. Lily might physically want him enough to
break her engagement to another man to satisfy her curiosity, but
she'd never once actually said she would be willing to marry him as a
consequence. Jeremy would have kicked his own sentimental arse had
he been physically able to do so.

It was Lily's turn to reach for Jeremy and have him shy away from
her touch.

"So, you do not wish to marry Townsend, but you're unwilling to marry me," his words came out as more of a statement than a question.

"That's not—Jeremy!" Lily stamped her foot in frustration, feeling all the world like a child, but not caring. This was beyond exasperating. What had happened to all of the warmth and flirtation from earlier? "You are not listening to me."

Lily witnessed the exact moment he boarded up his emotions from her and she felt the loss as keenly as she had when he'd failed to show up for their dance at the Lucklows' ball.

She recognized the look; it was the one he'd worn at his father's funeral—the one he used to protect himself and his emotions.

"Oh, I think I am hearing you quite clearly. You don't want Townsend, but I'm an insufficient replacement. You satisfied your curiosity in my bed and now you can move on." He turned on his heel and made to leave the chamber, but Lily snagged his sleeve.

"Stop!"

He whirled on her and the look in his eyes made her snatch her hand back. She wasn't afraid that he would strike her—she'd never in her life feared he would ever do her physical harm—but the look in his eyes was that of a wounded animal, and one never quite knew what those were going to do.

"I will not be made a fool," Jeremy snarled. "You've danced just beyond my reach for years. I was stupid to ever believe that you could have wanted more from me than a good tupping. I've never been anything more to you than your brothers' friend and your plaything." Lily winced at his harsh words. "You've had your fun and gotten a fool to propose to you in the process. You must certainly be proud of yourself because this is, by far, the grandest farce you've ever pulled, Lily."

Lily's throat began to close with emotion. Was he so blinded by his feelings of inadequacy that he couldn't see how much she had always cared for him? That he'd also made himself deaf to her sincerity? Mrs. Hallsworth's advice came rushing back to her.

"Why do you continually believe yourself inadequate?"

"Amn't I, though?" Jeremy began stalking Lily across the room, backing her against the bedpost. "I'm unworthy of anything but your lust."

Lily shook her head in denial and, when her spine connected with the bedpost, the marquess' engagement ring fell from her hand with a metallic thud and rolled away unnoticed.

"Whatever gave you that idea?" Lily demanded.

"It has always been as clear to me as the knowledge that I would one day become Baron Shefford."

"Which is something else for which you do not feel up to snuff." That stopped Jeremy's tirade. He stood over her, his chest rising and falling with his heavy breaths, but said no more. Lily took her opportunity to elaborate. "You knew you'd be Baron Shefford one day, but you weren't ready for it when it happened – no one was. Your father's passing was tragic, Jeremy, but no one could have done anything to stop it. Don't punish yourself for assuming your father's title. It's why you haven't redecorated your chambers; you're feeling guilty for moving on.

"You should know that you *are* good enough. You aren't afraid of hard work; you are fair, honest, and kind. Your tenants love you and your father taught you well...he lives on in you." Lily risked placing the flat of her hand over Jeremy's pounding heart. "That is precisely why you *are* good enough for me, Jeremy Balfour. You're a good man. And if you think you're not good enough for me because you don't have a grander title, then you're also daft...though I'm willing to overlook that one, tiny flaw." Lily's expressive mouth tilted into a smile, though Jeremy barely registered it in his racing mind.

"What are you saying?"

"I love you, you silly man. I think a part of me always has. You're my dearest friend, you've always been my protector, and I know for a fact that you care about me too. What more could I ask for in a partner and husband?"

Jeremy thought he felt his heart stop. "You will marry me then?"

"No," Lily said, a twinkle in her emerald eyes. "Not unless you give me a proper proposal and *ask* if I would like to spend the rest of my life with you instead of *telling* me it's what I'm going to do. I've had just about enough of people telling me what I'm going to do with my life."

Jeremy could have howled with pleasure at her words. She loved him. A weight had been lifted from his heart and it was finally allowed to soar. He bent his head to kiss Lily, but, before he could do so, there was a tap on the door. He pressed his forehead to hers with a groan.

"We've waited years," whispered Lily with a grin, "we can wait a little longer." She pressed her lips to his in a tender, fleeting kiss before ducking beneath his arm and answering the door. She was careful to only open it a crack so whomever it was wouldn't be able to see inside the room.

"Lady Stratford," Jeremy heard Mrs. Hallsworth greet her. "Viscount Sommerfeld is here to see you. If you *happen* to see Lord Shefford, would you please advise him of our guest? I cannot seem to find him anywhere."

Jeremy rolled his eyes at his housekeeper's insinuation. Though she was correct that Jeremy was, indeed, sequestered in Lily's chamber, she needn't make her knowledge so obvious.

Lily thanked Mrs. Hallsworth and told her she would be down shortly before she closed the door and turned back to Jeremy.

"Georgie is here."

"So I heard," Jeremy said, closing the gap between them in three great strides. Cupping the back of her head, Jeremy pulled Lily against him and slanted his mouth over hers in a deep, possessive kiss. She sighed and his tongue delved between her lips. Her small hands fisted in the front of his linen shirt a moment before she pressed him away from her.

"We can't keep Georgie waiting," she panted.

"I don't care." Jeremy bent to claim her mouth again, but Lily kept her arms locked.

"Well I do," she laughed lightly. "Come along." And with that, she turned, opened the door just wide enough to scan the hallway, and waved for him to follow her once she was sure they were alone.

"We're going to finish that later," Jeremy grumbled beneath his breath as they descended the stairs side-by-side.

"I'm counting on it," Lily sang lightly as she led the way into the parlor.

Little minx.

They found Lily's brother reclining on one of the sofas, staring out the sun-filled window at the street with its carriages, riders, and ladies in their frippery walking small dogs. Everyone seemed to be taking advantage of the unseasonably warm spring day.

He turned at the sound of the door and a wide grin split his face at the sight of his sister and best friend.

"Lily," he greeted his sister warmly and embraced her before turning to Jeremy. "How's your mother, Jem? Much improved, I hope?" They clasped hands in greeting.

"She appears to be on the mend." He looked down and gave Lily a warm smile. "She was in very capable hands while I made my way here from Kent." If he noticed the intimate way Jeremy looked at Lily, then he didn't show it.

"Indeed," Sommerfeld replied warmly. "Speaking of our Lily," he began as he turned to his sister, "I've some news for you regarding your, er, situation." His eyes darted to Jeremy, clearly unsure how much to divulge.

"It's okay, Georgie. I've told him we're going to break my betrothal to Townsend."

"Have you, now?" Sommerfeld looked back at him, his eyebrows flying to his hairline. Jeremy knew his friend was trying to gauge his reaction – elation, celebration, backflips of joy—but Jeremy schooled himself to remain impassive. It was best not to seem overeager just yet; especially because Jeremy recognized the look on his face.

It did *not* bode well.

"About the betrothal…" Sommerfeld rubbed the back of his neck.

Jeremy's stomach plummeted, but he remained steady and sidled closer to Lily to provide silent support for whatever brother was about to reveal.

"Did Father…did he refuse to consider it? Perhaps if I—"

"No," Sommerfeld shook his head. "Father just wants you to be happy."

Jeremy read the ensuing silence. "So, it was Townsend, then," Jeremy forced himself to utter. "He refused to allow your family to break the contract."

Sommerfeld nodded and dropped back onto the sofa with a weary sigh. He looked over at Lily, sadness and regret darkening his normally jovial countenance.

"The man is stubborn, to be sure. He seems determined not to give you up – whether or not that makes you miserable. I convinced Father to let me take him to the club, smooth things over with a few drinks, and then approach the subject gently.

"He's a man who is used to getting what he wants, Lily. I pleaded your case, but he would hear none of it. Even though it's more acceptable for a woman to cry off than a man, he still perceives it as an unacceptable slight and will not quietly release you from the obligation. He's threatened to sue for breach of contract if we attempt to pursue the dissolution. The Aldborough title is hardly something to sniff at, but Townsend's wealth and connections could drag this out for an exorbitant amount of time and bankrupt us long into when my future son takes over the title."

Out of the corner of his eye, Jeremy saw Lily wrap her arms around her waist. He placed an arm across her shoulders and guided her to the cushion beside her brother before she could become too unsteady.

"Does he have no care or concern for what she wants?" Jeremy's voice rose with his frustration. "He would condemn her to a lifetime of misery with him just to prove a point?"

George held out his hands palm-up in a gesture of helplessness. "Father spoke to him—offered him a handsome settlement to replace her dowry—but the man has no need for money. He just wants Lily."

He doesn't want Lily, thought Jeremy; *he just wants to make sure I cannot have her.*

Jeremy looked down at Lily, hoping she would forgive him for what he was about to say to her brother. There was no other way.

"You know the man better than I, Georgie," Jeremy began softly. "He seems to me to be a businessman at heart…would Townsend accept imperfect goods?"

George narrowed his eyes up at Jeremy while he attempted to process his friend's meaning. The moment the words sunk in, however, was very apparent.

Lily yelped in surprise as George shot to his feet – his cane clattering to the floor – and used his upward momentum to deliver a blow to Jeremy's jaw that caused his head to whip backward and his vision to flicker black. Jeremy staggered back a step and tested his jaw and teeth for soundness with a curse. It was rather unpleasant, but he would survive. He'd been struck far worse several times over the years and he had a good several stone on Sommerfeld. Not that he intended to hit Sommerfeld back, but it would have been a much more even match ten years ago. Lily, however, had no idea Jeremy wasn't going to retaliate and jumped between them instantly, a hand on each of their chests.

"Stop it, right now!" she demanded frantically, glancing between them. "I started it, Georgie. If you want to blame anyone, then blame me!"

"You?" Jeremy found the shock on Sommerfeld's face to be worth any soreness he'd experience later. He could well imagine Sommerfeld's poor, traumatized mind attempting not to picture all the ways in which his friend could have defiled his younger sister. He tried his damnedest not to smile at Sommerfeld's obvious suffering at the hands of his own depraved imagination.

Sommerfeld's entire body gave a dramatic shudder; he backed away from Jeremy, shaking out his hand. "You've just shattered any remaining pretenses I'd had about you being my sweet, innocent, baby sister, thank you very much."

"I'm a grown woman," Lily said by way of explanation and shrugged matter-of-factly. "It was bound to happen sooner or later."

"Yes well…" Sommerfeld looked back at Jeremy. "I had to do it, you know, for honor's sake. I did warn you."

"No offense taken," Jeremy replied, still trying to work out the kinks in his jaw. "I'd have done the same."

"As much as I'd like to call you my brother – because you really *would* be marrying her now if I had more say—" Jeremy put a hand on Lily's arm, forestalling her protest at her brother's dictates, "—but Townsend refuses to break the contract. If we tell him Lily…" his next word choice seemed to cause him physical pain; "allowed you liberties, then that will only bolster his grounds for the breach of contract suit."

Jeremy cursed under his breath. He hadn't fully considered that. However, another idea came to him.

What if he turned Townsend's ire away from the Stratfords?

"Lily…" Jeremy said softly. He ran his hand down her arm and took her hand in his. "Might I speak to your brother alone, please?"

He saw her hesitate and knew she was torn between giving in to his request and frustration over the fact that she was, yet again, not going to be present whilst her future was being discussed. If his plan was going to work, however, Jeremy needed Lily out of earshot.

She'd never let him go through with what he planned if she knew.

"Please?" he repeated gently and punctuated his request with a squeeze of her hand.

"I've not given up yet," Sommerfeld added to his sister. "You shouldn't either."

Lily finally nodded and turned to leave the room. Jeremy waited until he heard the sound of her feet softly padding down the hallway before he spoke.

"You don't seem as hopeful as you're trying to let on," Jeremy said bluntly as he seated himself in the armchair across from his friend.

"I've been wracking my brain for days, Jem. You know I love Lily and I would do anything to see her happy, but I don't know how our family will be able to weather this one. I'd give my right arm if it meant she could live out her days in marital bliss, but our father cannot—*I* cannot—condemn us to the poverty and shame that would befall if we attempted to go toe-to-toe with Townsend in court. We're a wealthy powerful family, but few can compare to the marquess in connections. As soon as he starts throwing his weight and his gold around, there's little we'll be able to do. Breaking this contract means a great deal more than crying off; it could mean the dissolution of the Stratford name as respectable." Sommerfeld rested his elbows on his knees and propped up his forehead. "I just don't see a way around it. Lily is going to have to go through with it."

"No," Jeremy interrupted gruffly. His hands on the arms of the chair faded to white with his grip on the upholstery. "She loves me, George. Did you know that?"

His friend lifted his head a fraction and gave Jeremy a sad half-smile. "I did."

"How can I allow the woman who loves me to marry another man?"

"No offense intended, Jem," Sommerfeld began as he sat up and rubbed his palms on his buff breeches, "but if our family and men of business have not been able to find a loophole in the contract or persuade him otherwise, then I don't know how you're going to do so."

"Precisely because Townsend hates *me*. What if I were to divert his attention; take the brunt of it? I have a hell of a lot less to lose than your family."

"What are you saying?"

"I am saying that I go to Townsend and tell him the truth. I explain that I've compromised Lily and he will have to break the betrothal.

I'll take all the blame—say that I coerced her. No man of his ilk would go through with a wedding with the chance that another man's child could end up the heir to the marquisate; he's far too prideful to allow that, especially not when that child would be the offspring of someone like me."

Sommerfeld scowled in Jeremy's direction. "You did ruin her quite properly then, didn't you?"

Jeremy couldn't help but give a small smile despite the seriousness of the situation. "I'd like to think she did just as much of the ruination as I."

Sommerfeld shook his head and waved off any further descriptions. "You're my closest friend, Jem, but I think our days of sharing stories of our sexual exploits need to come to an end." Jeremy chuckled as his friend continued. "I'll do my best to support you in this plan of yours, and I'm sure my family will agree—though perhaps we should leave out the 'ruination' bit. They may never look at you the same way…I know I won't." George gave a sad, lop-sided smile.

"Thank you, George. I've just one favor to ask."

"Anything."

"Find out when Townsend will be at the club and get me in there. I believe if he's put on the spot in public and caught off-guard, then he won't have the opportunity to run to his men of business and ask for advice. We need to act fast if this is going to work."

Chapter Seventeen

Lily watched from her chamber window as Jeremy climbed into a hired hackney with nary a backward glance. He and George had remained ensconced in the parlor for quite a while before her brother had ducked from the townhouse without so much as a goodbye.

The men were up to something and Lily didn't like it.

She hadn't liked it when they were all children, and she liked it even less now.

While she cared for the thought of the boorish Townsend demanding she go through with the wedding less, George and Jeremy becoming secretive was an ominous sign. She'd learned long ago that it usually spelled trouble—and not the innocent kind.

Lily had tried to corner Jeremy after George's departure, but he dodged her with expert execution by shutting himself away with his mother and then sneaking off to his chambers when Mrs. Hallsworth kept her distracted with planning the transportation of Lily's and her mother's belongings back to their townhome. Now that Jeremy was back in residence and Abigail was on the mend, their presence was no longer necessary, but Lily had no doubt Jeremy had sent his housekeeper to assist Lily in packing as a way to keep her from confronting him.

That infuriating man.

"What shall I do with this one, m'lady?" Mrs. Hallsworth asked, tearing Lily's gaze away from the spot on the street where Jeremy had once stood. She turned to find the older woman holding up the shreds of what remained of the morning dress Lily had worn the other day.

The one Jeremy had torn apart in his desperate bid to get to her bare flesh.

Lily's face heated at the memory, as well as the fact that she was faced with very obvious evidence of what had transpired.

"I don't know if it can be mended," Mrs. Hallsworth said as she examined the split seams.

"Please, just dispose of it," Lily requested, then added, "Discreetly," to be safe. She didn't need her mother asking questions about the gown's fate.

The housekeeper nodded and rolled up the fabric into a bundle along with her ruined shift. Jeremy would destroy her entire wardrobe if they continued at this rate.

Lily went to collect her book from the nightstand when the toe of her slipper kicked a small object and sent it skittering across the floor. Dropping to her hands and knees, Lily reached beneath the bed and searched blindly for the object. She was about to give up when her palm connected with the small, heavy object. She knew what she would find before she opened her hand to examine it.

Townsend's ring.

Jeremy addled her brain so much that she'd nearly lost the jewelry twice in as many days.

The weight of Lily's situation settled heavily on her chest, forcing her to sit on the floor as she stared at the ring in her lap. Mrs. Hallsworth peered around the bed and found her there, contemplating the jewelry as a symbol for the fate towards which she seemed to be inexorably propelled.

"Where has Jeremy gone?" Lily asked the housekeeper without looking up from the ring. She'd given up all pretenses of propriety at that point.

"I don't know, dear," the older woman replied gently. "He bid me look after you while he was out. I'd expect him to be home soon; he's not likely to run off while Lady Shefford is still abed." Noticing what Lily was staring at, she added, "That's a lovely ring."

"Indeed," Lily muttered numbly.

It's a shame it came from the wrong man.

Jeremy and Sommerfeld clattered up to the steps of the gentlemen's club in the Stratford carriage. Sommerfeld had an acquaintance who frequented the card tables and his long hours were conducive to keeping watch for Townsend. A few short hours after leaving Jeremy's townhouse, Sommerfeld had sent him word that Townsend had arrived intending to take dinner at the club. Jeremy had left his mother's bedside, trading places with the countess, and gave instructions to Mrs. Hallsworth to keep Lily occupied. He'd then changed into more formal attire and hailed the first available hack to the Stratford townhouse. Everything was going to change that evening, and Jeremy was hell-bent on making sure Lily was free of this farce of a betrothal.

"Townsend's not likely to be warm and welcoming to me, not after our last conversation," Sommerfeld reminded him.

"We don't need him to like you," Jeremy responded. "We just need him to hate me more."

"That shouldn't be too difficult," Sommerfeld's tone was light, but the smile didn't reach his eyes. Jeremy knew his friend had deep reservations about the plan—about what a powerful man like Townsend might do when confronted with the situation—but Jeremy was determined. Laying the blame at Jeremy's own feet was the only way to take some of the liability and scandal away from the Stratford name. It might very well ruin Jeremy, but he hoped it would at least allow Lily to choose her own path.

They alighted from the carriage and strolled into the club where they found Townsend in the smoking room, surrounded by associates, cigars and brandy in hand. The pungent haze of dozens of varieties of cigars and pipe tobacco clouded the air. Mixed with the scent of leather, expensive spirits, and floral pomade, it created a rather close and cloying atmosphere.

"Remember," Jeremy said in a low tone as they affected an air of casualness and strolled in Townsend's direction; "feign ignorance and agree to whatever I say."

"I still don't care for this," Sommerfeld grumbled.

"If you want Lily free of this man, then you'll do as I say."

It was at that moment that Townsend spotted them over the shoulder of one of his companions. Jeremy watched recognition spark and flare in those pale blue eyes a moment before they froze into chips of ice.

"Townsend!" Sommerfeld, always brilliant at playacting, said in a convivial tone and held out his hand to the marquess. The older man eyed George's limb with all the thinly-veiled distaste one would a wriggling eel. Begrudgingly, he switched his brandy to his other hand and took Sommerfeld's proffered one, though he didn't bother to stand. They proceeded through the banal process of introductions with the klatch consisting of several of Townsend's business associates and fellow peers.

"You remember Shefford?" Sommerfeld asked.

"I do," replied Townsend cooly.

Jeremy clenched his jaw at the older man's obvious contempt. A slow breath through his nostrils allowed him to speak with a measure of civility.

"I was wondering if we might have a word," Jeremy ground out.

"I believe I've said all that I needed to say, thank you. I've made myself quite clear. Now, if you'll excuse me—"

"You want to hear what I need to say," Jeremy lowered his voice and fixed Townsend with a stare that dared him to say otherwise. The marquess narrowed his eyes and tossed back his drink.

"Very well." He set the glass down with a clink and pushed himself to his feet. "If you'll excuse us, gentlemen? Shefford, here, requires some financial advice."

Jeremy forced himself to ignore the comment and take deep, calming breaths. His fists clenched and unclenched at his sides.

Sommerfeld made a few parting comments before trailing after Jeremy and Townsend, following them to a small table and pair of ladder-backed chairs in the corner. Townsend flagged down a servant and requested another brandy.

"What in God's name is so important that you had to interrupt my meeting? I've had my word with you, Shefford." He fixed those icy blue eyes on Sommerfeld. "And I've certainly said my peace with *you*. Now, Shefford, if you've come as some sort of muscle to Sommerfeld's pathetic request to free his sister of the engagement contract, then you must have mistaken me for a man who is easily intimidated by brainless brawn." Jeremy crossed his arms over his chest, more than anything to keep his fists from striking Townsend.

"I've come to you as one man to another. I strongly suggest you consider Aldborough's offer of settlement to dissolve the betrothal while you can still get something out of it."

"Oh, do you now?" he quirked a brow and snatched his brandy from the servant. "I take it back. This should be amusing."

"You don't strike me as a man who would want to marry another man's leavings, Townsend," Jeremy said curtly. It pained him to speak of Lily thusly, but he had to strike a nerve and the best way to do so was on the man's level: trite and blunt.

The correctness of Jeremy's assessment quickly became apparent: Townsend froze with his brandy glass halfway to his mouth. Now Jeremy had the marquess's attention.

"What the devil is that supposed to mean, Shefford?" he demanded, setting his glass down hard on the table with a resounding crack.

"Exactly as it sounds," Jeremy continued. He did his best to ignore the anxious tapping of Sommerfeld's cane upon the rug. "Marrying Lady Lily Stratford would jeopardize the integrity of your name and lineage."

"Are you saying Lily allowed a man *liberties*?" hissed Townsend, his palms flat on the tabletop as he leaned toward Jeremy and George. The fire had sparked in his eyes once more. Now it was time to divert that blaze from the Stratfords and onto Jeremy, himself.

"'Allowed' and 'liberties' are relative terms. I would use 'coerced' and 'intercourse.'"

"You!" roared Townsend, seeming to have forgotten they were in the relatively crowded smoking room of one of the most exclusive gentlemen's clubs in Town—just as Jeremy had anticipated. "You shared a bed with my betrothed?" he demanded. His pale eyes grew wide and wild. "Was it before or after our conversation?"

"After, if you're insistent upon specifics," Jeremy replied with a lift of one shoulder.

Townsend whirled on Sommerfeld and snarled, "Did you know about this?" Just as they'd planned, Lily's brother shook his head and plastered on an expression of disbelief. "Were you knowingly selling me damaged goods and your conscience got the better of you? You knew you had no right marrying her off, but you couldn't bring yourself to tell me what a slut your sister was?"

Jeremy's hand darted out and twisted in the front of Townsend's jacket before he could stop himself. He wrenched the material around his fist and jerked the marquess to face him.

"Call me what you will, but leave the Stratfords out of this. I am the one who defiled your intended. She didn't want to, but I pressed her. Taking her to wife would only call into question the legitimacy of any heir she bore and you don't want that, do you?

"Agree to call off the damned wedding amicably and take your settlement. Do what you will to me. Try to bankrupt me. Slander my name. I've been a man and admitted to what I've done."

"Unhand me, you filthy peon!" yowled Townsend as he jerked himself free of Jeremy's grasp and snapped his jacket back into place. "How dare you?"

"Take the settlement," Jeremy urged, his tone rising. "Save the gossip that you weren't enough for a lady so she sought comfort in the arms of another." Townsend's feral eyes widened further. "That's right," Jeremy lowered his voice, "going around telling everyone Lady Lily Stratford slummed it with me when she could have had you *will* backfire. Maybe not at first, but if you do so, then I'll make damn sure your manhood comes into question."

"You bastard," spat Townsend.

Jeremy had been right to believe Townsend wouldn't accept an insult such as that. The end was in sight.

"I demand satisfaction!" the marquess cried between furious gulps of air. "Name your second and weapon of choice." He jabbed Jeremy in the chest, punctuating the voracity of his challenge.

A duel.

Jeremy had briefly pondered the possibility that Townsend would be so offended that he'd challenge Jeremy—even Sommerfeld had mentioned it—but Jeremy had been counting on Townsend's desire for self-preservation to prevent such a thing. Still, even having accepted the possibility, Jeremy's heart skipped a beat at the actual challenge.

"Sommerfeld will be my second. I choose pistols."

"My second will be in contact. Dawn tomorrow." And, with that, Townsend turned on his heel and stormed off, knocking into several bystanders on his way.

For the first time, Jeremy noticed how silent the smoking room had grown around them. Mouths hung agape and cigar cinders fell unnoticed to laps and floors. Sommerfeld cleared his throat softly.

"Jem…we should go," he muttered beneath his breath.

The two of them abandoned the smoking room—hearing the instant roar of chatter and wagers behind them as soon as they were clear of the door—and decided to loiter in the hall long enough so they did not run into Townsend while he waited for his carriage to be brought around.

"What in the bloody hell was that?" Sommerfeld demanded. "You were supposed to convince him to break the betrothal on decent terms, not offend your way into a *duel*."

Jeremy said nothing and turned his eyes to the intricately carved scrollwork on the crown molding.

"Bloody hell," Sommerfeld continued, raking a hand through his hair. "I know you're a damned good shot, but this is absurd. You're either going to be killed or be locked away for killing a marquess. Say something, man!"

Jeremy finally turned toward his friend as they exited the building. "The man is a snake. You heard how he spoke of Lily."

"Be that as it may," Sommerfeld said, hauling himself into the carriage, "how do you think Lily is going to feel about all of this?"

"She's not going to know."

"Oh, lovely. More secrets." He rolled his eyes heavenward.

"You know as well as I that she'd try to stop it," Jeremy bellowed, finally allowing his voice to convey the tempest within. "It's the only way. I don't care what happens to me; she will wither and die as that man's wife."

Sommerfeld released a great rush of air from his lungs. They rocked along in silence for what felt like an interminable amount of time.

"You do realize you need to survive this, right?" he finally spoke up.

"Why?" Jeremy gave a soft, self-deprecating chuckle. "You'll miss me too much? Lily will never forgive you for not taking the bullet for me?"

"No. I'm never going to be welcome at that club again and it's going to be damned boring having to stay home every night. I need someone to keep me occupied."

Chapter Eighteen

Jeremy returned home late that evening. He and Sommerfeld had shared drinks and stories of more lighthearted times at Stratford House until Townsend's second, a pale earl named Wexford about the same age as the marquess, arrived. As custom dictated, Jeremy was not present for the discussion of terms, rules, and location; however, he trusted his friend with his life. He had no choice but to.

Jeremy sat in the library, rolling a glass of brandy between his palms, waiting for Sommerfeld to finish the negotiations. Traditionally, the delay in meeting for the duel was to give the parties time to cool off and rescind; however, Jeremy doubted the marquess was a man to do that. He had slept with the man's fiancé, insulted his manhood, and, generally, done a decent job of drawing all of Townsend's anger upon himself and away from Lily and her family. The plan had worked, even if it escalated to a point of no return.

Jeremy wasn't concerned about his well-being—most of these duels ended in intentional misses or grazes as adequate satisfaction for a perceived slight. Worst case scenario, he might take a shot to the shoulder and recuperate in the country; leaving the public eye and gossips to cool down just long enough for it to be proper for him and Lily to marry. It was impossible for him to imagine any other outcome. He simply wouldn't allow it.

Sommerfeld returned to the library from his meeting with Wexford in the study. His face appeared more drawn and weary than Jeremy had ever seen it. He waited patiently as his friend poured himself another few fingers of brandy and took up the seat across from him.

"You seem to have rotten luck in picking enemies," Sommerfeld sighed before taking a deep swig of the spirits. Jeremy remained silent and waited for him to continue. "Townsend's physician will be in attendance. The location is a field within a copse of trees on the outskirts of the city – a popular place for these meetings, apparently, due to its dubious jurisdiction." Jeremy listened as he further described the location. The choice made sense since—although dueling was viewed as a way for the nobility to reclaim honor—it was illegal. The uncertain jurisdiction would make it more difficult to convict them of dueling if they were happened upon.

"And the pistols?" asked Jeremy.

"My father has a set of dueling pistols; they were given to him as a gift. I've offered them up and Wexford accepted rather than find somewhere to purchase them at this time in the evening. I've already sent a footman to have them taken to a cleaner and ensure they're in proper working order."

As if summoned by their conversation, Sommerfeld's father, the Earl of Aldborough, strode into the room, papers in hand. He nearly reached the sofa by the fire before noticing the room was already occupied. A tall man—where George had inherited his height—he'd grown slightly thicker around the middle in recent years. Though incredibly shrewd in business dealings, his hazel eyes still lit with un-abashed laughter in more relaxed settings—where Lily had inherited her easy, bubbling joy. His hair had faded from the dusty blonde Jeremy remembered from his childhood to a gray shot through with silver. There had been a great deal less of the gray when Jeremy's father had been alive. Like Jeremy's mother, the earl had taken the death of his oldest friend, Vincent Balfour, with a great deal of sadness and struggle. Jeremy knew he'd feel the same way if he suddenly lost George or visa-versa. All the more reason for Jeremy to survive the duel; he didn't want to put Sommerfeld through what the earl was enduring.

"George, Jeremy! I thought you were out for the evening?" Aldborough greeted them a moment before gauging the temperature of the room. "I'd ask to join you, but it seems as if this isn't the most jovial of meetings." Ever observant – where the persistently studious youngest Stratford sibling, Simon, had inherited his perceptiveness – the earl was an expert at extracting the truth from his children and businessmen, alike. Lord knew he'd caught George and Jeremy in lies enough times for them to realize another falsehood was useless. The younger men exchanged a look that confirmed that it was better now to tell the earl the truth.

"Please, do join us," Sommerfeld said as he rose to pour his father a drink as well. Aldborough folded his paper neatly and draped it across his knee as he sat in the only unoccupied chair and accepted the drink from his eldest son.

"Are you two going to tell me what trouble you've dug yourselves into this time, or am I going to have to whip it out of you?" He gave an easy, joking smile, so like his eldest son's.

"I've somehow managed to stay relatively clear of this mess," Sommerfeld began, absently rubbing his thumb along the lion's mane on the head of his cane; "although Jem, here, seems to have gotten himself into enough trouble for the two of us."

Aldborough set his glass on a nearby table and leaned forward. "Is it money? Legal?" He fell so naturally into the role of second father that it made Jeremy's chest ache. The words felt like molasses in his throat and he was unable to force them out. What would he do if Aldborough was disappointed in him for the reckless way he'd behaved? Jeremy did not know if he could handle it atop everything else.

"Jeremy's been challenged to a duel," Sommerfeld responded for him.

Aldborough's disbelief was instantaneous. "What in God's name— How on Earth did you manage that?" The papers fell unnoticed from his lap, scattering across the rug like best-laid plans.

Jeremy said the one word he could—the one word he hoped would – explain things above all else.

"Lily."

The earl's gaze narrowed for a fraction of a second before he sat back and stared Jeremy down with the eyes of an eagle. Jeremy fought the urge to fidget as if he were a boy again.

"Did George let slip our complications with the betrothal contract and you thought you'd take matters into your own hands? And now Townsend has challenged you to a duel?" questioned Aldborough after a few moments of silence. "Of all the rash, idiotic—"

"Actually," Sommerfeld interjected with a wince, "Jem is more the *reason* for the 'complications.'" Several heartbeats passed before Aldborough's eyes widened in comprehension.

"Oh. Oh, my." He scratched at his jaw, lost in thought, and then looked back at Jeremy. "Lily wants to break the betrothal to be with you, then?" Jeremy nodded slowly. This conversation was even more uncomfortable than he thought it'd be. "And you, Jem? What does that mean for you? Is there some…reciprocity? I'd hate to know she wanted to break this on a whim."

Jeremy took a deep breath.

"I love her, sir. I've always loved her." The words drained a weight of molten lead from his heart, relieving a greater burden than he'd realized possible. He hadn't planned on saying them; they'd risen unbidden to his lips. Now that they were out in the open, however, Jeremy couldn't wait to tell Lily. He wanted to tell her how much he cherished her; how much he looked forward to holding her each night and waking to her smile in the morning; how he didn't think he could live without her. "I realize it's a bit late for this and it's something I should have done years ago—I seem to be a bit addled with it comes to Lily—but I would be greatly honored if, once the matter of her current betrothal is resolved, you would give me your blessing in marrying her. I may not bring the title or the prestige Townsend does, but you can be damned sure I would give my life to see her happy."

Aldborough's brows rose nearly to his hairline. "Yes, well…that seems to be what you're doing getting yourself into a duel…" He sat silently, eyeing Jeremy for several minutes. Jeremy wasn't quite sure what to make of the grim line of the older man's mouth.

"Legally," Aldborough finally began to speak with slow, measured words, "I cannot consent nor give you my blessing to marry my daughter, whom I've already contracted to another." Jeremy's breath seized in his chest. "We made the betrothal contract because we believed we were making the most beneficial match for our daughter and, on some levels, we were correct.

"However," he continued; "as your father's lifelong friend, I can say that nothing in this world would make me happier. You're a good and honest man, Jeremy—you're your father's son, to be sure. You have made it clear you *are* willing to sacrifice anything for Lily. But,

God Almighty! What the hell took you so long?" he said with a laugh and took up his drink, relaxing back into his chair.

"Jem can be a bit thick," Sommerfeld laughed. "Fell from one too many trees as a boy."

"Sure would have saved a hell of a lot of trouble and money had you spoken up." Aldborough shook his head and took another sip of brandy.

It was at that moment that Jeremy truly realized how foolish he'd been to believe that the Stratfords wouldn't accept him as a son-in-law. They had never truly viewed their daughter as a pawn to be bought and sold or bargained away—they only wanted to provide her with the best life they could. They'd never thought their children too good to play with the son of a baron barely above the level considered to be genteel poverty. Not once had they ever looked down their noses at the hard work his father had taught him as a way of life. Jeremy had been stupid enough to project society's dictates upon people who were like a second family to him. Now, if he survived tomorrow, he might just be able to legally call them family.

Aldborough stood suddenly and held his glass aloft, looking down at Jeremy. "Son. You'd better survive tomorrow because I'll be damned if I have to draw up another set of engagement papers for my daughter. You'd best be the last."

Sommerfeld winked and stood too, holding his glass up and out like his father. Jeremy's heart felt full and content for the first time since his father's death the year before. He stood and held out his glass as well, joining the toast.

"Aim true," said the earl. "And return safely."

"In other words," added Sommerfeld, "try not to get your pretty head blown off."

*****

Several hours later, Jeremy rolled to a stop in front of his townhouse and disembarked the hired hackney. He tossed his fare up to the jarvey and mounted the stairs, letting himself through the front door and locking it behind him. A small stack of trunks was poised near the base of the stairs. Lily and her mother were packed to leave his townhouse in the morning.

Most of the household had long since retired; though he didn't doubt his valet was waiting vigilantly for his return. He found a shaft of light filtering through a window from a lamp in the street and used it to make out the time on his pocket watch. He had seven hours before he was to meet Townsend in the field outside of London.

Jeremy slowly climbed the stairs and paused at the top landing before ultimately turning toward his mother's chamber. No light shone from the crack at the base of the door, so she appeared to be resting peacefully. He briefly contemplated opening the door and looking in on her, but he knew if he woke her that she would be able to tell he was keeping something from her. Jeremy had to settle for being torn between embracing his mother one last time in case something went amiss at the duel, and not wanting to put her already frail health in worse jeopardy. He turned and strode down the hall to his chamber. To his credit, Charles was only slightly bleary-eyed from waiting up for his master. Jeremy allowed him to strip him of his jacket and boots, requesting that the valet have his greatcoat brushed and ensure that his best black jacket and green waistcoat were pressed and ready for him to ride out an hour before dawn. Duels were formal affairs and participants were expected to dress the part.

Once Jeremy was alone in his room, however, the silence became deafening. He knew he should sleep to remain sharp. He'd only had two glasses of brandy with Sommerfeld and that had been hours ago.

Still, his racing mind refused to calm itself and his body was restless. Recalling his conversation with Aldborough only made matters worse.

And sitting in the bedchamber that remained unchanged like a shrine to his late father did nothing to help his mood.

Lily had been right.

He'd had the opportunity to make his mark upon the barony. It had been a relatively short time since his father's passing, but there was truly nothing keeping him from making the home his own. He wasn't flush with cash, but he didn't exactly have pockets to let. The only thing redoing the room would do was make his position as baron feel even more tangible than it already was.

He'd believed himself unworthy of Lily, but that had proven to be miles from the truth.

Inheriting the barony so suddenly had been a shock, but that was his reality. Simply because he hadn't felt ready didn't mean he wasn't prepared. It didn't mean he was unfit. If his father had done anything, it was to teach him how to be a good lord and to do everything to take care of those around him.

Wouldn't it be appropriate that that same quality was what made him a man remotely good enough for Lily?

And if he could recognize his worthiness in that aspect, could he finally allow himself to embrace his role as Baron Shefford?

Jeremy knew he could do that, and so much more, so long as Lily was by his side.

As if of their own volition, his feet carried him out of his bed-chamber, through the antechamber, and down the hall. He was almost startled to find himself outside of the room currently occupied by Lily. This time, he noticed a very faint flicker beneath the seam of the door. It might be a candle by which one was reading or the fire dying after the occupant had fallen into the arms of sleep. Either way, Jeremy could not have prevented himself from turning the knob any more than he could have stopped himself from breathing.

The room was silent and the bed was made and unslept in. He found Lily curled up in the dainty floral armchair by the fire. She looked almost feline in that position with her feet tucked beneath her thin nightshift and her fists pillowing her head atop one of the arms of the chair.

Jeremy experienced a familiar pang in his chest.

She was his.

As long as he survived the duel and Townsend dissolved the betrothal…as he would no doubt do once his pride had been satisfied.

Against his better judgment, Jeremy stepped further into the room and quietly closed the door behind him. He walked over to where Lily lay sleeping and crouched down until he was level with her eyes. She looked like an angel in the arms of Morpheus, haloed in flickering firelight with her golden lashes fanned out upon her petal-soft cheeks.

"Lily, love," Jeremy whispered, half loath to wake her, but she didn't stir. He reached out and stroked the gentle curve of her cheek with his knuckles. "You look terribly uncomfortable, love," he said as she nuzzled against the warmth of his touch.

Jeremy leaned forward and gently, carefully, slipped his arms beneath her knees and shoulders. Gaining his footing, he straightened and lifted Lily against him, her forehead nestled against the pulse in his throat. He was nearly overwhelmed by the intensity of his desire when he was engulfed in her delicate scent of lavender.

Lily awoke to the sensation of floating.

No, she wasn't floating. Someone was carrying her. Someone strong, judging from the solid wall of his chest against which she was being held.

She blinked the drowsiness from her eyes and looked up to find the hard angle of a familiar, stubbled jaw.

Jeremy.

She reached up and cupped his cheek, savoring the warmth and scratch of his new beard.

"Where have you been?" she asked, her voice heavy with sleep.

He looked down at her and gave her his broad, cheeky grin when he saw she'd woken. A warm ribbon of awareness began to unfurl within her. He held her as if she weighed nothing, making her acutely conscious of his masculine power.

"It's comforting to know that you missed me."

"Of course I missed you, you silly man." She curled her arms about his neck and pressed her lips to his throat, inhaling deeply. The smell of brandy and a hint of cigar smoke clung to his skin, mingling with his usual scent of leather and soap.

And something entirely Jeremy.

She felt as much as heard him take a shuddering breath. He turned and carried her over to the bed, laying her down as gently as if she were a porcelain treasure. Lily, however, refused to relinquish him when he made to right himself.

"Lily," he chuckled and reached behind his neck for her hands.

Lacing her fingers together to gain a better purchase, Lily continued to hold on. She knew Jeremy could break her grasp if he cared to do so, but he allowed her to cling to him and looked down into her face with those dark, smoldering eyes of his. "Lily." This time, her name sounded more like a plea.

"Stay with me, Jeremy."

His eyes slid shut and he groaned, "I can't—"

"Of course you can," she whispered and lifted her face to meet his in a tender kiss that conveyed her desire. Jeremy's lips quickly soft-

ened beneath hers and he began kissing her back with surprising ferocity. He braced his palms beside each of her shoulders and deepened the kiss, claiming her with his pillaging tongue forcing its way
between her lips. Lily's moan of pleasure only seemed to spur him on
further.

One of his hands trailed down to roughly cup her breast through
her nightdress and her nipple puckered at the insistent contact. His
fingers rolled and plucked at the sensitive nub, sending ripples of
pleasure throughout her body and increasing the heat building in that
secret place at the apex of her thighs.

His hands flew to her hips and he began hiking up her nightdress.
Lily sensed his urgency and reached down to help him, lifting her hips
as he turned her and pulled her to the edge of the bed. That same
strength he'd demonstrated in carrying her to the bed was being put to
new, exciting use as he hauled her legs to either side of his hips,
pressing her molten core against the thick, straining ridge in his
breeches. Lily gave a tentative wriggle of her hips and Jeremy rewarded her with a hissing intake of breath.

"God, Lily I—I—"

"I know," she panted against his lips, interrupting him. "I need
you, too, Jeremy."

With a curse, he reached between them and yanked at the falls of
his breeches with impatient fingers. When his throbbing erection finally sprang free, he took himself in his hand and rubbed the blunt
head of his sex through her slick cleft.

"I don't think I can be gentle," he ground out.

"It's okay," she breathed, trying to convey her sincerity in her eyes.
When he still seemed to be holding himself back, she added words
from her new vocabulary, "Jeremy…I need your cock inside of me."

This seemed to snap any remaining restraint he might have had. He positioned himself at her entrance and, in one great thrust, he slid into her to the hilt, stealing the breath from Lily's lungs. He hooked an arm beneath each of her legs and pulled her toward him to meet each of his deep, desperate thrusts.

Gone was the tenderness of their previous meetings of the flesh. This was all about primal desire as his body pounded against her. Lily gasped for air as her pleasure mounted with each rough collision and glide of slick flesh on flesh. Jeremy leaned forward, tilting Lily's pelvis and gaining deeper access to her body. She cried his name at the new, thrilling sensation, the overwhelming, delicious fullness.

He dropped her legs and pressed a palm to her lips to soften her cries of mounting pleasure, and she hooked her ankles around his thrusting hips, keeping him close as he ground his pelvis against hers. His motions stroked her higher and higher until she shattered with muffled sighs and sobs against the slightly work-roughened skin of his palm. Jeremy's release followed soon after. With a series of sharp, digging thrusts, he spilled his hot seed deep inside her with a curse culminating in a guttural groan.

He released her mouth and braced his forearms on either side of her head. His eyes were screwed shut and the ragged air leaving his lungs matched Lily's breath for breath. Her legs loosened and she reached up to cup his face in her hands, placing a kiss upon the furrow in his sweaty brow and stroking his hair. A small moan, like the purr of a tiger, rumbled through his chest.

"That feels nice." His breathing was beginning to regulate and he looked up into her face. She smiled down her body at him and her heart skipped at the sight he made with the disheveled locks of his raven hair hanging over his face, his sated half-smile and dreamy dark eyes tempting her to sin all over again.

"Let's get more comfortable and I'll do it some more," she offered, and Jeremy did as he was bid. He slid from her body with a sigh and proceeded to pull his shirt free of his breeches and over his head. Lily stopped in her attempt to divest herself of her nightdress and, instead, enjoyed the way the firelight played on the planes of Jeremy's sculpted body; the swells of his arms and chest, the hard planes of his back, the ridges of his abdomen, and the generous muscles of his legs and backside as he finished removing his breeches.

Assuming she wasn't yet undressed because she needed assistance, he gently helped her finish untying the neckline of her gown and pulled it over her head. She then moved backward on the bed to make room for Jeremy's sizable frame.

"Come here," she beckoned softly as she lay back on the pillows. The ropes creaked beneath his added weight as he settled himself against the pillow of her milky white breast.

Jeremy's eyes slid shut as the delicious sensation of Lily's fingers and nails against his scalp overtook him. She tenderly stroked his head and hair, twisting the soft locks around her fingers and caressing his temples.

His palm covered the gentle swell of her stomach, his thumb skipping over the tiny valley of her navel as his hand moved in aimless patterns. He reveled in her softness and perfection.

For that short time, Jeremy allowed himself to forget what awaited him in the morning and, instead, focused on this woman. This gentle moment spent listening to the even, steady beat of her heart reaffirmed Jeremy's conviction that he would, indeed, give his life to ensure her happiness.

If this was not love, then he had no idea what was.

*****

Jeremy awoke from a doze a short time later. No light shone against the draperies, so it was still well before morning. The realization of what awaited him in only a few hours hit Jeremy in full force.

Gone was the blissful haze of his release in Lily's arm; reality returned with renewed strength. He lifted his head to find Lily asleep soundly, one arm thrown out to her side and the other resting above her heart. His heart gave an involuntary throb at the innocent image she presented. The irrational part of him wanted to lock the door, Townsend be damned, and curl up against Lily's naked body for the rest of their days. He knew, however, that that could never be. Not if they were ever to have a future she deserved.

Slowly, so as not to wake Lily, he pushed himself to a seated position and slid from the bed. Lily didn't stir. He took the edge of the coverlet and folded it over her so she would not catch a chill in his absence.

He located his breeches in the dim lighting afforded by the dying fire, pulled them on, and gathered the rest of his clothing beneath his arm. He paused with his hand hovering over the doorknob. Looking back over his shoulder, he realized he could not leave without kissing Lily one last time—for there was a definite possibility that it very well could be *the last time*. If that was his fate, then he wanted to die with the memory of her on his lips. Striding back over to the bed, Jeremy bent and placed a tender kiss atop her head, inhaling the scent of her hair and imprinting it upon his memory.

Lily woke when Jeremy left the bed, but she did not move. She'd watched him from beneath the fringe of her lashes as he donned his breeches. Her heart had soared when he'd turned back and kissed her, leaving an achingly sweet mark atop her head. He'd opened the door an inch and made sure the hallway was clear before taking his leave.

Lily then rolled over to the spot Jeremy had occupied; it was still warm from his body. She buried her face in the pillow and blanket, engulfing herself in his scent, and she drifted back to sleep, cocooned in the warmth he'd left behind.

Chapter Nineteen

The sound of boots traveling up the hallway woke Lily a few hours later. Judging from the darkness of the room, it was still before sunrise. She sat up and listened as the footsteps made their way down the stairs. The unmistakable deep timbre of Jeremy's voice filtered up through the floorboards, accompanied by a woman's response. They exchanged a handful of words before the front door clicked shut and the lock slid home. They'd been speaking too softly and were too far away for Lily to make out any individual words, but that only piqued her interest.

Jeremy had only returned home a few hours earlier; where would he be going at this time of the morning?

Flinging back the coverlet, Lily leaped from the bed and went to the window. She pulled back the edge of the curtain just enough to peer down into the darkened street, and what she saw made her blink hard and wonder if she was, in fact, awake.

Her family carriage with its matched set of four bay horses in jangling harnesses pulled away from in front of the townhouse.

It's strange enough that Jeremy would be leaving his house at this hour, thought Lily; *but what role did George play in all of this?*

For there was no doubt in Lily's mind that the carriage could be carrying none other than her eldest brother. No one else could have been Jeremy's accomplice in this odd behavior.

Lily spun from the window and found her nightdress lying haphazardly on the foot of the bed where it had been tossed a few hours prior. She struggled with it for a moment before pulling it over her head, then snatched her dressing gown and pulled it on as she flung open her door. Her bare feet tapped down the stairs and she became momentarily entangled in the skirt of her nightdress as she reached the foyer. There was no sign of the woman to whom Jeremy had been speaking. Surely she couldn't have gone far?

Lily peered into the parlor and found Mrs. Hallsworth, herself in a simple dress and no apron, her graying hair limned in sickly yellow from the glow of the street lamps outside. Her hands were clenched together in front of her lips as she stared out the window. Lily could have believed the housekeeper was lost in fervent prayer.

"Mrs. Hallsworth?" Lily inquired as she entered the room and tugged her dressing gown closed with the sash about her waist.

The older woman gave a startled little jump and turned to Lily. She dropped her hands from her mouth but continued to hold them clasped in front of her.

"My—Lady Lily. I didn't wake you, did I? I apologize—"

"You didn't wake me," Lily replied slowly as she took in the haggard condition of the normally prim and proper housekeeper. She'd been woken and dressed in a hurry. Her neckline was askew and her hair, rather than being tied in her usual knot, was pulled back with loose strands hanging wildly here and there. A sense of dread began to bloom in the pit of Lily's stomach.

"Mrs. Hallsworth…where has Jeremy gone?"

The older woman glanced out the window before turning her gaze to her clasped hands. She did not reply.

"Please, Mrs. Hallsworth," Lily's voice began to rise. Something was not right. "What is the matter? Where has he gone?"

"I shouldn't say…"

Lily reached out and took the older woman's hands in her own. They were cold as ice. The indecision present in the housekeeper's eyes when she finally met Lily's gaze only caused Lily's panic to bubble more furiously.

"Please. I cannot help him if I don't know what is happening," Lily pleaded.

Mrs. Hallsworth shook her head. "His valet…my nephew, Charles…had me woken when he realized what was going on." The housekeeper hesitated again. "There is to be a duel."

"A what?" Lily exclaimed, dropping Mrs. Hallsworth's hands. A numb frigidity began to settle in her limbs. "George? My brother? What has he done?"

The housekeeper shook her head and it was her turn to take Lily's trembling hands. "Lord Shefford. He's been challenged to a duel. The viscount is his second."

The thought of Jeremy's life in danger caused the edges of her vision to blur. She forgot how to breathe. This moment of panic felt worse than any she'd ever experienced in a crowded ballroom; quite possibly because she knew there was a distinct chance that she'd just shared her last moments with Jeremy. Lily wavered for a moment before injecting steel into her spine.

What would Jeremy do in her position?

"Where?" Lily croaked. "Where is this duel to take place?" she demanded more loudly.

"You can't be thinking of following him? He'd never forgive me for allowing you to interfere or put yourself at risk."

"Mrs. Hallsworth," Lily breathed, squeezing the woman's fingers; "you're sorely mistaken if you think I'm going to stand by and let Jeremy risk his life." What cruel God would allow them to finally find one another only to rip him from her hands? "If you don't tell me, then I'll find your nephew and he won't know a moment's peace until he gives me the information I'm after. You've known me my entire life, so you know what a hellion I can be."

The woman's lips thinned into a fine line of indecision. "Very well," she finally said, much to Lily's relief. "He'll not forgive me... and it'll likely cost me my position."

"You know as well as I that would never happen," Lily said, encouraging the older woman with a firm squeeze of her hands.

"They believe this to be men's business and that it must take place if the families are ever to move on in peace." Lily gave a grim nod. "Let me rouse a footman to accompany you."

"There's no time!" Lily hissed, fairly dragging the woman up the stairs. "We cannot risk waking the entire household and alerting my mother or Lady Shefford." Lily was struck by a thought that halted her mid-step. "Does she know? Does his mother know about the duel?"

Mrs. Hallsworth shook her head and Lily turned to continue up the stairs. Lily knew, if Jeremy were mortally wounded, she would feel as if her soul had been torn from her body; his mother, however, would surely succumb to her weakness and cease to have any reason to live. Jeremy needed to come out of the duel unscathed...for more than just his own sake.

He had to.

"Have your nephew hail a hackney and give them the directions," Lily ordered as calmly as she could manage. "Then come and help me dress. Quickly!" The housekeeper nodded in agreement and turned toward the back stairs leading to the servants' chambers.

Lily burst through the door of her room and immediately began divesting herself of her robe and nightdress. In her frantic state, Lily became entangled in the fabric. Her jerky movements only served to make matters worse and a frustrated sob tore from her throat.

She released the dress and closed her eyes, taking a succession of deep breaths and counting each one. She was no good as a supportive presence to Jeremy if she gave into hysteria.

She had to get to Jeremy. She couldn't let him go through with the duel. It wasn't worth his life. She didn't know what she intended to do, all she knew was that she couldn't stand idly by as he made such a dangerous wager.

Twenty minutes later, Lily had donned the only dress that remained unpacked, a pale purple morning dress entirely unsuited for rapid travel. Mrs. Hallsworth had retrieved a hooded traveling cloak from Lady Shefford's wardrobe and draped it over Lily's shoulders.

"You should cover up, there's a chill in the air," the housekeeper said in a motherly tone and tied it beneath Lily's chin.

She walked Lily outside where they found Charles, Jeremy's valet, speaking with the young hackney driver. Rather than allow the valet to hand her up into the vehicle, she turned to the jarvey.

"You've been given directions?"

"Yes, mum," he doffed his cap as he replied. He couldn't have been more than twenty years of age—no doubt working an undesirable shift while he was still learning the ropes. Lily reached beneath her cloak and pulled a coin from the small, hidden pocket sewn into the waist of her gown.

"There's a crown for you if you get me to my destination as fast as you can drive, Mister...?"

"Hobbes, mum." The young man's watery eyes widened at the coin. "Doyle Hobbes."

"Mr. Hobbes. There will be another crown if you can get me there before dawn. Understand?"

He nodded vigorously and Lily tucked the coin back into her pocket. She allowed Charles to help her up the step and she settled into the seat.

"Do be careful," Mrs. Hallsworth nervously called up to her. "Lord Shefford will never forgive me if something happens to you."

"Don't fret," Lily said, pasting on a braver smile than she felt. "Jeremy knows me better than to believe I would have allowed anyone to stop me."

The hackney jolted into motion with a cluck of the driver's tongue and a sharp flick of his whip. They gained speed quickly in the nearly abandoned street. As young as he was, Hobbes seemed to know the roads quite well and avoided the ones which would be crowded by shopkeepers and vendors on their way to market.

Lily pulled her hood up over her hair as they rocked along. They had to get there in time. She had to stop Jeremy from throwing himself in harm's way for her. She had to see for herself that he was okay. And if he wasn't...

Her fists tightened in the voluminous fabric of the cloak as she screwed her eyes shut and counted her breaths.

Sommerfeld hopped down from the Stratford carriage and Jeremy followed shortly thereafter, stepping into a ground fog so thick it obscured the earth. The warm days and cooler nights caused a mist to rise from the nearby pond and creep over the grass, making it seem as if they floated along toward the bobbing orange lanterns held aloft by men whom Jeremy assumed were Townsend's second, Wexford, and the physician.

The whole scene looked ethereal, felt surreal—as if Jeremy were watching the events unfold from afar. Introductions were made just as the first tentative blush-colored fingers of dawn reached above the horizon and tinted the sky above the trees. Enormous knotty oaks stretched high above them and the forest, curiously, formed a near-perfect circle for their group; as if Mother Nature herself were backing away from the events which habitually unfolded in this secluded place.

The Pond, as this place had been so cleverly dubbed, apparently had quite the reputation for providing a secluded place for such exchanges. Duelers were unlikely to be interrupted by snooping men of the law, so disagreements could be settled, pride could be satisfied, and reputations could be restored in this eerily peaceful place.

Sommerfeld handed over the silver engraved dueling pistols—newly cleaned—to Townsend's second for inspection. The man looked as if he hardly knew which end fired the shot and Jeremy fought the absurd urge to laugh at the absurdity of it all. Meanwhile, Townsend stood separate from them, hands on his hips, impatiently watching the waiflike fog drift over the surface of the pond. He hadn't so much as looked at Jeremy or acknowledged his and Sommerfeld's arrival.

Jeremy refused to allow this to ruffle him. Instead, he focused on the discussion of the seconds. The number of paces was agreed upon and the length was marked out by a sword brought by Townsend on the far edge of the pond. Sommerfeld, ever his Pickwickian self even in these severe conditions, refused the proffered second sword and, instead, stabbed his lion's head cane into the earth for Jeremy's boundary. Jeremy rolled his eyes, but he secretly appreciated the slight bit of levity, even if no one else found it amusing.

The eastern sky began to bleed from navy to lavender, then blush and honey. Most of the lanterns were extinguished and set aside. Jeremy eyed his opponent, noting the obvious quality of the black clothing the marquess had chosen for the occasion. Similarly dressed, the only color Jeremy wore was in the waistcoat he'd commissioned a couple of years back to precisely match the hue of Lily's eyes. If she'd noticed at the time, then she hadn't said anything. Jeremy quite liked it and found the choice fitting for the circumstances.

God, did he want to see Lily—to hold her again. On the chance that he was killed here in this damp field, he was determined to carry the memory of her scent, the taste of her lips, and the sound of her laughter with him to his grave. He would die knowing she was free.

Aldborough had already given his son the paperwork the marquess would need to sign to dissolve the betrothal. The documents lay safely in the pocket of Sommerfeld's coat. He trusted his friend to ensure Townsend signed those papers after his pride was satisfied, regardless of what the outcome meant for Jeremy.

"Shall we get this started then?" quavered the ancient physician, glancing at the lightening sky. Jeremy was half surprised the old man had any medical knowledge outside of the Dark Ages.

"Yes." Wexford cleared his throat. "The *points* have been set," he said and cast a disdainful look at Sommerfeld's cane. "The rules are as follows: Participants will each stand beside their designated points, turn to face one another, and, at the dropping of the kerchief, both will fire. This will continue until first blood or until the challenger has determined he is satisfied. Is this understood?"

Townsend and Jeremy both nodded. Sommerfeld took that as his cue and stepped forward to hold open the ebony box containing the loaded dueling pistols. Townsend chose his first and Jeremy took up its mate. The weight of the weapon was heavier than any other gun he recalled having held. He stared for a moment at the intricate floral carvings before curling his fingers around the grip.

"To your points," Sommerfeld said. He led Jeremy to his cane sticking up from the soft earth. Jeremy stood with his back to Townsend, doing his best to tune out the discussion behind him and, instead, focused on his friend. Sommerfeld stood off to the side and held his hand out to Jeremy.

"Good luck, my friend," Sommerfeld whispered with a sad smile. "I hope all of this is worth it."

Jeremy clasped his hand tightly in response. "Lily is worth it."

"I hope I never fall in love," chuckled Sommerfeld. "If you're willing to face a pistol for it, then God only knows what my fool self would do."

There was a soft click from behind Jeremy. He might have disregarded it were it not for the sound of a woman screaming his name.

Jeremy released Sommerfeld's hand and spun on his heel to see Townsend's pistol leveled at him from less than halfway up the field.

A crack of pistol fire sliced through the peaceful dawn and Jeremy dropped face-first to the damp earth.

Chapter Twenty

A guttural male scream pierced Lily's skull, nearly blinding her with panic and terror.

Jeremy.

She could think only of reaching him.

She'd paid the jarvey to drop her off some distance from the field, far enough away that they wouldn't hear the jangle of tack or bouncing wheels on the rutted dirt path. Doing her best to ignore her nausea—the hackney hadn't been sprung for such rough terrain—she ran as quickly as her gown and shoes would allow before she gave up and kicked the slippers aside. She'd run barefoot for a great deal of her childhood in the country, after all, much to her mother's chagrin.

Lily had hiked up her skirts and hurtled onward, the hood falling back from her head and her blond hair flying out behind her as she dashed along as quickly as her inappropriate clothing would allow. She followed the directions the driver gave her and, as the sun began to fade to a warm gold, she heard men's voices from up ahead. She slowed her pace and did her best to manage her breathing. Foregoing the worn footpath, she ducked beneath tree limbs and over logs, snagging her skirts and hair on grasping branches, ignoring stinging scratches upon any bits of exposed flesh, and finally came up against a clump of untamed bushes. The brush was just thick enough to conceal her if she replaced her hood and wrapped the dark fabric of the cloak around her.

She'd watched from across the small pond, barely able to restrain herself, as the men each went to their separate halves of the field. She quickly spotted Jeremy's dark head beside her brother's unmistakable height.

Lily attempted to catch her breath and prepared to stand and do whatever it took to stop the duel from taking place. She watched as Jeremy and George exchanged words and clasped hands when a motion out of the corner of her eye caught her attention. What she saw as she peered through the foliage made her heart freeze mid-beat.

Townsend's tall black-clad figure advanced up the field in several quick strides. He turned and stood, legs braced apart, and leveled his pistol at Jeremy's back. Lily half stumbled, half jumped to her feet as a scream tore itself from her lips.

There was the echoing crack of a pistol being fired.

Jeremy was lying in the grass.

Her knees gave way and the bushes clawed at her arms and tore her cloak on her way down. She gasped for air through her clenching throat and leaned upon her palms, now filthy and bleeding from catching her weight against the rough earth.

The gut-wrenching sound of a man's bellow of pain pierced through her panic, driving Lily to her feet and propelling her through the bushes.

She ran without registering what was going on, without caring about the others present, thinking only of getting to Jeremy while he still breathed. As she came to the scene, however, she didn't see what she had anticipated.

Both George and Jeremy lay on the ground, but it was George who was bleeding. Rather profusely, as a matter of fact. Lily's shock-induced numbness began to wear off. And her mind registered what had happened.

George had been shot.

That meant...

She turned just as Jeremy launched himself to his feet and spied George cursing through gritted teeth, attempting to apply pressure to the wound in his lower thigh. Then, Jeremy's wide eyes caught hers and Lily felt the world stop. She'd believed he'd been wounded or dead. Now, he stood towering over her. A commotion behind him caught Lily's attention as Townsend threw his single-shot pistol to the ground and turned on his heel to dash away.

"Go!" Lily panted; "I'll see to George."

Jeremy whipped away from her and flew after Townsend. Lily sprinted, slipped, and skidded to her knees beside her elder brother. The blood, startlingly red in the early morning light, seeped through the seams between his fingers soaking a large stain in the leg of his charcoal breeches and dripping to the grass in a steady trickle.

She covered his hands with hers and pressed the weight of her body onto his thigh. Soon, she too was covered in her brother's hot, thick lifeblood. George groaned in pain at her added weight and loosed a violent string of curses, but he didn't push her away. His face paled—from blood loss or pain, Lily could not tell.

"Georgie," she sobbed in a thick mixture of fear and relief. He was alive, but she knew he wouldn't be for long if the bleeding couldn't be staunched.

The physician.

Duels had to have physicians present for the injuries, did they not?

Lily looked over her shoulder and found an ancient, stooped man standing in the middle of what was supposed to have been the dueling field. He looked lost or entirely befuddled by what he'd just witnessed.

"Are you the physician?" Lily cried. She could feel dampness seeping through the knees of her dress and she did her best to convince herself it was the dew on the grass. The old man looked at her, mouth agape and eyes wide. "Are you the physician?" she asked, more forcefully this time. Panic edged its way into her voice. "My brother is injured," she stated the obvious, hoping it would shock the physician back to his senses. "Please, tell me what I am to do." The man blinked his rheumy eyes and seemed to recall where he was.

"A tourniquet," he finally croaked and made his way over to where George lay. "We must make a tourniquet and tie it off above the wound to staunch the blood flow." He carried with him a small black satchel. Undoing the clasp, he fumbled around through vials and bandages but seemed to find nothing sufficient to tie around the girth of her brother's thigh, muscular from regular riding excursions.

A tourniquet.

Lily wasn't sure she could tear off a big enough piece of her skirts to create a sufficient one. George swallowed hard and her eyes were drawn to the bobbing knot of his cravat. That was it.

"Your cravat, George!"

"My what?" he hissed through his clenched jaw.

"Your cravat. I need to untie it and use it for a tourniquet."

He nodded once in understanding. Lily counted to three before removing her hands from his leg and clumsily began to work at the intricate knot. Her blood-slick fingers slipped and streaked George's jaw and coat in his blood, but she was finally able to unwind the long strip of fine fabric from his neck.

"Lie back," the physician ordered George. Her brother did so reluctantly, and Lily worked the fabric beneath his leg and created a loose knot a few fingers' widths above where she believed the wound to be.

"He'll have to remove his hands," said the physician, "and you'll have to pull it as tight as you possibly can. I'd help, but my fingers have not the strength they used to."

"Bloody brilliant," George panted. Leave it to him to make snide comments while they were trying to save his life.

"It'll hurt," warned the old man. "But it needs to be tight or he'll lose more blood."

Lily nodded in understanding.

"Ready George? Release your leg when I tell you to."

He jerked his understanding and clenched his jaw. "Get on with it."

Lily took a bracing breath and focused all her attention on the cravat.

"Now," she commanded.

A rush of blood escaped the void left by George's hands, but she yanked on the ends of the cravat as quickly and as hard as she could, earning a furious bellow from George. He dropped his head back to the earth and repeatedly slammed a fist on the ground. She knew his fiery curses weren't actually directed toward her, but it didn't make her ears burn any less. She tightened the makeshift tourniquet further until the physician told her it would do, and then she tied off the ends in a tight succession of knots.

"Good, good." The physician nodded his approval at her work.

Lily sat back on her heels and saw the wound for the first time. She swallowed back bile at the gaping hole and glimpse of splintered white bone and ragged sinew. She nearly pressed her fingers to her lips but stopped before she covered her face in George's blood.

"That bad, eh?" George ground out, seeing her expression. His pallor had continued to worsen, but Lily was careful not to show him her level of concern. The usual jovial flush was completely gone from his high cheekbones and his breathing had become more labored.

She took some folded bandages from the physician and pressed them over the wound, trying her best to still her trembling fingers as she did so.

"It's not terrible," Lily tried to reassure him as she nonchalantly wiped the coagulating coating of blood from her hands onto the grass. George unscrewed one eye.

"You look as if you're going to vomit. Please, be a dear and turn the other way, thank you."

Lily scoffed at him and took his blood-drenched hand in both of hers. George's fingers gripped her hand so tightly it made her knuckles ache, but she let him hold onto her. He closed his eyes and clutched the grass with his free hand.

Lily tried to shield him from her sinking suspicion that she was his lifeline to consciousness as his breathing grew more labored and his joints began to tremble uncontrollably.

*****

Jeremy tramped down his contradictory urges to both berate Lily for following them to the dueling field and yank her into his arms and never let the clever woman go. The sight of Sommerfeld lying on the ground in a rapidly expanding puddle of blood caused Jeremy to hesitate, but he knew his friend was in as good a hand as any.

Jeremy sprinted off after the retreating Townsend—both men's boots skidding on the damp grass as they advanced. There was no sign of Wexford; no doubt the coward had fled as soon as Townsend's murderous intent became evident. It was a true friend who ran rather than be complicit in such a plot...

The marquess didn't make it more than a couple of large strides before Jeremy launched forward and caught the slimmer man about the waist, tackling him to the ground and knocking the wind from both their lungs. Jeremy flipped Townsend over with a fist knotted in the neck of his shirt and finally got to do what he'd wanted to for every moment of the last few weeks: he was able to show Townsend that, occasionally, brawn could beat cunning...as a matter of fact, it could beat the cunning right out of a man. Jeremy braced one boot on the ground for purchase and hauled back his arm.

The force of his fist on the marquess's face caused the man's head to bounce off the earth with a dull thud. He got in a couple more blows before Townsend's hands flew to Jeremy's throat and he used Jeremy's weight against him. Kicking off the ground with strength no doubt earned from countless hours spent riding recklessly through public parks, he rolled Jeremy off of him and began getting in a few good blows of his own. One punch caught Jeremy's ear, causing a deafening ring to echo in his skull.

"I will not be bested by the likes of you," Townsend spat, his icy eyes wild.

Before Townsend could land another strike on the side of Jeremy's skull, Jeremy caught him in the stomach with a well-placed knee and then kicked, sending him sprawling backward and skidding several feet before coming to a stop.

Jeremy rolled and pounced, pressing his forearm to the marquess's throat. Townsend clawed at his sleeve, but Jeremy only leaned more of his weight across the other man's esophagus.

Gone was every shred of dignified, aristocratic composure Jeremy would have sworn oozed from Townsend's very pores. In its place was a red-faced screeching coward who would shoot a man in the back rather than face him in a proper duel; a man who would force a woman into a miserable loveless marriage, not because he wanted her, but because he didn't want anyone else to.

Something whistled through the air and landed nearby with a dull clatter.

"Filthy bastard!" bellowed Sommerfeld. He'd pulled his cane from its earthen sheath and aimed for Townsend's head, though his prone position didn't make for the best angle. "Bash him bloody for me, Jem!" The last sentence died on a grunt of pain and Sommerfeld, having exerted himself too far, lay down once more.

Jeremy turned his attention back to the struggling marquess. His eyes were bulging and bloodshot; bloody spittle seeped from the corner of his downturned mouth.

"You pathetic little prick," Jeremy spat. "You'd have killed me in cold blood just to have me out of the way."

"Unhand me," Townsend choked out.

"You've lost the upper hand, Townsend," Jeremy replied, maintaining his pressure on the other man's throat. Townsend struggled harder, but the murderous glint in Jeremy's eyes only burned more brightly. "You've lost your chance at satisfaction and you've only ended up making a fool of yourself. Now you'll have lost your pride as well as your bride."

Townsend's eyes glittered and he let out a strangled sound that resembled a cackle. "That's where you're wrong, Shefford. I was never going to release her from the contract."

Jeremy was so taken aback by the admission that he slightly slackened his hold on Townsend's throat. The marquess gasped for more air and continued, a maniacal smile on his face. "I'm going to wed her, bed her, and take joy in the image of you rotting in hell, thinking of me fucking her every single night." His grotesque gurgle of laughter died quickly at the sound of a pistol hammer being drawn back.

"I suggest you do as he says, Townsend," came Lily's flat, icy voice from above them.

Jeremy looked up to find that she'd retrieved his discarded—still primed and loaded—dueling pistol from where he'd dropped it in the earlier chaos. She held the weapon in both hands, elbows locked, sights trained on Townsend's skull. Covered in her brother's blood, she looked like some sort of battlefield archangel, haloed in the rising sunlight.

Moving slowly so as not to startle Lily into pulling the trigger, Jeremy leaned back and rocked to his feet. Townsend gulped air and tugged at his compressed throat as he sat up. Lily's sights remained trained on his head the entire time.

"And why would I do that?" he croaked viciously. "You probably don't even know how to use that thing."

"You'd be on the losing end of that bet," Lily replied evenly.

"I'd listen to the lady," Jeremy added as he sidled over to Lily and dabbed at a cut on his temple, rubbing the fresh red blood between his fingers. "I taught her myself. Her aim is better than most men." Seeing the seriousness in their faces, the redness blanched from Townsend's complexion.

"You wouldn't. I'm *Marquess* of Townsend – a peer of the realm!" He staggered to his feet. Lily wasn't drawn by the quick motion and she stayed calm and focused, training the pistol at Townsend's chest. She remained ever-level and steady.

"Jeremy is a peer as well, or did that conveniently slip your mind when you attempted murder? When you shot my brother, a viscount, and heir to the Earl of Aldborough?" Lily arched a brow. "Perhaps you'll find it more acceptable if I shoot *you* in the back?"

"You'll be hanged!"

"And who would believe a sweet young lady like me would do such a thing?" Lily asked matter-of-factly.

"Shooting accidents happen all the time. You really would be free of the contract then," Jeremy added flippantly to Lily.

"Lay down the weapon!" Townsend demanded, his voice rising to an unholy level. For all his bluster, Jeremy noticed the fire in those ice-blue eyes was beginning to morph into fear.

"Not until you sign the papers dissolving the betrothal." Lily remained steadfast and Jeremy's heart swelled fair to bursting with pride over this brave, determined, woman—*his* woman.

Townsend glared at the two of them as if he might cause them to burst into flames. He knew he'd been caught.

"George has the papers," Jeremy said.

"Retrieve them; I'll watch Townsend."

Knowing better than to second guess a woman holding a firearm, Jeremy backed up the few paces to where Sommerfeld was lying, the physician sitting nearby monitoring his pulse in his wrist.

"How are you, Georgie?" Jeremy noticed for the first time his friend's sickly pallor and the amount of blood soaking through his breeches. Jeremy's stomach plummeted into an icy pond.

"Lovely," Sommerfeld replied through chattering teeth. "I could swim the Channel, but I'd settle for a bottle of brandy."

"You don't seem fine."

"A bit of shock," the physician interjected. "We need to get him back to Town so the leg can be properly tended to. The shot will have to be removed and the leg needs to be set."

"See? Something to look forward to." His fists clenched and un-clenched as if he were testing the sensation.

"It's going to be okay; we'll get you home and stitched up—right as rain."

"Papers," murmured Sommerfeld through clenched teeth. "If I die from this and you don't even get the bloody papers signed then I'll haunt you both for the rest of your miserable lives."

Jeremy shook his head and carefully riffled through the inner pockets of his friend's coat. He located the long, thin box containing the thick stack of rolled parchment, sealing wax, quill, and ink that would set Lily free.

Keeping an eye on Lily to make sure she had Townsend under con-trol, Jeremy grabbed one of the remaining low-burning lanterns and returned to where she still held him at bay. He unfolded the thick stack of papers and prepared the quill, holding both out to Townsend.

The marquess eyed the implements through his swollen eyes as if they were venomous, but snatched them from Jeremy when Lily made a little jerking motion with her chin. The quill scratched furiously across the parchment and Lily felt her heart begin to lighten. She watched from the corner of her eye as Jeremy used the lantern to soft-en the sealing wax. Dripping it on the space below Townsend's signa-ture, Jeremy motioned for him to press into it his ring with the Townsend crest. Lily's heart soared as he did as he was bid and Jeremy stepped back to her side, parchment safely in hand. He carefully rolled the contract and tucked it into his breast pocket.

Lily hadn't realized she'd begun to shake until Jeremy wrapped his hands around hers and gently forced her to lower the pistol. He tugged it from her fingers and replaced the hammer.

"I hope you and your little slut are happy, Shefford," screamed Townsend, emboldened now that his life was no longer on the line. "I'll be sure to tell everyone how she let you mount her like a bitch in heat."

Lily's heart thumped wildly, but more so when she saw the stoic expression on Jeremy's face. It worsened when a cool half-smile tilted his lips.

She knew that look.

It wasn't a good one.

"No, Townsend, I don't think you will." Jeremy took several slow steps around the marquess and began to circle him like a predatory cat. Lily didn't think she'd ever seen his dark eyes burn as they did at that moment. She watched as he caught George's discarded cane on the toe of his boot and, in one fluid motion, kicked it up and snatched it out of the air.

"You see, if you happen to say a single disparaging word about Lily or the rest of the Stratford family, then I'll be forced to pay you a visit. No amount of money can protect you from me and I know, deep down in that pitiable excuse for a soul, you know this. I do, however, hope you have a lovely trip back to London. You may want to seek medical attention for your head first, though."

Townsend opened his mouth to speak, but, before he could, Jeremy swung a vicious backhanded blow with the silver lion's head tip of George's cane and connected with the side of Townsend's skull with a sickening crack. The man was unconscious even before he crumpled to the ground.

Chapter Twenty-One

There was little time to celebrate the dissolution of the betrothal because Lily and Jeremy's attention turned immediately to George. His skin had taken on a waxen quality and a sheen of sweat coated his brow; his trembling had increased to an uncontrollable degree.

"George?" Jeremy knelt at his friend's side. His glassy green eyes stared unblinkingly at the sky. Jeremy reached out and shook his shoulder. While Sommerfeld's head tilted in his direction, he knew his friend didn't see him. He was lost in a haze of pain, shock, and blood loss. "Stay with him," Jeremy said hurriedly, pulling Lily down beside him. "Don't let him fall asleep."

Lily stroked her brother's forehead and nodded. Jeremy heard her begin speaking to George as he rose and dashed off through the trees to locate the carriage. His blood roared in his ears as he ran. He had to get George proper medical treatment and something to dull his pain. Aldborough would never forgive him if he got his son killed.

Jeremy would never forgive himself.

He caught sight of the Stratford coach, the driver standing on the ground and adjusting a strap for one of the harnesses. Jeremy gave a sharp, piercing whistle through his teeth as he grew nearer. The horses' ears pricked at the sound.

"The viscount's been injured. We need to get him back to the city as quickly and gently as possible." The man nodded and vaulted up into the driver's seat. Jeremy instructed him to turn the carriage and pull it up as close to the copse of trees as he could without getting mired in the damp earth—Sommerfeld would surely die if they got stuck out here in the country.

Crashing back along the path, Jeremy returned to the clearing. He found Lily talking to her brother, asking him questions, patting his face and his hands, doing all that she could to keep him from slipping away—even if he remained unresponsive. Her voice continued on steadily, but Jeremy could read the panic in her verdant eyes when she looked up at him.

"George," Jeremy said loudly. His friend's eyes tracked the sound. "We're going to lift you. We have to get you to the carriage and back to Town. It's going to hurt like hell, but it's just the two of us so you need to help as much as you can."

Together, Jeremy and Lily pulled him into a sitting position. If his dead weight was any indication of the help he was capable of giving, then this was going to be bloody awful. Jeremy slipped Sommerfeld's arm over his shoulders and hooked his hand beneath his other arm; Lily did the same on his other side.

"I'll take the brunt of his weight," he told Lily. "You just help keep him steady and make sure his injured leg remains clear."

Lily nodded, her mouth set in a determined line. He thanked God that she was strong and not the squeamish type.

"We stand on the count of three," Jeremy continued, bracing his legs to take on Sommerfeld's weight. The three of them rose as one and Sommerfeld hissed his pain through gritted teeth as his leg shifted. They steadied themselves and gained their footing. He listed toward Lily—being the shorter of the two and the one on the side with his injured leg—but Jeremy tugged him back.

"Lean on me George," Jeremy said calmly. "Lean on me." He did as he was asked to the best of his ability and groaned deeply as they began to make forward progress through the clearing.

Jeremy didn't bother sparing a glance at the prone body of Townsend, but he heard the physician attempting to revive him after his blow to the head. Though it was the least of his concerns at the moment, a loud snore assured Jeremy he wouldn't be hanged for murder anytime soon.

Their progress was slow and jerky. Jeremy took on his friend's weight each time he stumbled and strained under the burden of keeping his bum leg elevated when the white-hot blaze of pain grew too much. Concerningly, his trembling was rapidly becoming body-wracking shakes.

"Just a little further, George; you can make it," Jeremy encouraged his friend. Sommerfeld's chest heaved with the effort to push through the pain and exhaustion, but he continued. To Lily's credit, she remained vigilant and steadfast, helping her brother as much as she could and ensuring they weren't caught up by any branches or other natural debris. She whispered continual encouragement to both Jeremy and her brother.

Her voice gave Jeremy strength, even as his hope for his friend flickered with every passing minute.

Finally, the tree line broke and they found the carriage waiting. The driver bounded down from his perch and ran to assist them. To his credit, he didn't seem overly surprised to find Lily in their company. He took Lily's place at Jeremy's side and, together, he and Jeremy were able to make a chair for George with their arms. They lifted him and carried him the last several yards to the carriage. Lily dashed ahead and threw open the carriage door as wide as it would go so they would have an easier time loading him in.

She cringed as George was jostled in the process, eliciting a deep, heart-wrenching groan from her injured brother, but there was nothing to be done. They had to get him into the carriage and back to London as quickly as possible. His life depended upon it. Together, they helped lay George down on the forward-facing seat before the driver jumped down and scrambled back up to his perch.

"Please—drive as swiftly as you can, but avoid as many ruts as possible. We cannot jostle him over much."

"Yes, m'lady." The driver tipped his hat and gathered up his reins.

Jeremy's hand reached down from the carriage to help her climb up into the vehicle. The small space was even more cramped with George's long frame sprawled out as much as possible to keep his injured leg straight. He lay with his head on the bottom cushion, the top of his head against the side of the carriage. His torso took up the entirety of the cushion with one leg bent up and resting. The other leg was stretched out across the carriage and propped on the opposite seat. Lily sidled in and gently lifted George's head, placing it in her lap. Jeremy took the only unoccupied space on the opposite cushion beside George's foot. As soon as they were settled and the door was latched, Jeremy pounded on the roof of the carriage. They jerked into motion.

Lily smoothed back a blond lock of her brother's hair from his sweat-drenched forehead. The glazed look floated back into his eyes and he focused on something unseen over her left ear. Her panic began to rise once again.

Not George.

She couldn't lose George.

To lose him would be as devastating to her as losing Jeremy.

"We'll be home shortly, Georgie," she said, trying to keep the tremor from her words. They hit a bump in the road and the carriage rocked and creaked around them despite its springs. He gave a strangled groan and his eyelids fluttered shut.

"George?" He didn't open his eyes. "George!" She patted his cheek and a sob wedged itself deep in her throat. Jeremy reached across the carriage and took her bloodied hand in his.

"He's still breathing." His voice was steady, but Lily recognized the concern in his eyes. "Maybe unconsciousness is a blessing. We can travel more quickly and he'll feel less pain."

Lily gnawed on her lower lip and looked down into George's face. Perhaps Jeremy was right. The lines of agony were erased from George's face, though his waxen appearance and the dark circles beneath his eyes were evidence of his grave condition. A tear slipped free from her eye and fell to George's cheek. She wiped away the moisture with her thumb, but it was quickly replaced by another. Jeremy's fingers squeezed hers in an attempt at comfort, but both of them knew there were no words to make it better.

The congestion of the streets became worse the further they traveled into London. The city had come alive with the passing morning; more and more people going about their business created a hindrance to their progress. Meanwhile, Lily cradled her brother's head, occasionally placing her fingers below his nose to test for breath and swiping at tears running in trails down her cheeks. She murmured to him under her breath, knowing he was beyond hearing, but attempting to reach him anyway.

Jeremy seethed.

That shot had been meant for him. He should be the one injured and bleeding.

Not George.

Not him.

And Lily?

The entire carriage ride, Jeremy had vacillated between wanting to throttle her and desperately wanting to kiss her and thank her for her impulsiveness. She should never have put herself in harm's way, but he was lucid enough to realize that, without her, he might be dead. If Sommerfeld had still been the one to sustain the injury, he never could have helped him and pursued Townsend at the same time. Either the marquess would have escaped and never broken the betrothal, or Sommerfeld would have expired right there in the dew-dampened clearing. There was a distinct possibility that his friend might still meet an untimely end, judging from his sickly pallor and ragged breath, but he never would have made it this far without Lily.

Sommerfeld's wound wept a slowly growing puddle of blood onto the floor of the carriage. The tourniquet had helped staunch the heavy flow, but only a physician's training and proper tools would be able to mend it. He felt sick to his soul with helplessness as he watched his friend's life melt away with each drop of blood, filling the atmosphere within the carriage with the strong stench of iron.

Finally, Jeremy could take it no more. He threw open the carriage window and stuck his head and shoulders into the fresh air. Spying a ragged boy with filthy hair and ill-fitting clothing, Jeremy whistled and called him over to the carriage. The boy hesitated, perhaps being warned away from strange lords in carriages trying to lure him in only to never be seen again.

"Can you run fast, boy?" he asked the urchin. The child nodded. "Do you have a good memory?" He nodded again. Jeremy reached into his pocket and pulled free a crown. "Will you run a message for me?" The child's eyes grew even larger than the glinting piece of gold.

"Yessir," he squeaked and nodded again.

"I need you to go to Stratford House just up the road; it's the big white one with columns a short distance from the park. The Earl of Aldborough lives there."

"The big one wif the black metal fence?"

"That's right," Jeremy praised the boy, reassured that the child would recognize the distinctive wrought-iron fence in front of the townhouse. "Go 'round to the servant's entrance near the stables and courtyard, tell them that Baron Shefford sent you. Tell them Sommerfeld is injured and to send for a physician. We will be there as soon as we can. Understand?"

The boy nodded his head again and reached his grubby hands up to take the coin. "Stratford 'ouse. Black fence. Shefford sent me. Sommerfeld 'urt. Need a physician. Be there soon," the child repeated dutifully.

"Good lad. They'll feed you something in the kitchens and then I'll make sure to give you another coin for your services when I arrive." The child's face lit up—whether at the food or mention of more coin, Jeremy wasn't sure.

"Yessir!" The boy snatched the coin and took off at full tilt, dodging pedestrians, startling horses, and disappearing amongst the din of London. Jeremy would have gone on his own—they were only a few blocks away—but he didn't dare leave Sommerfeld and Lily alone; God forbid the worst happened.

Jeremy folded his wide frame back into the dark carriage. He caught Lily watching him, her shining green eyes flickering in the dim lighting.

"D'you think we'll make it in time?" she asked him softly.

"I hope to God we do," he replied as George's tremors worsened and his teeth began to chatter.

Chapter Twenty-Two

Lily still stood, forgotten, in the center of the parlor several hours after their arrival at her family's townhouse.

Jeremy had leaped down from the carriage even before they came to a complete stop. Stratford footmen had already been posted on the stairs and rushed to greet them. Evidently, the street urchin had done well in following directions.

The footmen reached in and gently pulled George from her lap; she felt a pang in the vicinity of her heart as his soft locks of hair slipped from her fingers and the weight of him was removed. They brought him in as swiftly as they could. Even from where she sat out in the carriage Lily could hear her mother's hysterical cries at the sight of her eldest son's condition. Her father's commanding, yet shaken, tone cut through the din as he barked orders. Lily barely registered Jeremy's face as he filled the door of the carriage.

Silently, he held out his big hand to her, bloodied knuckles and all. She took it and allowed him to help her down, steadying her as her muddy foot got caught in the hem of her dress. He quietly and quickly led her up the stairs and into the house

Lily felt as if she was watching a frantic parody of a play. She recognized the comforts of home, but the frenzied nature and dashing about of a household with a dying heir was wholly unfamiliar. Jeremy showed her into the parlor where they would be out of the way of the noise and chaos. Before he could speak to her, however, Lily heard her father shout for Jeremy. She watched as Jeremy's countenance hardened, bracing himself to explain just how this had all come to pass. Before he turned, he tucked a stray lock of hair behind her ear.

And there she stood.

There she remained.

She listened as the house became quiet, save for the occasional sounds of servants gathering hot water, linens, and anything else the physicians requested.

Then the screaming started.

Lily clapped her hands over her ears and sank to the floor – heedless of the mud and blood she smeared over the expensive rug.

Lily didn't need to be told that the physicians had begun to dig around inside George's leg to remove the lead shot and repair what they could. They'd set the bone and finish staunching the bleeding. The guttural cries echoed throughout the halls of the townhouse before a deafening silence fell. Lily screwed her eyes shut and prayed that George had been drugged or his body had once again blessed him with unconsciousness. She took sickening solace in the fact that there was no scramble of servants—no wail from her mother—so at least the doctors were continuing their work.

They wouldn't do that if there was no hope for George, Lily told herself, again and again, hoping she would believe it a little more each time.

Her heart continued to pound as she rose to her feet and clenched her trembling hands against her chest. She felt simultaneously overheated and chilled, alert and exhausted. Not knowing what to do with herself, she continued to stand, and stand.

Until Jeremy came to find her.

He appeared in front of her, silent as a cat—or Lily was too far gone in the tempest of her thoughts that she hadn't heard him enter. It could have been minutes or hours; time no longer felt real. Her first thought upon seeing Jeremy was how drawn and exhausted his features were. The persistent stubble on his jaw had made its customary appearance, but a new furrow had dug its way between his brows, and lines bracketing his mouth made him appear far older than his years. He'd doffed his black coat and now wore only a stained emerald green waistcoat and shirtsleeves rolled up to his elbows to reveal his strong forearms. He ran a hand through his overlong ebony hair as he approached her. His appearance told Lily the worst had happened. Reading the panic in her eyes, Jeremy rushed to assuage her before she could collapse.

"George is resting. He should live if there is no infection."

Lily felt her knees buckle in relief, but Jeremy was there to grab her, as he always had been…as he always would be. He held her against his side with one strong arm around her waist. A suffocating wave of emotions crashed over Lily. Everything she'd fought so hard to keep at bay battered her, pounded over her in a nauseating hurricane.

She couldn't breathe.

She went to lift her hands to her face, but she saw the black and brown smears of blood and dirt coating them and stopped. A sob escaped her lips as she scrubbed furiously at her palms, trying to wipe them on her skirts and the ruined cloak she'd borrowed from Jeremy's mother.

He caught her hands in his and shushed her. She choked on a sob and the dam broke. She wrapped her arms around the solid wall of Jeremy's broad torso and buried her face in the warmth of his neck. He enfolded her in his arms without a moment's hesitation, crushing her to him and pressing his lips to the top of her head. He swayed and murmured soothing nonsense into her hair, trailing his palms up and down her spine.

When Lily could finally keep more than a gasp of air in her lungs, she tilted her head back and looked up into Jeremy's face.

"I—I thought I'd lost you," she managed to speak between sobs. "But you were alive…and then I thought I was going to lose George." She was stating the obvious, but it was the only way Lily could help herself sift through the myriad of emotions hammering away at her. "It's all my fault."

Jeremy shook his head and gripped her upper arms. "Don't you ever feel that any of this was your fault. Townsend is the bastard who chose to handle things as he did. Nothing drove him to that but his greed and pride." His tone was severe, but his eyes were warm and fathomless. Lily managed to catch her breath a bit when faced with the sure security of his presence.

"Now," he continued; "You're a filthy mess, so a bath might seem in order." Lily elicited a sound somewhere between a laugh and a sob as Jeremy used his thumbs to caress away her tears. "Your father is talking with the physicians and your mother is sitting with George. I heard her order a tub be brought to your rooms."

"Do you think they blame me for what happened to George?" she asked as Jeremy wrapped his arm about her waist once more and began to lead her up the stairs.

"As much as it terrified me to look over and find you bolting across the clearing, the truth is that George would have died were you not there. I could have died. If they blame anyone, it ought to be me," he replied matter-of-factly, but there was an undercurrent of bitterness tinting his words. "I'm the one who named him as my second; I'm the one who goaded Townsend into a duel in the first place."

The echoes of George's screams of pain would haunt Jeremy to his dying day. When the earl had called upon him to help hold George down so the physicians could do their bloody work, he'd viewed it as penance for putting his friend in such a position. He was one of the few men strong and heavy enough to accomplish the task. Though George fought him, cursed him, wild-eyed and incoherent, violent with pain, Jeremy had taken it all. He deserved it. Even if he lived with the memory forever, he only hoped George was past the point of remembering what he'd been forced to do.

"You? But why would you intentionally do such a thing?" Lily asked, snapping Jeremy back to the present.

He looked at her seriously, the dark fire in his eyes, intense.

"Because I'd die before I saw you unhappy." The words took the very breath from Lily's lungs. Her lips tried to form words, but they seemed to die away before she could use them. "Which chamber is yours?" Jeremy asked, looking up and down the hallway. Lily gestured with her hand, trying to ignore its coating of gore.

Instead of releasing her, Jeremy led her to the door and opened it for her. Inside, the deep brass tub steamed with hot water and filled the room with the scent of dried lavender soap, solving Jeremy's secret ponderings about from where, exactly, the intoxicating aroma originated. Assuming she'd be too exhausted from the ordeal to properly dress for the day, her maid had laid out a clean nightshift and dressing gown for Lily.

Lily gave a small sound of pleasure from somewhere deep within her throat. She deftly untied the lacings at the neck of the cloak and it fell to the floor in a puddle of filthy cloth. Jeremy froze in the doorway, torn between the realization that he was under the earl's roof with George lying near death only a few rooms away, and his crippling desire to care for Lily. She was clearly in shock and distraught over what had transpired—and rightly so. She was struggling to wrap her mind around it all. She'd nearly witnessed the death of one of her brothers.

She had looked so frail when he found her still standing exactly where he'd left her in the parlor. Trembling, muddy, and covered in blood, she resembled a wounded baby bird. He'd always had a strong urge to protect her, but none more so than at that moment. He longed to hold her against him and form a wall around their peaceful moment in time—he wanted to create somewhere where she could never be hurt, would never be forced to bend to anyone else's will, where she wouldn't be judged for not fitting into any sort of mold.

Jeremy stepped into the room and pressed the door shut behind him. Lily didn't turn at the sound of him closing the door; nor did she when he took the dainty wooden chair at her writing desk and wedged it beneath the knob to prevent any unpleasant intrusions. He needed to make sure Lily could relax undisturbed; that they could have a few moments of peace and sanctuary to recover from what had happened.

Jeremy walked up behind Lily and swept the fallen curls of golden hair from her pale neck. His lips ached to press a kiss to the thrumming pulse he saw there, but he held himself in check. This wasn't about seduction; he was there to care for her.

He began unlacing her gown and helped her step free of the garment. He noticed with some surprise that she was not wearing any shoes, but asking what had happened was irrelevant. They were gone, and her feet were scraped and muddy. Her petticoats and corset came next until she was bare and perfect in front of him. His groin gave a powerful throb, but he ignored it. Instead, Jeremy took her hand and helped her step into the tub and lower herself into the steaming water.

"That's it, love," he whispered when she lay back and closed her eyes with a sigh. Jeremy took his turn at lady's maid and began plucking as many pins from her tangled hair as he could, collecting a small pile of the maddeningly tiny implements in his hand and setting them on her vanity. He unbuttoned and slid free of his hopelessly destroyed waistcoat and dropped it to the floor. Stripped to his shirtsleeves, he rolled the cuffs up higher past his elbows and tried not to take too much notice of Lily's soft, pale, glistening curves reclining in the tub.

Taking up a washing cloth, he knelt beside the tub with the intent to wash her hands and the salty sweat and tears from her flushed cheeks. Jeremy soaked the cloth in the warm, scented water and carefully wiped at her face. Encouraged by her sigh of pleasure, he continued his gentle machinations on the graceful curve of her neck. Her hair was next. He grabbed the nearby pitcher and, tilting her head back, he cascaded the warm water through her long, golden locks. Creating tantalizing silver rivulets along the hills and valleys of her breasts and shoulders.

Jeremy dipped his arm in the water to retrieve her hand. He gently caressed and scrubbed away the grime, letting it melt away along with the awful memories of the day. He wiped the perfect crescents of her nails and cleaned the small cuts and abrasions on her palms. She giggled when he scrubbed at her feet—still ticklish after all these years. Jeremy couldn't have stopped his grin had he tried.

When she was sufficiently scrubbed and pink, Jeremy retrieved the large bathing cloths and helped her stand. She glowed in the firelight, flushed rosy from the warm water. She appeared more at ease, but emotionally drained and physically exhausted. Jeremy wrapped a cloth around her shoulders and patted her dry. He lifted her from the tub and set her on her feet.

"I'm not fragile, you know," Lily smiled as she continued to towel herself off. Her spark was returning; a good indication to Jeremy that she was coming round. He snatched another cloth and draped it over her head, scrubbing as one would after bathing a dog. "Stop!" she laughed and batted at him. She lifted the cloth from her head and peered up at him from a curtain of molten gold.

"I don't know if the bath helped," Jeremy said. "Now you just look like a drowned rat."

"If I look like a drowned rat, then you're the only one to blame," she retorted with a smile and flipped her hair back from her face, squeezing it out with the cloth in her hands.

Jeremy found even this mundane gesture to be highly erotic. In fact, Jeremy didn't think there was a thing she could do that didn't endear her to him or make him fall more in love with her—her unconscious grace and the easy way they were comfortable around one another. And now she was free.

Jeremy cleared his throat and fought the urge to adjust his trousers. She needed to rest. He needed to cool off. They both needed to recover.

"I should go," he said softly.

Lily's heart sank and she reached out to catch his bare forearm as he turned. The crisp hairs there tickled her palm. "Must you? I…I don't want to be alone just yet."

Jeremy heaved a heavy sigh. "I shouldn't, Lily…"

"Just stay until I can sleep. I need you to hold me, Jeremy."

The words nearly killed him on the spot. How could he say no?

"I need to bathe." He gestured lamely to his soiled clothing, the blood and grime filth drying on his skin. Lily quirked a brow at him.

"I see a tub and some clean linens—the water is still warm if you don't mind sharing it."

Realizing he could come up with no further excuses, Jeremy began untucking his shirt from his trousers. He pulled the garment over his head and tossed it off to the side. He spied Lily watching him with unabashed admiration, causing a fresh wave of arousal to rush to his groin.

"You're enjoying this far too much," he chuckled.

"When you've spent as many years as I wondering what was hidden beneath your clothes, then staring is only natural."

"Then you understand why I cannot take my eyes off of you," Jeremy's voice was a deep rumble in his chest. Her barely perceptible shiver of excitement stoked his arousal. "I had to play maid, so you'll need to play valet," he said, dropping onto the edge of her bed. "I need assistance removing my boots."

Tucking the corner of the linen toweling beneath her arm, she gave a mock curtsey and sank to her knees in front of Jeremy. He swallowed hard at the image she presented. Barely clad and on her knees before him. How many fantasies had he experienced which included this exact scenario? No less than a dozen came to mind in an instant.

They worked together to slip the tight-fitting leather from his calves. Jeremy tossed the boots to the side and stood, slipping off his trousers and smallclothes as he went. Stepping into the tub, he submerged himself in the lavender-scented water before she could catch sight of his entirely inappropriate arousal.

When he broke the surface and swiped the sopping hair from his eyes, he saw Lily – still holding the toweling cloth around her—pacing the room and gathering his clothing. "What are you doing?" he asked, scrubbing at the remnants of George's blood on his knuckles – some of it may very well have been Townsend's as well, now that he thought of it.

"You're unbelievably messy," Lily said as she laid out his shirt and waistcoat. "You shed clothes as you walk like a snake sheds its skin."

"I don't believe I've ever been likened to a snake before," Jeremy replied, scratching at a particularly stubborn bit of grime.

"Very well. Breadcrumbs. It's like you're leaving breadcrumbs; I need only to follow your clothes to find you."

"Naked," he flashed her a wicked grin.

Lily's cheeks warmed, but she didn't shy away. Instead, she grabbed the remaining washing cloth, soaked the corner in the water, and gently dabbed at a spot on Jeremy's temple. "You've been hurt." The cloth came away tinged pink and brown with blood.

"I'd hardly call it an injury." Jeremy took the cloth and wiped at the small cut, thinking of George's grave wound and current, precarious state. To call this an injury hardly felt just. Still, her concern touched him deeply. "I'll be just another moment or two," he assured her. "Get comfortable and I'll join you presently."

Lily turned and continued drying herself. Jeremy rinsed, stepped from the tub, and patted himself dry. He found Lily reclining beneath the coverlet, bared from the waist up; her dusky nipples puckered against the chill of the air. She was staring pointedly at the toweling cloth in his hand—the one he'd been about to drop to the floor. Jeremy hesitated and, rolling his eyes, he folded it into some semblance of neatness and draped it over the side of the tub. He cocked an eyebrow at Lily.

Better?

She nodded once and smiled.

Suddenly, however, Jeremy was faced with a new conundrum. How to get into Lily's bed without giving into his body's forceful need to touch her, caress her, taste her? He'd wanted to comfort her, hadn't he? What kind of a man was he that he couldn't restrain himself and just hold the woman he loved when she needed comfort?

But, bloody hell, how he needed *her*. Somewhere, in the back of his mind, he recalled learning of this phenomenon, where those who'd been in life-threatening situations craved a reminder that they were alive—that they'd been alive. And wasn't sex just the perfect way to accomplish that?

No matter how badly he ached, Jeremy steeled his resolve to respect Lily and simply hold her...as innocently as a man could whilst naked in bed.

Before his arousal could become too *apparent*, Jeremy strode over to the bed and settled himself beneath the coverlet. Lily instantly sidled up to him, nestling her shoulder beneath his arm and the tender curve of her cheek against his chest. She hooked a leg over his thigh when he tugged the coverlet up to cover her bare shoulder. She purred as she settled in and the sound cut a sizable slice in Jeremy's resolve.

Rather than act upon his desires, he spoke in a low, gentle tone and told her of George's injury; how the doctors had given him drugs for the pain, removed the shot from his leg, and done what they could to repair the damage. He was careful, however, to omit the fact that George had suffered considerably in the process, that Jeremy, himself, had been called in to help hold him down as the physicians did their gruesome work. As long as a fever didn't strike, they expected George to survive.

Though they had seemed hopeful that George would walk again, Jeremy had recognized the false bravado of men unwilling to admit to the imperfections of their craft. It would be a long and tenuous road, but Jeremy silently vowed to do everything in his power to help his friend. He knew deep down that he'd never be able to repay George for the unwitting sacrifice he'd made.

What Jeremy did tell Lily seemed to reassure her. She wanted to see her brother as soon as possible and Jeremy promised to accompany her if she wanted him to.

"I love you, Jeremy," she whispered after several minutes of warm silence, her soft breath tickling the dark whorls of hair on his chest.

Those words made his heart feel fair to bursting all over again. He knew he'd ever tire of hearing her say them, especially because – coming from Lily—he knew they were the honest, most innocent form of truth. She was handing him her soul to do with what he wished and that kind of trust struck him hard in the gut.

"If you ever talk yourself into another duel, however," Lily continued; "I may have to kill you myself."

Jeremy chuckled. "I wouldn't put it past you. I was not joking when I told Townsend you were one of the best shots I've ever seen."

Lily grew quiet and spent a few thoughtful moments running her nails over the ridges of his abdomen.

"Do you think he'll leave us alone now?" Jeremy stiffened—of course, she was referring to Townsend.

"Not only did he disgrace himself today, but he now knows I make no idle threats. I'll do whatever I have to to protect you, Lily. I always have and I always will."

She pushed herself into a seated position and stared down at him, her long golden locks creating a shimmering curtain around their faces.

"Why do you say such things? Do you find so little value in your own life?"

"I say them because I mean them," Jeremy replied in earnest. "I say them because I love you, Lily Stratford. I always have…I will until my dying breath…and I will do absolutely everything in my power to make sure you are happy and content. Believe that I will never take you for granted and I'll spend the time I have left proving to you that you are my entire world."

Lily's heart thudded against her ribs. Jeremy loved her. A part of her had known as much, but to hear the words from his lips made her soul soar to new heights.

"I love your laughter and joy," Jeremy continued, tucking a curl behind her ear and drawing her in with his molten chocolate gaze. "I love your grace and kindness." He smiled broadly. "And I will happily buy you every lamb in Kent if you will agree to be my wife."

"Now that," Lily breathed, "is a proposal."

Epilogue

A quiet wedding ceremony took place that summer in a small stone parish south of London. The bride was resplendent in a simple gown of ivory lace and pearls, her golden hair woven through with little blue blossoms, and carrying a full bouquet of Kentish wildflowers. The bridegroom was dashing in his stark contrast to his intended, with his raven-wing hair slicked back and well-fitted black formalwear. Many would remark upon the stunning couple in the years to come, but more would tell of the groom's unabashed pleasure at the sight of his bride—a delight that seemed only to grow as the years went on.

The best man stood beside the groom at the altar, but a footman remained nearby and ready with a chair and crutches in case the tall, blonde man's injured leg gave way. His determination to fulfill his duties overshadowed any pain or discomfort and, instead, he leaned heavily upon his lion's head cane. He was thinner, paler than before his injury—the fever and pain had taken its toll on his handsome features and sharpened them—however, nothing could dim the joy in his eyes at watching the union of his best friend and sister; the joviality in his tone as he clapped the groom's shoulder and was finally able to call him "brother."

The mothers of the bride and groom sat together in the front pew, foregoing the traditional seating arrangements and opting instead to hold hands and swipe at tears of joy as they watched their children forever unite their families and undo past errors in judgment.

The vows were recited in front of a very slim congregation bathed in the morning sunlight filtering through the red, yellow, and blue hues of the stained-glass windows. Family and a smattering of friends were in attendance but, had there been a hundred guests instead of fifteen, it was doubtful the smitten bride and groom would have noticed. The vicar, having known the couple their entire lives – even baptized them—presented a joyful ceremony. The groom gifted his bride with a dainty gold band set into which was a single, clear, brilliant emerald—to match her eyes, he would later tell her. The kiss at the conclusion of the ceremony was, perhaps, a bit more enthusiastic than some of the more conservative attendees would have cared for, but the joy was infectious and quickly replaced any shock. Their love and elation were palpable; perhaps amplified because they were finally free to share their affection after so many years of keeping it hidden.

Gossips would whisper about the sudden marriage—a mere matter of months following the dissolution of the bride's betrothal to another man—but the romance of their love story, the depth and duration of their affection, made it clear that they'd been destined for a true love match. The romantics in the powder rooms at balls who were drawn to such tales far outweighed those whose venomous tongues would wish to denounce such obvious love.

Nature graced their union with a warm, sunny day for their wedding breakfast, which had been moved out of doors into the gardens of the bride's familial country home to take advantage of the fine weather.

The groom winked as he fed the bride a bite of toast coated in a thick slathering of strawberry jam.

Did you enjoy Jeremy and Lily's story?
The next book in "The Stratford Family" series is available now! Find George's story in
Saving the Viscount — an enemies-to-lovers, forced proximity, steamy Regency romance.

Follow Kelsey for updates:

Instagram - @authorkelseyswanson
Facebook - Author Kelsey Swanson

Acknowledgements

This book wouldn't have been possible without the constant love and support of my family. Thank you to my husband for supporting my dreams when I disappeared into my laptop and books, for being my rock when I need it most, and for reminding me to find the silver lining. Thank you to my son for believing I hung the moon and stars (I hope you feel the same way when you one day realize your name is in this series…I *swear* the character was named years before you were born). You are my sunshine, my only sunshine. To everyone who helped me discover my own voice and style as a writer: you're the real heroes here because I know you've sat through some questionable content. Carolynn, Caitlin, and Annie: you may not have had a direct hand in beta-reading this particular story, but your guidance in the past helped me tremendously in discovering who I was and I will never forget it. Nathan: my long-suffering friend who wasn't afraid to critique my writing (even though it certainly wasn't always your taste), helped me when I had meltdowns about formatting and computer issues, and for being a sounding board for so many aspects of my life. Also, you lose the game.

ABOUT THE AUTHOR

Author, wife, mother, animal lover, and owner of an obscenely large To-Be-Read book stash; Kelsey is an Illinois native. She fostered her love of reading and writing after a heart condition sidelined her childhood. Her passions continued to develop long after surgery restored her health. To this day, it's difficult to find her without a book in her hands. She dove headfirst into the romance genre (perhaps) a bit earlier than the recommended minimum age and became rather adept at disguising her reading material. Once exposed to the glittering world of historical romance, she was forever changed. Her love of writing and all things British translated into her future collegiate studies in both English (with an emphasis on Brit Lit) and History (mainly British and European). She would go on to earn Bachelor's Degrees in both English and History, as well as a Master's Degree in English. She finished penning her first novel fresh out of high school and has never looked back. When she's not reading or writing, she's usually watching reruns of her favorite shows or streaming just about any true crime show; obsessively collecting architectural designs, crafts, and recipes on Pinterest; or sketching, crocheting, cooking, and spending time with her family. She is a diehard supporter of the Oxford Comma and is glued to the TV whenever le Tour de France is on. The Baron's Folly is her first published novel.

Kelsey loves to hear from readers! Find her on social media, or email her at authorkelseyswanson@yahoo.com. Reviews on Amazon and Goodreads are always appreciated!

Made in the USA
Monee, IL
11 June 2025

18949435R00166